BLOOD

HUNTER

THE VAMPIRE'S MAGE SERIES

BOOK 3

BY C. N. CRAWFORD

Blood Hunter

Book 3 Of The Vampire's Mage Series

Copyright © 2016 C. N. Crawford

ISBN-13: 9781520307008

Edited by Tammi Labrecque
Cover art by Rebecca Frank
Interior design by C.N. Crawford

www.cncrawford.com

Contact the Authors:
cn@cncrawford.com

Twitter: @CN_Crawford
Facebook: cncrawfordauthor

First Edition

Printed in the U.S.A

Also by

C. N. CRAWFORD

The Vampire's Mage Series
Book 1: *Magic Hunter*
Book 1.1: *Shadow Mage*
Book 2: *Witch Hunter*

Demons of Fire and Night
Book 1: *Infernal Magic*
Book 2: *Nocturnal Magic*

The Memento Mori Trilogy
Book 1: *The Witching Elm*
Book 2: *A Witch's Feast*
Book 2.1: *The Abysmal Sea*
Book 3: *Witches of the Deep*

For Michael and his awesome hair

1

$\mathcal{R}$osalind pushed through a tall oak door, leading to the Gelal Field just outside Lilinor's walls. The waxing moon hung in the sky like a god's eye, washing the shadowy landscape in silver. Even though she'd been in Lilinor for two full weeks now, she still hadn't become accustomed to the utter dominance of the moon over the kingdom.

A perfect home for creatures of the night.

But it was Caine's home. Not hers.

Her footsteps crunched over a dirt path. Lined with myrtle trees and sycamores, it meandered down a hill in gentle curves. The wind rustled through the leaves; nearby, a raven cawed.

In the crook of one arm she carried a wicker basket. She'd filled it to the brim with fresh-baked corn muffins, butter, and a jar of honey. Steam from the muffins warmed her arms as she walked, a small smile curling her lips. The idea of sneaking out of the castle thrilled her—plus tonight would nearly resemble a normal night. Food, wine, gossip. What more did she need?

At least she had her friends here in this city of darkness.he was supposed to meet Tammi and Miranda at the old Temple of Nyxobas. Aurora had said she might stop by, too.

Since arriving in Lilinor half-dead, Rosalind had hardly seen her friends—and that was probably because she hadn't wanted to leave her room over the past two weeks. For one thing, she'd been avoiding Caine. Whenever she thought of him, the first thing that sprung into her mind was his divine beauty. The softness of his kiss. The gentleness of his fingertips over her skin.

And the second thing to spring to mind was the image of him brutally slaughtering her parents while she watched.

The cognitive dissonance was a little too much for her to handle.

But it wasn't just Caine that kept her locked in her room. She also had to deal with the lunatic spirit in her head—Cleo, her batshit crazy second soul. Since Rosalind had fought her cousin weeks ago, Cleo's voice had only grown louder. And the iron ring no longer kept her quiet.

Half the time, Cleo's thoughts drowned out Rosalind's own. Mostly, Cleo begged to see Ambrose, to touch the vampire lord. And when she didn't want to touch him, she wanted Rosalind to light him on fire.

And yet ... out here, in the fresh air, her second soul had mostly muted. Maybe, when insomnia and Cleo's thoughts ripped her mind apart, she could creep out to nap among the bluebells and sycamores.

Rosalind inhaled the rich scent of jasmine and followed the curving path that wound down the hill. Her silky gown slid against her legs as she walked, and she pulled a black cashmere shawl tighter around her shoulders. At the bottom of the hill, she spotted the stone ruin—a forgotten temple—and her pace quickened. Somewhere in there, Miranda and Tammi waited for her.

As she neared the arched doorway, a murder of crows took

flight from one of the crumbling towers. Shivering, she crossed into the temple—if it could still be called a temple. The ruin no longer had a roof, and moonlight washed over tall grasses and wildflowers.

"Rosalind!" Miranda and Tammi called out in unison.

Rosalind grinned. "Hello, my dears!"

Miranda and Tammi sat below an arched window, with a spread of food laid out before them: cheese, bread, grapes, a bottle of wine, and a few glasses. Around the blanket, bluebells and white poppies dappled the grass.

Rosalind joined them on the crimson blanket, folding her feet beneath her. "I'm starving. Sorry I'm late."

Tammi straightened, flicking her pale hair behind her shoulders. "Not to worry. I've been drinking all the wine."

From her seat on the grass, Rosalind surveyed the old hall. Only three walls remained, and six cracked columns formed a sort of aisle. Vines clung to the stone surfaces, as if trying to reclaim nature's territory.

Miranda leaned over to hug her, enveloping her in the scent of the ocean, and Rosalind smiled. *This is what it's like to have a sister.* "Have you been waiting long?" Rosalind asked.

"Only ten minutes," Miranda said.

Rosalind dropped her basket in the center of the blanket. "I brought some muffins."

Tammi shook her head, frowning. "I'm not hungry."

Miranda wore a wreath of wildflowers threaded with seashells. She picked up the bottle of wine, and filled a glass, handing it to Rosalind. "How's your extra soul? Is Cleo still messing with your thoughts?"

Rosalind groaned. "A little obsessed with Ambrose's dead body. The woman needs a cold shower."

"Or maybe she needs to get laid," Tammi said.

Rosalind frowned. "Not gonna happen here."

"Ambrose might be technically dead," Tammi said, filling her own glass, "but he *is* hot as hell. I wonder if he likes sharp teeth and creepy, empty eyes."

"Oh, stop," Rosalind said. She eyed Tammi's hair—the pale blue of starlight—and her glimmering eyes to match. "You're not creepy. You look beautiful, honestly."

Tammi's eyes lingered on Rosalind for just a little too long. Her friend's body went completely still, and she ran her tongue over her teeth.

Rosalind looked away quickly. *Okay, that look was a bit creepy.* Shaking it off, she turned to her twin. "What do you think of Lilinor?"

"It's beautiful." Miranda plucked a bluebell, and began threading it into a poppy's stem. "But I'm not sure we belong here. Apart from Aurora, most of the vampires can't look at us without thinking about our blood."

"I know," Rosalind said. "That's why I suggested we meet up outside. In the palace walls, there's always a vamp sniffing around."

Tammi emitted a low growl.

Okay. That was creepy, too.

Miranda pulled a seashell from her pocket, threading the poppy's stem through it. "All the vampires resent us."

"Us? Why?" Rosalind asked. "We're neither as glamorous nor as powerful as they are."

Miranda tied a pair of stems in a knot. "Haven't you noticed? Human women are here only as servants. As courtesans. Nothing more. Demons are supposed to use us. Not work with us like equals. And we have the ear of the king."

Tammi twirled her glass. "Honestly, the three of us don't belong anywhere. You're both an unholy combination of mage-spirits and gods-blood. I'm some kind of human-demon abomination created through your family's unholy magic. None of this was meant to be. Basically, we need our own world at this point."

It was true—they didn't really belong anywhere. Yet somehow, with Tammi and Miranda here, Rosalind felt like she *was* at home. Even here in the city of night, where everyone wanted to drink their blood.

"I feel like I belong with the two of you," Rosalind said. "Both of you are my family, and that's all I need to be happy. As long as we can avoid dying at the hands of vampires."

Miranda plucked another wildflower. "After we serve our purpose here, we'll just have to make our own tiny little kingdom, the three of us. We'll get a little house by the water, and we'll build a magical shield around it, and we can sit around reading books. I can paint landscapes. You can…" She frowned at Rosalind. "What do you like to do?"

"I used to be into demon hunting. Guess I need a new hobby."

"I'll read romances and sew amazing dresses for us," Tammi said, brightening for a moment.

Miranda pointed at Rosalind. "Muffin-baking. That's your new hobby. You bake the muffins, Tammi reads to us by the fire, and I can paint portraits of us all. Caine can visit us if he wants. He's a demigod with an extra soul, so he's an abomination, too."

Tammi raised her glass. "We will call it Abominatania! Only the godsforsaken may enter."

Rosalind bit into one of the muffins, relishing the buttery taste. "I don't bake muffins. Ambrose has instructed Caine's fae cook to send us these." Every day, an aggrieved vampire showed up at her door with a steaming basket of meat pies, bread, cheese, and pastries.

"This is from Caine's cook?" Tammi asked. "Another reason to invite him to Abominatania."

"No," Rosalind said sharply.

"Why not?" Miranda asked. "He's just like us."

"Um, because he crucified our parents in front of us?"

"Oh, that." Miranda waved a dismissive hand. "Well, they did ruin his life. They chained him to a wall in the basement for a year."

Rosalind's heart clenched. "True."

"When our parents gave him the extra soul, he went insane." Miranda shook her head. "And our parents ruined *our* lives too. For years, anyway. We could have been together that whole time. We could have had a family. But they were mad for power. So maybe they got what they deserved."

Tammi sipped straight from the wine bottle, then wiped the back of her hand across her mouth. "And I thought my family was screwed up."

Miranda reached out, touching Rosalind's hand. "Well, we have each other now. Let's not dwell on the past."

Rosalind smiled faintly, her thoughts circling back to Caine. *Maybe he had a good reason to kill my parents.* They'd chosen to imprison a shadow demon—a demigod, in fact—and they'd nearly destroyed his mind. Of *course* a demigod would seek vengeance. That's what demigods did when they were wronged.

Still, it didn't change the fact that he had a disturbing habit of keeping the truth hidden. He'd known all along what had happened to her parents, and he'd never told her. And clearly, he was still keeping his darkest secrets buried deep. What terrible revelation was coming next?

From outside the temple walls, the faint tinkling of bells whispered on the wind. The sound sent a shiver up Rosalind's spine.

2

$\mathcal{F}$ootfalls made her turn her head, and she saw Aurora crossing the grass with a silver flask in her hand. She wore a beautiful nectarine dress that hugged her slender figure. "There you are."

"Aurora!" Rosalind smiled. "I'm glad you could join us."

Aurora took a sip from her flask. "Sometimes I forget this place is here. No one worships in the temple anymore."

Rosalind pulled her shawl close, still listening to the tinkling bells. "What's that noise?"

"What noise?" Aurora asked.

"The bells." Rosalind held up a finger until she heard it again. "There. Did you hear it?"

"Oh." Aurora nodded at one of the half-collapsed walls. "The Garden of the Dead. I've *got* to give you a tour. It's right over here."

Rosalind stood. *The Garden of the Dead. Now this I need to see.*

Aurora led her to another tall window, open to the air.

As Rosalind approached, her gaze landed on a moonlit cemetery. She clutched the crumbling stone windowsill, gazing out at the small necropolis. Crooked, old statues of angels and dragons jutted from the ground. Scattered around the cemetery stood yew trees. Even from here, she could see flecks of color decorating their boughs.

"The garden of the dead," Aurora said in a hushed voice. "When you hear the bells, it's the spirits, speaking to us."

The hair rose on the back of Rosalind's neck. "Who is buried here?"

"Courtesans, mostly, but some vampires too," Aurora said. In a heartbeat, she was over the windowsill. "Let me show you."

Rosalind followed after—landing not quite as gracefully, dust clouding around her.

Aurora started down an old gravel path that meandered between the graves, and Rosalind hurried to catch up. As they walked, the sound of tinkling bells grew louder.

Aurora pointed to an ornately carved obelisk towering over most of the other stones. "That's Old Willard's grave. From what I gather, he was a sexy little minx in his prime. The personal concubine of Lady Albintheen."

"How did he die?" Rosalind asked.

"Of old age. Lady Albintheen kept him youthful by feeding him her blood. But there's only so long that can go on. Eventually, his heart finally gave out over his dinner of lamprey pie."

"Right."

Before Rosalind could ask another question, Aurora was already hurrying toward another cluster of graves, surrounded by a small iron fence.

"These are the Aspinwall Sisters." Aurora shook her head "Mind you, they weren't actually sisters. Everyone called them that because they dressed identically. Same hair. Same clothes. Same makeup. Same knickers. The vampire they served, Otto Aspinwall, had a bit of a thing for twins."

"Oh." Rosalind grimaced. "Is he still alive?"

"Nah. Quite tragic, really. Otto was obsessed with his twins. Loved their blood. Loved the weird role playing twincest shit they did. And one night, when they got him a little too excited, he totally lost control to the blood-hunger. Drained them both. He was inconsolable for weeks. Then, he just gave up and went through a portal to the sunlight."

Rosalind winced. "Charming. I didn't know vampires committed suicide."

"Not often."

Rosalind ran her fingers over a rough stone, webbed with moss. "So, are there funerals for the dead concubines?"

Aurora shrugged. "For the ones who were loved. They get funerals and gravestones, and the rest are... sort of jumbled together in unmarked graves."

"And what are the funerals like in Lilinor?"

"They're called feasts of the dead. The ceremony opens a gateway to the afterlife, so the dead don't end up trapped in the House of Shades." She turned to Rosalind. "Others give their souls to Nyxobas, and they get stuck in the shadow hell—especially those who die at the hands of a vampire. Bottom line: don't take a vamp as a lover. It tends to end in death."

"Surely death among the vampires isn't permanent?"

"It usually is. Ambrose doesn't permit the creation of new vampires without his permission. And Caine doesn't allow bone-conjuring or necromancy."

The neared a strangely enormous yew. Great boughs, large as tree trunks, curved over them in a canopy. Ribbons and streamers, now faded by the weather, hung from them like Spanish moss. Keepsakes decorated every branch: ribbons and jewelry, tiny framed pictures, notes and letters. Some of them hung intertwined with the ivy that snaked around the trunk.

Tiny, silver bells hung from the branches.

A breeze puffed the branches, and the bells rang softly in the darkness. Rosalind shivered. *The dead may whisper to us, but we can't know what they're saying.*

Under the canopy, Aurora reached up to pull down a blue ribbon, tied to an old skeleton key. She unfurled it, and read out loud. "Samuel Stocktown."

"Another concubine?

"I have no idea. Most people buried in this cemetery get their name hung from a branch. Some are vampires, killed in battle or by the sun. And some are human, like you." Aurora pointed to a large mound. "But most humans are buried there, in the common grave. No one remembers their names. Humans die so easily."

Loneliness welled in Rosalind's chest, and a cold wind whipped over her skin. Under the tinkling bells, a faint scratching noise rose floated on the breeze. "What is that scraping?"

"Ah. Those are the vamps Ambrose buried alive." Aurora shot her a sharp look. "So don't go digging around the roots of the yew, unless you have a death wish. Though I kinda get the feeling that you do, sometimes."

Rosalind's mouth went dry. Suddenly, she had a strong urge to get away from the terrible noise. She turned back to the gravel path that lead to the Temple. "Let's go back to the muffins and wine. This place is giving me the creeps."

Miranda was right: humans could never be at home here in Lilinor. Maybe humans and vamps were equal in death, but not in life. As far as she could tell, humans were basically here as sex slaves. And every now and then, a vampire might lose control to his blood-hunger and suck one dry.

If she and her friends stayed in Lilinor too long, there'd be nothing left of them but a few ribbons and bells on a yew.

Ambrose... Cleo whispered. *Touch me again...*

"Shut up, you lunatic," Rosalind muttered.

"I didn't say anything," Aurora said. "You talking to the voices in your head again?"

"If only there was some way to get Cleo so drunk she would just fall asleep."

"Why don't you just give her what she wants?"

"Sleeping with Ambrose, you mean?"

"Sure. Why not? I'm sure he'd be game."

Rosalind's nose crinkled. Apart from the fact that Ambrose creeped her out, she was pretty sure that wouldn't be enough for Cleo. Cleo wanted her to slaughter him, too. *Best leave that part out.*

At the top of the hill, Rosalind climbed through the windowsill. As they crossed the grass to Tammi and Miranda, she hugged her shawl closer. The cemetery had totally unnerved her, like she'd seen a certain vision of her future.

Still, the sight of her sister gently threading a wildflower wreath calmed her nerves, and she pushed the memory of the graveyard to the back of her mind.

Aurora plopped down on the blanket. "I misjudged. I don't think Rosalind liked the Garden of the Dead."

Rosalind sat next to her, then snatched up her glass of wine. "As much as I enjoy visiting dead courtesans, the sounds of vampires scratching in their coffins was a little weird."

"You need to be careful," Miranda said, still working on a wreath. "Sometimes, what's buried doesn't stay underground."

Rosalind sipped her wine. "Maybe we should choose a new picnic spot next time. Not sure I like eating cheese next to a mass grave for prostitutes. Nothing against prostitutes. It's just a little sad. No one even remembers who they are, or what their lives were like."

"And where do they bury the abominations?" Tammi's red nails dug into the flesh of her arms. She was definitely not handling this demon thing well.

"Are you okay, Tammi?" Rosalind asked.

"I'm *fine,*" Tammi said through clenched teeth.

Miranda threaded a final wildflower into a seashell, then lifted the wreath, handing it to Tammi. "This will ease your mind."

Visibly relaxing, Tammi ran her fingers over the petals. "It's pretty."

Miranda dropped the other wreath on Rosalind's head. "And this one's for you. I can make another for you, Aurora. The bluebells will bring peace to your heart and mind. The ivy is for Druloch, Rosalind's lord. The white poppies are for the god of night. Aurora and Tammi's god."

Maybe it was a placebo, but with the wreath on, Rosalind felt her muscles relax. She let out a slow sigh. "And what are the seashells for?"

"Those are for Dagon, my god. They tie you to me." Miranda smiled. "You see? Drew wants you to be his queen. He wants a magical Stepford wife. But this is the only royal crown you need."

Rosalind shivered at the mention of her cousin. She could only hope she'd never see Drew again, or she'd end up his obedient little slave.

Tammi's hands tightened around her own wreath, her knuckles white. "Erish still haunts my dreams. Her face hovering over me as she turned me into a demon in Drew's castle. I hate Drew just as much. I really want to rip out his throat. I *need* to feel his hot blood run down my chin, down my throat." She breathed deeply, in and out through her nose. Her silver eyes drilled holes in Rosalind.

Aurora leaned back on her hands, staring at Tammi. "I think I know what you're feeling."

14

Tammi's vision seemed to clear, and a horrified look crossed her face. Clutching the wreath, she rose and sprinted off toward the castle without saying another word.

Rosalind stood. "What was that?" she asked, more to herself than to anyone else. Something told her not to run after her friend. Tammi needed to be alone.

"That," Aurora said, "was blood-hunger. Guess she really does have a demon body."

3

*H*ugging herself, Rosalind padded down a dark hall as quietly as she could. Candlelight danced over the flagstones; every flicker of light and shadow seemed to make her jump.

In the rest of the world, daylight was the most powerful protector against vampires. But in Lilinor, a land of eternal night, the vamps had free reign in the shadows.

Granted, Ambrose had given the vampires strict orders: anyone who harmed the human mages would suffer a traitor's death. Rosalind wasn't clear *precisely* what a traitor's death involved, but it probably involved an initial round of medieval torture, followed by a living burial in the Garden of the Dead.

But shadow creatures had ways of committing their worst deeds under the cloak of darkness, when no one was watching, so Rosalind wasn't taking any chances. She'd hidden anti-vampire weapons all over her body: hawthorn stakes strapped to her thighs, iron knives in sheaths under her dress.

Miranda was right: the vampires *did* resent them. Rosalind had seen a few too many bared fangs and darkened eyes as she walked past. And it wasn't like a human could go unnoticed here. In fact, as she walked past each of these doors, the vamps inside would be perking up their ears at the sound of her beating heart.

Their nostrils would hungrily sniff at the scent of her sweat, the blood pumping beneath her skin.

And just maybe—when she got to Tammi's room—her friend would be just as eager for her blood.

But Rosalind was going to stop by anyway. Tammi had no clue how to fight, so Rosalind wasn't too worried for her safety. And Tammi needed a friend now more than ever.

As she walked down a particularly dark hallway, a door to her right slammed open. Rosalind whirled. There, just inches from her, stood a platinum-blonde vampire. Blood dripped down her chin onto a white gown, and her eyes blazed red. "I thought I smelled something."

"Sorry, lady. I'm off limits. Ambrose's orders."

The vamp snarled. She didn't look like she wanted to back down. *Blood hunger.*

Rosalind's muscles tightened, and she turned to walk on. Before she could take another step, the vampire grabbed her by the hair, dragged her into the room, and threw her down hard on the stone floor. Rosalind's knees smacked onto the flagstones, and she fell forward onto her hands.

Rosalind reached for one of the stakes at her thigh. Just as she lifted the hem of her dress, the vampire picked her up again—this time by her throat—and slammed her against the wall. Powerful fingers pressed into Rosalind's neck, cutting off her air.

A dark-haired male vampire stood behind the blonde, his expression almost bored. "Whose courtesan is this?"

Rosalind kicked the female in her ribs, and the vamp dropped her. In the next second, Rosalind had a stake gripped firmly in her fingers. Slowly, she straightened. *I really don't want to fight two at once, but I will if I have to.*

"I'm no one's courtesan," she said through clenched teeth. "Like I said, I'm off limits."

The male vamp stepped closer, running a long finger over Rosalind's shoulder. "You're not dressed like one of the whores."

Rosalind stepped away from him, grimacing. "That's not why I'm here. I'm a mage. I work with Ambrose and Caine."

The female bared her fangs. "Ah. She's one of the humans Ambrose is forcing vampires to serve." She spat on the floor.

The male growled. "I'm a lieutenant in Ambrose's army. I'm one of his trusted advisors. I will not fetch your sandwiches, little girl."

Rosalind clutched her stake tighter. These two vamps seemed a little jacked-up on blood, or perhaps meth. "Okay, well, thanks for the chat. I'm going to be on my way."

The female took another step closer, boxing her in. "You must think you're pretty special, little human. Traipsing around with the king and our general like you're someone important. But deep down, I promise you, Caine and Ambrose don't think of you any differently than they do the other human whores. When they're done using you, you and your sister will be working in our harem, or buried under the ground. Just two more bodies for the whore pit."

The male grinned. "Esmerelda. You do get feisty after drinking." He nodded at a passed-out girl, propped up on a chair.

Rosalind's stomach tightened. "Thank you for your concern, but after I'm done with Ambrose, I'm out of here."

Neither of these vamps seemed particularly worried about the hawthorn stake in Rosalind's hand.

"Believe me," Esmerelda said, her eyes burning red. "Caine, Malphas, and Ambrose have been through many human females, and all of them thought they were special. None quite as arrogant as you, but that will make your downfall all the more delicious." She leaned in closer, stroking Rosalind's hair a little too forcefully.

"I know Ambrose said I can't kill you, so I won't. But I want you to know that demigods like Caine and Malphas see you as nothing more than tits and ass."

The male frowned. "What else is there to human females? Besides the blood, I suppose."

Esmerelda patted Rosalind's head, like she was a dog, and smiled sweetly. "If I were you, I'd make sure your door is locked tight at night, or you might find yourself splattered across the cobblestones. Just like you did to that ker queen." The smile faded from her lips. "Let's go, Darren."

Esmerelda turned, stalking out of the room, and Darren followed.

"Darren is a stupid name for a vampire!" Rosalind called out after them. *Okay, so I don't always come up with the best comebacks.* She leaned back against the wall, then slipped the stake back under her dress. *Best to give Esmerelda and Darren a few minutes to clear out before I cross into the hall.*

While she waited, she surveyed the enormous, octagonal room: the tangle of bloodstained bedsheets on the four-poster bed, the gargoyles in arched alcoves. Starry lanterns hung from the ceiling. Then her gaze returned to the pale form slumped in an armchair, and she jumped. *I forgot there's someone else in here.*

Rosalind took a step closer, eyeing the vampire—no, a human. A curvy brunette, dressed in cherry-red high heels, a black corselet. Blood dripped down her neck, and white powder dusted the tops of her breasts.

That would explain why the vamps were so jacked up.

Rosalind stepped closer. Was she even still alive?

Leaning down, she tapped the woman's shoulder, but she didn't move. "Hello?" She lifted the girl's chin. Slowly, sleepy green eyes opened. Rosalind held the girl's chin up, so she wouldn't pass out again. "Are you okay?"

Drowsily, the girl straightened. "Where are Esmerelda and Darren?"

"They left."

She pressed a hand to her throat. "Oh, thank god. They nearly drank me dry. They're supposed to replenish me with their blood after, but frankly I'm glad they left. They get a little out of control after a few lines."

Rosalind glanced at the white powder. "Right. They seemed a bit excitable."

The girl's eyes drifted closed again.

"Do you need medical help?" Rosalind asked.

The girl straightened, blinking her eyes. "Sorry. I'm kind of tired."

Rosalind frowned. "Seems like a dangerous line of work."

The girl shrugged. "You get used to it."

"Feeding the vampires?"

"Yeah. I'm just hoping the incubus takes a shine to me instead of the vamps." She blinked her eyes. "He doesn't require blood. I've never seen him, but I heard he's super hot. And he's, like, a demigod. Only thing is, everyone seems to fall in love with him, which is kind of sad."

Rosalind schooled her face into disinterest. "He's fond of courtesans?"

"Aren't all demons? They're bred to use our bodies. It's in their DNA—or whatever demons are made of."

"Right."

The girl held out a hand. "I'm Bridgette."

Rosalind took her hand, smiling. "Rosalind."

Bridgette arched an eyebrow, taking in Rosalind's silky gray dress and the plunging neckline. "They let you dress like that?

In a fancy gown, like a vampire?" Her forehead crinkled. "How come I haven't seen you in the harem?"

"I'm not a courtesan."

Bridgette's eyes widened. "So what are you?"

"A mage. Sort of. But I don't think I'll be staying here forever." Rosalind cocked her head. "Where is the harem anyway?"

Bridgette sighed. "They keep us below ground, near the armory. That's how little they're threatened by us. They don't even lock up the weapons. Then they send for us when they need blood or sex. We're not allowed to roam freely." She hugged herself, shivering. "And I'm constantly freezing, since vamps don't understand heat—or that, like, sometimes it's nice to wear sweatshirts and pajamas. They always have us dressed in this crap." She snapped the top of a sheer thigh-high stocking.

"How long have you been here?"

Bridgette bit her lip. "Let's see, two years? Right after I graduated from college."

Rosalind's eyebrows rose. "So... how did you end up here? Was it your choice, or were you abducted?"

"My choice. I graduated from college with, like, over half a million dollars of student loan debt, and an art history degree that no one seemed to care about. I couldn't even get a job at Starbucks. And I felt like, I'm either gonna jump out a window or join the demons. Probably not the best decision I ever made." She hugged herself, her eyes glazing over. "Sometimes I see the courtesans leave the harem, and they just don't come back."

Rosalind had a pretty good idea why. *More bodies for the whore pit.* "Aren't you scared of the vamps?"

"They're not supposed to kill us, but only because they think of us as a limited resource. It's not like they have empathy. I guess most of them are no worse than a drunken frat boy, apart from the blood drinking." She rubbed her arms. "Ambrose is different than most. He terrifies me. He just walks into a room and I want to run the other way. There's something really dark about him."

Ambrose, Cleo whispered. Rosalind could feel her body responding to the name, her skin warming. "Can you change your mind? And return home?"

Shivering, Bridgette rubbed her arms. "Are you kidding? They're very secretive about Lilinor." Her eyes glistened in the dim candlelight. "I'm never getting out of here alive."

"Maybe there's a way around it."

Bridgette smiled sadly. "I like your optimism, but I think I'm stuck here. Still, you're a mage, right? If you ever figure out a spell to fix the weird alpha male shit going on in this place, I'll owe you big time." She bit her lip. "Not sure how I'd pay you back, except I make really good red velvet cake."

Rosalind smiled. "Don't underestimate the allure of red velvet cake." She pulled off her cloak, handing it to Bridgette. "Here. Keep yourself warm."

Bridgette's brow crinkled. "Are you sure?"

"Of course. I've got more, and you're freezing down there. Take it."

Bridgette smiled, wrapping the shawl around her. "Thank you. Come visit us some time, if you can."

Rosalind smiled, turning to the door. "I will."

She crossed to the door. As she pulled it open, a sigh slid from her. She was living among people who viewed humans as a sort of subspecies. A resource. Slaves, even, who should walk around in skimpy underwear and live in a freezing basement—and above all, keep their mouths shut.

How many courtesans had Caine entertained over the years? And did he really think of her the same way? As a toy to use and discard when he was done?

Her fingernails pierced her palms. *Why does it matter?* It wasn't like Caine was her boyfriend—far from it. Their shared history was dark and twisted.

Yet she felt herself drawn to him, like a magnetic pull that tugged at her core. In fact, as she walked farther down the hall, she glanced at the painting of Lord Byron. The route she'd taken to Tammi had led her right by Caine's room.

The hair rose on the back of her neck. Had that been an accident?

Or am I as enthralled by Caine as Cleo is by Ambrose?

4

As she drew closer to Caine's room, the shadows seemed to thicken around her, climbing up the walls. The temperature dropped, and goosebumps rose on her skin. In the sconces, the candle's flames waned, nearly snuffing out.

He's here.

She considered turning to run, but something stopped her. That magnetic pull, she supposed. Pulse racing, she hugged herself and took a few steps back, pressing her back to the wall. The cold stone bit into her skin through her thin gown. *Maybe I can just hide in the shadows.*

A silver aura, scented of thunderstorms, twisted past her. She froze.

As Caine turned the corner, his icy eyes bored into her.

She swallowed hard. *So much for hiding in the shadows.*

A faint smile curled his perfect lips, and he slowed his gait. His soothing aura caressed her bare arms, warming her body. As he moved toward her, electricity seemed to charge the air between them.

This is what it feels like to be in the presence of a demigod. She'd been avoiding him for weeks, and seeing him so close felt like a punch to the chest.

Her breath caught in her throat as she took in his stunning contrasts: The dark lashes that framed his pale eyes. Sharp cheekbones above the gentle curves of his mouth. Soft skin over steely muscles.

Standing so close to Caine was an exquisite sort of pain, a sharp heat deep in her chest.

It would be so easy just to reach out from where she stood against the wall, and touch that beautiful face, to feel his skin, to press herself against his body.

So easy to kiss his perfect lips, to drag him into his bedroom and rip his clothes off, to feel his hot mouth against hers.

And that is probably what all those courtesans thought—the ones who fell in love with him. She tightened her fingers into fists to stop herself from reaching for him.

Her throat tightened. How many other women had thought they were special to him over the centuries? She'd be an idiot to ignore what Esmerelda had said. *I will not be just another body for the whore pit.*

You have interesting desires, Cleo whispered. *You want to bed the man who murdered your parents?*

Rosalind's heart skipped a beat, and she sucked in a breath, trying to gain control.

Caine studied her carefully. "Have you been waiting for me, just outside my room?"

She shook her head. Heat raced through her body, and she could hardly think straight.

He looked amused. "Your pulse is racing. Something wrong?"

She swallowed hard, willing her heart to slow down. Yes, she wanted him—but she didn't want him to realize how badly. It would give him too much control over her. She schooled her face to calm. "My pulse is always fast. It's a medical condition. Anyway, I was just walking past your room."

"So this little encounter is purely a coincidence." He arched a disbelieving eyebrow.

"I'm on my way to see Tammi."

"You've been avoiding me. Until now, when you've come to my room with your heart racing."

Rosalind's forehead crinkled. "Don't be ridiculous."

"You couldn't avoid me forever, whether you wanted to or not. Tomorrow, Ambrose wants us to work on the daywalker spell. You, Miranda, and me."

"Fine."

He cocked his head, owning her body with his gaze—up and down. "I see you're well-prepared for a fight."

She crossed her arms. *How does he know that?* "Can you see through my clothes?"

"I could if I concentrated—and it's a tempting thought—but I don't need to. I can see the outline of the weapons strapped to your thighs." He brushed his fingertips over the hilt of one of her knives.

She glanced down at his hand, her heart beating frantically. Had she never noticed before the strength in those large hands? She could imagine them tracing up the inside of her thigh…

She tightened her jaw; her cheeks warmed. *Get a grip, Rosalind.*

She was pretty sure Cleo was making this harder than it needed to be. "I need the weapons. Despite Ambrose's edict, the vampires aren't fond of me."

"Of course. You were a Hunter."

"That, and Ambrose has told them to bring me food, like they're my servants. I know how they think of humans—we're supposed to be slaves, dressed in lingerie. Some of the vamps apparently think we exist to fulfill every demon desire."

He narrowed his eyes. "Do you view any of them in particular as a threat?"

"I don't think so. They seem well-aware of Ambrose's edict. But they believe my place is in the harem, and they're particularly affronted about the muffins."

"Would you suggest that Ambrose stop sending you food? I do remember how lustfully you attack your meals. I can't imagine you turning them away."

"Let's not be drastic," she said. "Ambrose can keep the food coming, and I'll just keep the weapons strapped to my thighs."

Even as she struggled for control of herself, a new idea began to form in her mind. She wanted Caine. Badly. And maybe there was a way to use that desire to her advantage...

A seed of an idea began to germinate, taking root in her mind. Was it Cleo's thought, or her own?

A wicked smile curled Caine's lips. "Why do I feel like you have a second option in mind?"

Her chest heated. A vision bloomed: Caine's fingertips running up the inside of her thigh as she sat draped over his lap. She wore nothing but lacy, black underwear, and her back arched as he stroked her skin, his fingers moving higher and higher up her leg...

Her heartbeat thundered, so loud she was certain the entire hallway could hear it. And she was sure Caine could see the blush creeping into her cheeks.

Still, that one tempting idea began to bloom in her mind. Let the damn vampires think she was a courtesan—Caine's courtesan. After all, wasn't it an advantage to let your enemies underestimate you? Caine had taught her that.

She couldn't quite decide if it was genius, or if she was driven by Caine's overwhelming beauty. But the more she thought it over, the more it seemed to make sense.

She exhaled slowly, and tried to compose her thoughts. "The other option is that I let them think I'm a courtesan, I suppose. Just to stop them from deciding they need to kill me. Let them think I'm as harmless as any other courtesans—the ones who live by the arsenal of weapons no one bothers to lock up."

His eyes darkened, and heat radiated off his body. Just standing near him was turning her on. Her obvious arousal was embarrassing, and more than that—it was drawing out his incubus instincts.

Cleo's aura stroked her ribs. *Tell him what you want him to do to you—where you want him to touch you.*

Rosalind licked her lips, staring up at Caine. "Maybe they could think I was your courtesan. To play down my real power."

Boxing her in, he pressed his hands to the stone wall on either side of her head. He smelled amazing, and she had the strongest impulse to press her mouth against his neck.

"Is that really what you want?" he asked.

Excitement prickled over her skin, and she took a deep, steadying breath. His sweater was a thin, gray wool, and she wanted to stroke his muscled chest under the fabric. *Where do Cleo's thoughts end and mine begin?* Surely she hadn't been this crazy before Cleo had started taking up real estate in her mind.

She gazed up at his perfect face. What was the point in denying herself? "I think it's a good idea."

Her stomach fluttered. Could he see right through her?

Caine lowered his face to hers. "And what do you want me to do to you?" he whispered.

"You know," she said.

"I want you to say it out loud."

His powerful aura licked at her skin, and heat shot through her. Already, her back was arching. *Sweet heavenly gods, I'm in trouble.*

29

"Just kiss me, in front of the vampires." She swallowed hard, trying to think clearly. "It's only for their benefit, of course."

He leaned in closer, his breath warming the side of her face. "I see. We need the vampires."

His magic curled from his body, reaching down the corridor in silver tendrils. Within seconds, the hallway doors creaked open. Vampires began creeping into the hall, slipping through the shadows like ink through water.

Dozens of gleaming eyes locked onto Rosalind.

"We're not alone now," Caine whispered into her ear.

Her pulse was racing out of control, and she tried to slow her breathing. Her skin grew hot. She was getting dangerously turned on, and she had the mortifying feeling that Caine was enjoying his control over her.

He leaned in, skimming his teeth over her throat. At the contact, her thoughts became muddled. All she could process was that her legs seemed to be opening against her will. Slowly, he trailed kisses up her neck, until he stared into her eyes once more. There was a certain ferocity in his gaze, and she was sure he was holding back.

He ran his thumb over her lower lip. "Tell me. You want me to kiss you properly?"

Cleo's aura simmered. *Why are you denying yourself what you want? You'll be dead someday. Get it while you can.*

Oddly enough, the dead mage's words made a strange amount of sense. "Yes," she said simply.

His eyes slowly slide slid over her body, as if he were was undressing her with his eyes.

Then, he traced his fingertips down her arms and gripped her wrists. He raised them above her head, pinning them to the wall. Helplessly, she gazed up at his cold gray eyes, completely mesmerized. Her blood roared through her veins.

So this is what it feels like to be in the thrall of an incubus.

Caine leaned down, pressing his warm lips to hers. His kiss grew hungry, his lips parting, and a low growl rose from deep in his chest. As he kissed her, his grip tightened on her wrists, as if he was losing a little of that control.

His muscled body pressed against hers, and she opened her mouth to him. His tongue brushed against hers, and fire shot through her belly.

As his mouth claimed hers, she lost all sense of time and space, no longer sure where her body ended and his began, only that she wanted more of him.

Slowly, he ran his hands down her arms. His hands skimmed lower over her body, until he was grabbing her ass and, pulling her closer into him.

She needed more of him, didn't even care that they were standing before a crowd of vampires.

Just when she thought she could no longer remember how to speak, he pulled away, with a nip at her lower lip. Her legs turned to liquid.

Caine took a deep breath, his eyes now black.

Rosalind wanted to strip off her dress right there and throw him to the floor. *Gods, I need him now.*

He stared into her eyes. Soft as a feather, his fingertips skimmed up her body again, sending shivers through her. The gentleness of his touch was pure torture. She'd seen him fight before—brutally, viciously—and she'd never have expected such a predatory creature to be capable of such a soft touch.

She gasped as he traced his hand higher, grazing her breast over her silk dress. Her breath hitched in her throat.

This was a strange sort of agony. She wanted him now, wanted to wrap her legs around his hips, and yet he moved so painfully slowly, like he had all the time in the world.

31

Gently, he trailed his thumb just over her hardened nipple. The silk strap of her dress slid down her shoulder, and he leaned in again, kissing her neck. A dizzying warmth surged in her as he grazed his teeth along her throat.

A low moan escaped her throat, and she felt his muscles tense in response, like he was struggling to keep control.

She needed the hardness of his body pressing against her. She was ready to beg him to run his tongue all over her body.

She wrapped her arms around his neck, opening her eyes. Over Caine's shoulder, her gaze landed on Esmerelda. The vampire eyed Rosalind with a satisfied smirk.

Suddenly, Rosalind's stomach tightened, and her blood cooled instantly.

Another body for the whore pit.

The phrase rang in her mind, and Rosalind's cheeks burned. *Gods below.* At the sight of Esmerelda, her blood cooled instantly.

As Caine raised his face for another kiss, she forced herself to tilt her head away. She desperately wanted his mouth on hers again, but one more look at the redhead dampened her excitement.

She'd needed them to underestimate her, but she wasn't sure she wanted to subject herself to a full blown display of humiliation in front of Esmerelda.

"I should go," she managed.

A tendril of hair stuck to her damp cheek, and Caine brushed it away.

His breath warmed the shell of her ear. "If you don't want them to think you've got above your station, you need to let me end our encounter. Don't take this personally." He brushed his thumb over her collarbone again, then whispering, "Don't take this personally."

Casually, he released his grip on her, stepping away. With a completely composed expression, he sighed. "On second thought, I'm not in the mood."

Rosalind could feel herself turn red, and she pulled up her dress. The vampires stared at her, eyes wide. Surely her heart was beating loud enough to entice all of them. Suddenly, she had a deep desire to crawl back into the shadows and hide.

And there was Caine, cooly strutting away, completely unruffled. Like he did this all the time.

And, realistically? He probably did.

Esmerelda snickered behind her hand, and Rosalind crossed her arms in front of her chest. A large blond male leered at her hungrily, licking his lips.

Time to go, she thought.

Just as Rosalind took a step to leave, Caine pivoted, glaring at the vampires. "You do realize she belongs to me. I might not be using her now, but she is mine alone. Only I may touch her. Is that clear?"

Rosalind's head was spinning, and she could hardly string a coherent thought together.

As she hurried away from the vampires, she stared at the floor, ignoring Esmerelda's victorious smirk. *Nothing more than tits and ass,* she'd said. *I hope you can lay off now, Ginger Vamp.*

She shivered as she stalked down the hall, away from the hungry eyes of the vampires. *Well, that's not how I expected my night to go.*

Could she blame Cleo for that little episode? If she didn't find a way to get control of Cleo's influence, her second soul would drag her into a whole lot of trouble. The woman clearly had no boundaries.

5

Outside Tammi's door, Rosalind took a deep breath, trying to forget the feel of Caine's fingertips skimming over her skin. When her pulse had slowed to a nearly-normal rate, she knocked on the door.

Her muscles tensed as she waited for a a few moments. *How do you ask your best friend about her blood hunger?* This was definitely a situation she'd never had to handle before.

She knocked again, a little louder. After a few more moments, the door swung open. Tammi's eyes were wide, blazing like stars. Her long silver hair tumbled over a thin black dress. Her skin was milky white.

"What?" she asked irritably.

Nothing, just...do you want to drink my blood? Rosalind cleared her throat. "You ran off quickly at the picnic, so I just wanted to see how you were doing."

"I'm not in the mood to be around other people." Tammi crossed to a small dressing table, and sat on a stool in front of it. She narrowed her eyes at her own reflection, her entire body tense.

Rosalind stepped inside, glancing around the room. Steel-gray fabric draped over the bed, and candles flickered from a chandelier. The dressing table stood against the stone wall, complete with a mirror. Tammi sat in front of it, gazing at her own reflection. She picked up a hairbrush and began brushing her tresses. "I'm not the same anymore," she said with a low growl.

Rosalind sat at the edge of Tammi's bed, her fingers curling around a blanket. "Not the same how?"

"Not the same," Tammi snarled. "Hungry."

Rosalind's mouth went dry. "Maybe I should go—"

Tammi's face contorted with rage, and she flung her hairbrush at the looking glass. She whirled, lunging for Rosalind. In the next moment, her teeth were on Rosalind's throat.

Without thinking, Rosalind flung her friend off, then punched her in the jaw.

Tammi stumbled back, a shocked look on her face. Rosalind stood, holding out her hands to the side. *Easy, girl.* Tentatively, she took a few steps back toward the door. She had plenty of sharp demon-hunting weapons, but she didn't want to use them on Tammi—nor did she particularly want her throat ripped out this evening. "I don't want to hurt you, Tammi. I'm just going to walk out of the room."

Apparently no longer capable of human speech, Tammi growled. Her sharp teeth glinted in the candlelight.

Rosalind took another step back. *Easy does it. Nearly at the door.* If she made any sudden movements, those pointed teeth would end up buried somewhere in her flesh.

Tammi snarled, and the sound rumbled through Rosalind's gut. *Not really Tammi anymore.* She took another step back, and spoke in her most soothing voice. "I'll just leave you to... brush your hair and stare in the mirror. Everything is fine."

She fumbled behind her for the doorknob until her fingers touched the silver. *Got it.* She turned the knob and yanked open the door. *Freedom!*

But just as she stepped into the hall, Tammi lunged again, knocking her to the stone floor.

"Stop it!" Rosalind lifted her hips, grabbing Tammi by the hair to pull her off. She rolled on top of her friend, pinning her arms to the floor. Tammi roared, baring her teeth.

"I said stop it!" Rosalind yelled. "Get a hold of yourself, woman!"

Tammi blinked, as if suddenly awaking. Slowly, her fingers unclenched from Rosalind's hair.

Footsteps echoed off the ceiling, and Rosalind looked up. Darren was walking toward her, flanked by two blond male vampires. The blonds looked distinctly like medieval Danes, with braided beards. They strode on either side of him, carrying spears.

"I thought I heard a kerfuffle." Darren's voice rang off the stone ceiling. "Is it just me, or was this human supposed to remain unharmed, under orders from Ambrose?"

"Not just you, sir," one of the Danes said. "She's one of the mages."

Rosalind released her friend's wrists, and Tammi rose slowly. Rosalind saw only fear on Tammi's pale features now.

"It's okay," Rosalind said. "Everything is under control." She stood, smoothing out her gray dress.

Darren stepped closer. "What's wrong with your ker friend? And what on earth is she doing here? I thought we killed all the keres."

Tammi crossed her arms. "I'm not a real ker. I was human, but some dickhead turned me into a ker. And now I want…" She ran her tongue over her teeth. "I have different cravings."

"Of course," Darren said. "Blood hunger?"

"Do keres drink blood?" Rosalind asked.

"Sometimes." Darren sniffed, wiping the back of his hand under his nose. "They don't require it. But this one isn't really a ker, is she? She's a new creature. A human given a new life as a demon."

Tammi's face fell. "Just like a vampire."

Darren looked at her. "If I'm not allowed to hurt the human whore, then you certainly aren't. What are we going to do with you?"

Rosalind glared at him. "She's new to this. She doesn't know how to handle it, but she'll get things under control."

Darren steepled his fingers, looking to the ceiling while he considered the situation. "Novice demons like Tammi are unpredictable and volatile. They must be trained. There's a place for them—the Abzu. I'm sending her to speak to Ambrose, but I imagine he'll send her on to the Abzu."

Rosalind frowned. "How long would she have to stay there?"

"As long as it takes for her to gain control of her impulses. There's a cleansing ritual, some training. A novice must prove herself before she is released. Hard to know how long that will take." He sniffed again. The cocaine seemed to have irritated his nose. "Not everyone has the self restraint that I do."

Tammi crossed her arms. "Will I get blood there?"

"Yes."

She ran her fingertips down her chest, still eyeing Rosalind hungrily. "When do I go?"

Darren nodded at the two Danes. "Aldrich and Rodney will take her to Ambrose."

Without so much as a final glance goodbye, Tammi stalked down the hall, barefoot. Aldrich and Rodney hurried to flank her.

Darren's gaze turned to Rosalind, slowly taking in her body. He stepped closer, his gaze lingering on a tear in the shoulder of her gown. "I've heard that Caine has claimed you as his concubine, and no vampires may enjoy your womanly delights."

Rosalind's stomach turned. *Gross.*

She took a step to move around him, but he blocked her path. "I'm not finished speaking to you." He seemed transfixed by the torn dress, and he ran a long, pointed tongue over his lips. "Have you noticed that the most beautiful things are also the most fragile? How tempting it is to touch that which breaks easily."

Okay... "Right. I actually have to go somewhere else now."

Darren stared down at her. "Aren't you supposed to be working on a daywalking spell? I thought that was your whole purpose here."

"You're one of Ambrose's trusted advisors, aren't you? I'm sure he's filled you in."

Darren tapped a long finger against his mouth. "He's been promising us that spell for a while, and yet I haven't seen anything materialize."

"Maybe I don't like the idea of demons like you having more power than you already have."

She'd read about what could happen when humans meddled in nature. When wolves hunted caribou, they culled the weak. If humans tried to protect the caribou by shooting the wolves, it backfired. Diseases spread and took out entire herds. Any major changes to one species could mean devastation to another. Nature had its own balance.

"What are you talking about?" he scoffed. "We're *meant* to dominate humans. That is nature's way."

"Maybe vampires are meant to have limitations, to keep things in some sort of balance so they don't completely destroy humanity."

"Fine." Darren's pupils flashed with red. "But it won't be *all* vampires. Just those here."

Her thoughts whirled. She really *didn't* want to give vamps like Darren and Esmerelda more power over humans.

On the other hand— maybe daywalking vampires could act as a counterbalance to Drew's power. Without a powerful enemy of his own, Drew could turn half the human race into blood-drinking demons like Tammi. And the other half he'd probably sacrifice in the Brotherhood's fires, just to keep the Hunters happy.

The unholy alliance of witch and witch-hunter.

She shrugged. "Perhaps it's a *lesser of two evils* situation, but you're not doing the vampires a great PR service by blocking my path right now."

Darren cocked his head. "Lesser of two evils, hmm? And is that how you feel about Caine?"

Now he had her attention. "What are you talking about?"

"He's not the only powerful demon in Lilinor who wants your nubile flesh. I'm sure you can see Ambrose wants you, too. He sends you food; Caine does not. Yet you've chosen Caine. A hunter choosing an incubus. Is he merely the lesser of two evils, or have you been lured in with his incubus charms, like so many before you?"

Rosalind frowned. "Ambrose wants me?"

"Don't think you're special. Demons are drawn to humans like moths to a flame."

Ambrose... Cleo's words screamed in her skull. *I want him to burn, yet I remember the feel of his bare skin against mine.* An image burned in Rosalind's mind: Ambrose's hands cupping Cleo's pale breasts, leaning in and kissing her neck, his mouth hot on her skin. A wave of pleasure rushed through her body, and she nearly groaned.

"Not now, Cleo," she snapped.

Darren's eyes widened, as if Rosalind was suddenly the scary one. "Cleo?"

"Never mind."

"I suppose you've amused me for long enough. But if you're here to create daywalkers, do it fast. Whether or not Ambrose desires your flesh, he will only indulge you for so long." He turned, stalking off past her.

Cleo's aura roiled in her mind. *He brought me a wreath of blackthorn. He kissed my throat, his hands clutching my body—*

"Yeah, I get it, Cleo!" Rosalind's voice echoed off the ceiling.

Where was that wreath Miranda had made for her? That thing had actually subdued Cleo's ranting.

He brought me the sweetest wine—

Rosalind turned back to Tammi's room and pushed open the door. She snatched the wreath from the floor and frantically pulled it onto her head, sighing as Cleo's voice faded in her skull.

6

In the apple orchard, the sound of violins drifted on the evening wind. The air hung thick with blossoms. I pulled open my dress, letting the spring air kiss my bare skin, waiting for him to come to me...

But the air chilled, and a storm wind rushed over my body.

Now the air fills with the smell of gangrenous flesh and rotting wood. An intruder lurks in here.

Wake, Rosalind. Wake and see it.

Rosalind's eyes snapped open. Tangled in her sheets, she slept in her thin silk nightgown next to her sister. Milky daylight streamed through the edge of the closed curtain.

Something wasn't right. The room smelled terrible, and when her eyes adjusted her heart thundered against her ribs.

Daylight. There is daylight in Lilinor.

That alone was very wrong. The sun didn't shine in the City of Night. She sat upright, her panicked gaze landing on Miranda.

But Miranda wasn't alone.

Crouching on her sister's chest was a gaunt figure. White light gleamed off his bald head, the color of unbaked bread. The creature had no mouth or ears—just two slits for a nose, and gaping black eyeholes. He smelled like the bottom of a grave.

Before she could reach for him, the creature wafted away like black smoke on the wind—so quickly that Rosalind had to wonder if it had just been the remnants of a dream.

She glanced down at her pillow. She'd been sleeping on her half-crumpled wildflower wreath, while Miranda's crown still rested on her head. Rosalind rubbed her eyes, trying to clear the fog of sleep from her mind. *What was that thing?*

Her gaze trailed over Miranda's throat; at the sight of an iron necklace, Rosalind's adrenalin surged. It looked like the charmed necklaces Drew used to control people. Around the metal chain, colored magic swirled into the air—gold, silver, blue...

Rosalind ripped the thing from Miranda's throat, examining it. The exact same type of thin iron chain the keres had been wearing in Maremount—a collar of sorts. And Drew's strange magic was all over the damn thing. He couldn't be in Lilinor, could he? Either way, he'd be able to control anyone wearing one of the chains.

Miranda's eyes opened, and she sat up. "What's going on?"

Rosalind shook her head, still gaping at the necklace. Had the creatures gone after anyone else, or just Miranda and Rosalind?

Whatever the hell was going on, there had clearly been some sort of breach of Lilinor's defenses. Maybe Drew's strange magic allowed him to open portals without permission.

"What's happening?" Miranda asked, still blinking.

"There's daylight in Lilinor." Rosalind threw off her bedcovers. "And Drew might have seized control. I need to warn people."

Rosalind rushed for the door. She flung it open, then raced through the corridor, her heart thrumming. Where *was* Ambrose? Sometimes he slept in the White Tower, but not always.

But she knew exactly where to find Caine—one floor up, next to the painting of Lord Byron.

She pushed through another door into the stairwell, her pulse racing. Her feet pounded the stairs as she raced up. This had to be Drew's doing. No one else could use that type of magic—apart from Erish, but she was locked safely in the dungeon. Wasn't she?

Rosalind pushed through the door at the top of the stairwell. The sunlight streaming through the windows looked so *wrong* here. How many chains had the demons distributed?

Rosalind opened a door to one of the rooms. There, sprawled over a bed, lay Esmerelda. An iron chain hung around her neck. She rushed to the next door, turning the knob. A muscular, blond vampire lay in the middle of the stone floor. Another iron chain.

Rosalind's throat went dry. The demons could have hit the whole city.

She turned, sprinting for Caine's room. Her bare feet pounded over the stone floor, and she screeched to a halt at the painting of Lord Byron. Frantically, she flung open the door to Caine's room.

In the center of a silver bed, Caine lay wrapped in his bedsheets, his chest bare. His thick black lashes rested against his cheeks. At the sight of his beauty, her heart skipped a beat. For just a moment, she forgot why she'd come, letting her eyes linger over the tattoos that snaked over his muscled chest. The moon and stars, the strange thin dagger on her forearm... Together, the symbols were like a map of his life—one she couldn't quite read.

She blinked to clear her mind, and her gaze moved up his body...to the iron necklace on his throat. Tendrils of magic—blue, gold, and silver—wafted off the iron.

Drew was here, and every demon in Lilinor might be mind-controlled by him.

She rushed to Caine's bed, then jumped up next to him to rip the necklace from his throat.

With a growl, Caine's eyes snapped open. The next thing she knew, he'd flipped her onto her back. The back of her head landed on his pillow, and he gripped her hair with one hand while the other pinned her own hands over her head.

How had he managed that so quickly, without hurting her?

Her pulse raced as his hard body pressed against hers. Through the thin silk of her nightgown, she could feel his warm skin, his powerful body. *So that's what happens when you wake up an incubus from a deep sleep.*

He inhaled deeply and laced his fingers with hers.. "Rosalind. You're not wearing your ring. Isn't that dangerous if Cleo takes over your mind?" He leaned in close, his breath warming her neck. "But maybe now isn't the time for me to ask questions like that."

"I don't wear the ring anymore," she whispered. "It doesn't work."

His leg pressed between hers, and heat flooded her body. *Focus, Rosalind.* She swallowed hard, trying to clear her mind. "I came here to warn you. There's been a breach of Lilinor's defenses—some creatures that can disappear like smoke. They've clamped iron chains on everyone. I just ripped yours off. And the city is flooded with daylight."

He blinked hard, as if trying to clear his mind, and released his grip on her. He sat up, glancing at the window. "Daylight." He raked his hand through his hair. "Seven hells."

"Daylight, and mind-control." She held up the necklace. "These are the same chains Drew used on Tammi and Miranda in Maremount. They're charmed with his magic. He'll be able to control anyone wearing one."

Caine jumped from his bed in a blur of silver, suddenly completely alert. "We need to get to Ambrose."

"Where does he sleep?"

"That's anyone's guess. Sometimes in the Ishtaritu hall, sometimes in..." Caine's golden skin paled, and a look of complete horror crossed his face. "The White Tower."

Suddenly, Rosalind understood. *Ambrose's open-air lair.* Ambrose often slept there, beneath the stars. If the creatures had slapped a collar on him, he'd be burning to death in his bedsheets right now—a charred body in the blazing sun.

"Come with me." Caine held out his hand, and she stepped closer to him, folding into his embrace.

He began chanting the teleportation spell, and she joined in, feeling his electric aura rush over her skin.

When she opened her eyes, they stood in Ambrose's tower room. Sunlight blazed between the open vaults, but not a single smudge of ash stained Ambrose's sheets. Relief washed over her, and she heard a sigh slide from Caine.

"Thank the gods. He's not here. But I want to find him now. As lord, he'll be the primary target for the demons."

Rosalind grabbed his arm. "Maybe we can use magic."

"For what?"

"Hang on." She crossed to one of the tall, peaked windows, gazing out at Ninlil Castle. The cobblestone courtyard below was ringed with rickety stone towers; they pierced the blue skies, each crowned with a sharp spire. A fountain stood in the center of the courtyard.

From here, Caine and Rosalind had a view of all the living quarters, and she would be able to direct the spell into each of the rooms. "I used a spell in Maremount," she said, "to free the prisoners and take their necklaces off. We can do the same here—a spell for bending iron. We'll need to work together, to make it as strong as possible. It'll save us hunting around the whole fortress for Ambrose."

He shook his head. "No. Ambrose is the priority. If we use a spell—"

The opening of courtyard doors interrupted him, and Rosalind's heart skipped a beat. From each of the doors, vampires walked into the sunlight, moving as silently as wraiths. Smoke rose from their skin.

"The iron spell," Caine said. "Now!"

Her heart hammering, Rosalind began chanting the spell for warping iron. Caine joined in with her, their magic curling together in swirls of silver and green.

Is it too late? Before they could get to the end of the spell, flames sparked around the vampires' bodies. And yet they still moved steadily forward like blazing viking funeral boats.

Caine stopped chanting and raised his hands to the skies. His silver aura whipped from his body, streaming to the heavens.

What is he doing? Whatever it was, Rosalind needed to stay focused until she could get the damn necklaces off the vamps. Once freed, they could plunge into the fountain to douse the flames.

Her heart clenched as the smell of burning flesh reached her nose, yet she kept chanting.

Even as the vampires burned, an eerie silence enshrouded the courtyard. Not a single voice cut the quiet. The vampires simply walked onward into the light, pouring from the doors, skin blazing in the hot sun. Black plumes of smoke curled into the air.

Rosalind could feel Cleo's dark delight. She *liked* this.

Watch the little vermin burn... Cleo whispered.

Rosalind felt sick. *Crazy twat.*

If she wanted this to work, she'd have to block out the chaos on her mind, the warring emotions. With all the mental focus she could muster, she directed Cleo's vernal aura around the iron collars. At last, the metal necklaces twisted from the vamps necks, and fell to the cobblestones with a loud clang.

And that was when the screaming began.

Agonized shrieks ripped through the air, and the vampires staggered, limbs blazing. A few dove for the fountain, but most stumbled blindly, in too much pain to save themselves.

By her side, Caine's aura intensified, rippling over Rosalind's skin in a staggering burst of power. Rosalind glanced at the sky; somehow, Caine's magic was forcing the sun to set. The setting sun stained the sky a deep, blood red, but rays of sun still washed the city in gold.

I can help him. Rosalind closed her eyes. With Cleo's help, she launched into a spell for Mishett-Ash, the god of storms.

Her stomach flipped at the power of the magic whirling around her body. An icy aura froze her skin. With trembling legs, she chanted louder, calling on the god to bring his storm winds to Lilinor. Another aura rushed through the air, briny and wet.

Miranda. Somewhere in the fortress, Rosalind's twin was working her magic, too.

The sun sank lower, dipping just behind one of Ninlil's spires, and still, rays of sunlight streamed around it.

Rosalind closed her eyes, repeating the Angelic words to lure a storm into the skies. As she chanted, thunder rumbled over the horizon, and the hair on the back of her neck stood on end. Fat drops of rain fell on her skin, drenching her hair and clothes. The storm's power rolled through her body.

From the courtyard below, the screams quieted.

Softly, Caine touched Rosalind's arm, and she opened her eyes. All around her, Cleo's aura swirled in the air, mingling with Caine's.

Rosalind's entire body shook, and her eyes rose to the sky.

49

Not only had she called a storm over the city, but Caine had somehow turned the daylight to night. The sky over Lilinor was pure midnight black. Lightning cracked in the sky, casting pale light over the sodden piles of gray ash littering the stony courtyard.

Hundreds of vampires had wandered out to their deaths in just a few short minutes.

Across the fortress, shouts rang through the halls. At least they'd saved most of the city.

Still, with all the carnage below, Rosalind's knees had gone weak. She turned, leaning against the wall, and let herself slide down the cold stone.

From behind her, Caine spoke in a low growl. "You saw Drew's magic on the necklaces?"

"Yes. It's either him or Erish."

"I'm going to stab them to death with their own ribs."

"Did you see Ambrose out there?"

He shook his head. "No. He's safe for now. But I'm going to find him."

"How did the creatures get in here?" Rosalind asked. "And how did they get from room to room so fast?"

"Drew must have found our portal. And somehow, Nyxobas let him open it." He frowned. "What did the creatures look like?"

Rosalind shuddered. "The one I saw was missing a mouth and ears. Its flesh was gray, like a corpse. And it smelled like a grave."

"Alu demons," Caine muttered. "They belong to Nyxobas. They can travel on the wind, and disappear at will like smoke. They're extremely rare."

Rosalind's mouth went dry. "Maybe they're not demons. Maybe they were human until Drew turned them." She rose, unsteady on her feet. "And he's probably still in the city. Lurking in the shadows, planning his next move. We need to find him."

"Not you. You're too valuable, and I need your magic to keep the sun out of our city. If Drew made the sun rise once in Lilinor, I'm sure he can do it again." He glanced up at the dark sky. "I need you and your sister to draw on your magic to keep the sun down. Under the cover of darkness, the entire vampire army can operate swiftly and hunt for Drew."

"Fine." Dizzy, she leaned against the wall, trying to focus. "But I don't understand. I didn't hear you chant a spell for the night. You just raised your hands up and magic burst out of your body."

"It's a demigod privilege. Gods-magic. You won't be able to do the same. Ask Cleo for a spell."

Cleo's aura whipped around Rosalind's head, throwing her off balance. Rosalind rested her head in her hands. *He brought me a wreath of blackthorn...*

Caine gently grabbed her elbow. "You look like you're about to collapse. After we get Drew and his demons out of here, we need to heal your mind. With powerful magic like we're using, Cleo will take over."

Rosalind looked at his face, so close to hers, and Cleo whispered, *A beautiful man draws you into his spell like a moth to a flame.*

Rosalind stared into his eyes. "I know."

7

With Cleo's whispers ringing in her skull, Rosalind sprinted through the halls, her bare feet pounding the cold flagstones. She thundered down the stairs, pushing through the door into her own hall.

Miranda stood outside the bedroom door, still in her nightgown. "Rosalind!" Her face had gone pale. "I tried to stop it! I tried to help you call a storm!"

"I know!" Rosalind hurried to her sister. "We need to work together. I need you to chant with me." She pushed open the door into their room and, as soon as Miranda was inside, bolted the door behind them.

It's not enough, Cleo whispered. *If Drew wants to kill you, he'll find a way.*

Rosalind's hands shook, and she gripped her hair to steady them.

No way to be safe, Cleo snarled.

"Rosalind!" Miranda shouted. "Focus! What spell do we need to do?"

Seal the door, Rosalind, Cleo whispered. *He'll come after you. He'll find you.*

Shaking, Rosalind turned to the door and raised her hands, and she let Cleo whisper a spell through her lips. *"Ezebu, utuk xul daltu."*

The green aura surged around the room, sealing the door, and Rosalind let out a slow breath.

Miranda touched her arm. "What spell do you need my help for?"

"We need to make sure the sun doesn't rise again," Rosalind said, crossing to the window. Total darkness still covered the city. "Our second souls will know the spell, according to Caine. And we have to appeal to Nyxobas."

Shouts pierced the air. Rosalind flattened her palms against the window, listening to the rain hammer the cobblestones below. Then silver, gold, and blue magic unfurled into the air, lighting up the courtyard.

Drew. He was still here, still weaving his sadistic spells.

Below, more vampires stumbled into the courtyard, necklaces glinting in the light of the magic.

Rosalind's heart thudded, and her gaze flicked to the sky. Through a break in the storm clouds, the sky had brightened to a deep indigo.

He's raising the sun once more.

Rosalind's breath caught in her throat. "The sun's coming back. Chant with me. Help me appeal to Nyxobas."

Miranda slid her hand into her twin's, and together they launched into a spell for night.

Margidda Nyxobas, ed Nanna...

Their green and blue auras curled through the window, spiraling up to the brightening sky. As they chanted, Miranda's watery aura washed over Rosalind's skin, soothing her muscles. Using magic with her own twin felt powerful, and strength coursed through her body.

Sisters. Together. Like we were meant to be.

Rosalind closed her eyes, entreating Nyxobas to hide the sun once more. As she chanted, an image rose in her mind: a man with a ivory skin, black hair and eyes like starlight.

Nyxobas.

His powerful aura surrounded her. She could almost lose herself in the darkness, if she let herself. She could almost fall into the abyss...

Her body trembled at the power of the magic's spell, and she forced her eyes open again. The sun had set once more, the sky darkening to a deep, midnight blue. She glanced at the courtyard again—at the vampires still stumbling through the doors, dazed—and felt as dazed as they looked. The powerful magic had completely drained her body, and her knees nearly gave way. She wasn't sure she'd be able to conduct another spell if she wanted to.

"Look." Miranda pointed out the window at a human man, clad in tight black clothes. "A Hunter."

Behind the man, more humans poured from the doors, weapons drawn. The vampires stood there—dazed, completely defenseless.

Rosalind swayed, her body shaking. Even through her fog of exhaustion, one thing rang clear in her mind. "They're going to slaughter them," she whispered.

As Rosalind stared, unsteady on her feet, a dark-haired Hunter stalked over to a female vamp wearing only a thin red nightgown, and grabbed hold of her long auburn hair.

"We need to do something," Miranda said.

Before Rosalind could launch into another spell, one of the courtyard doors exploded with silver magic. In a blur of silvered light, Caine sped over to the Hunter's side. His black eyes burned with an animal ferocity. The ghost of dark wings rose from his shoulders.

Rosalind's heart thudded at the sight of him. This was Caine, without the mask of humanity. And he was terrifying.

It took him less than a heartbeat to grip the Hunter's throat. Another beat for him to rip the human's head from his body, blood spraying in a crimson arc. Caine whirled, his hands finding their way to another Hunter's neck.

"Or maybe we don't," she murmured. Where Caine was, Ambrose was sure to follow. Caine wouldn't be here if he hadn't already saved the vampire lord.

"Caine against a few dozen Hunters," Miranda said. "My money is on the incubus."

Sure enough, Ambrose was next through the shattered door, black magic curling from his body.

Out in the courtyard, the vampire lord tilted back his head, and roared. The sound rumbled through Rosalind's bones, imbuing her with primordial terror and a desperate need to flee.

Still, she stayed rooted to the spot, watching the action unfold.

A female Hunter threw a stake at Ambrose, and he caught it deftly, hurling it back at her. It struck its mark right in the woman's chest, and she fell to the ground.

"And now we just watch the slaughter," Miranda said.

Rosalind watched, her jaw open, as Caine and Ambrose ripped through the Hunters, tearing out hearts, cutting off heads. Blurs of silver and black, breathtaking in their graceful savagery, leaving crumpled corpses in their wakes.

Ruthless predators, with the speed of gods, they seemed to have the courtyard entirely under control. Caine tore out the heart of the last remaining Hunter, tossing it on the ground.

Then—from nowhere—multi-colored magic burst around

Ambrose. In the next moment, his body was gone.

Caine paused, still gripping the heart. Blood dripped down his arm, and he stared at the place where his king had stood.

Rosalind's heart skipped a beat. *Drew found a way to get to Ambrose after all.*

The shadows behind Caine's shoulders thickened into powerful, black-feathered wings. Caine tossed the heart to the ground, then beat the air with his wings, lifting into the sky.

Rosalind's heart jumped into her throat. "What the hell just happened?"

"Drew just stole our king," Miranda said through clenched teeth. "And Caine is going to find him."

As Caine took flight, Rosalind's gaze flicked back to the vamps. They were moving among the Hunters now, circling each other like feral creatures. Tendrils of blue, silver, and green magic curled from their necklaces.

Darren prowled around another vampire—a petite brunette, her fangs bared. With a loud roar, Darren pounced, leaping onto the woman and ripping into her neck.

Rosalind's stomach churned. "Drew is using the vampire army against itself."

Where is Aurora? Frantically, Rosalind scanned the courtyard, and caught a glimpse of her friend stumbling over the grass in a singed nectarine-colored dress.

Exhausted or not, if Rosalind didn't act now, Aurora could be killed by another vamp any moment. Her heart hammered. She'd have to use her last reserves of magic on another rendition of the iron spell. "We can use the iron-bending spell again," she told Miranda. "Will you help me?"

"Of course. Are you sure you're up for it? You look completely exhausted."

Rosalind gripped the window sill harder, steadying herself. "We don't have a choice."

"How are we supposed to help all of them?"

"I can direct the magic to the right places." She glanced at her sister. "Can you start the spell?"

Miranda launched into Angelic, her briny aura trickling over Rosalind's skin. Rosalind joined in, watching as their magic curled into the courtyard. The auras curled together in perfect whorls of blue and green, and she was struck once again by how *right* it felt to work together with her twin. Like being home.

She focused on channeling the magic around the vampire's necks, starting with Aurora. The metal around her friend's neck began to twist, and—

A thundering boom interrupted her thoughts, and she whirled.

Standing in her doorway, with magic bursting from his body, was Drew.

Her betrothed.

The world seemed to fall out from under her feet. In a rush of power, his aura rushed over her skin, disorienting her with a flood of sensations: soft moss and the smell of leaves, gravel, wind and water trickling over her body. With all this powerful magic at his fingertips, he'd be nearly impossible to fight.

Not to mention that she had nothing left in her system.

But I have to try.

He was here to slaughter her friends, and he wanted to own her like property—to use her for breeding his terrible, incestuous Atherton progeny. She'd do anything she could to keep him away from her.

"My dear betrothed," he cooed.

Rosalind's adrenalin surged, and she scanned the room for the nearest weapon. Her gaze landed on the silver pike resting near her bed. She hurtled across the floor to the weapon, snatching it from the ground. Heart pounding, she whirled.

Drew was right behind her. She swung for his head, hoping to bash in his skull.

Without breaking a sweat, he lifted a hand, catching the pike in his grip.

Her stomach flipped. *Not good. He has some kind of superhuman strength.*

With a placid expression, Drew twisted the pike, knocking her backward onto the bed. In the next heartbeat, he was on top of her, pressing his powerful fingers around her neck.

He squeezed. She kicked him in the groin, and he grunted. Still, his fingers tightened, crushing her throat.

She shot a panicked glance at Miranda, who threw a knife at Drew. The throw should have buried the blade in his skull, but Drew ducked in blur of whirling auras. The knife plunged into the wall.

Rosalind kicked him in the stomach, and he grimaced, locking his gaze on her. His fingers clenched harder around her throat.

He stared at her, eyes flashing with licks of red, green, and silver fire. "You haven't even seen the real magic yet. Do you want to feel it? Inside you?"

"Get off of her!" Miranda threw a second knife, but Drew's free hand whipped into the air, snatching it. He pressed the blade to Rosalind's throat, then looked up. "If you take another step closer, Miranda, I'll slit your sister's throat. If you utter one syllable of Angelic, I'll slice through to her spine before you can draw another breath. It's a better punishment than you both deserve, after your betrayal."

Rosalind's breath left her lungs. "What do you want, Drew?" she choked out.

He stared down at her, arching an eyebrow. "You. Under my control. And now, I'll show you both the real magic. You'll be ever so impressed." Still pushing the blade against her throat, he slid his hand down the front of her chest, pressing it against her stomach. His fingers grew cold as ice, and a chill spread through her. Glacial cold filled her ribs, freezing her skin, icing the inside of her mind.

Dread tightened her heart. Her body was no longer her own.

Drew dragged the knife lower, pointing the tip just over her heart. "Stand," he said to Rosalind. His voice seemed to come from the inside of her own mind, and her skull filled with icy eddies of his magic.

Slowly, he backed away, still pointing the knife at her chest. Against her will, she felt herself stand. She stared right at him. Somewhere, deep under the icy chill of his magic, her mind churned with horror.

How is he doing this—a type of magic only possessed by demons?

He hadn't put a collar around her throat—yet he could control her.

"What are you doing?" Miranda shouted.

Drew stroked Rosalind's hair. "You keep quiet. or I'll force her to walk right into my knife." He leaned closer, whispering into Rosalind's ear. "Turn around."

His voice reverberated from the base of her brain. A part of her mind screamed in outrage, but her body followed his command, his frigid magic snaking around her skull.

Drew stepped closer, sliding his arm around her waist and pulling her in tighter against his body. His fingers traced up and down her side, running over her ribs. With his other hand, he pressed the blade against her throat, nicking her skin.

"You're probably hoping that monster you're fucking will come to save you," he purred. "He won't. I've sent the alu demons after Ambrose. Right now, your incubus is protecting his king. He's not here, protecting you. Now you know where his priorities lie. I told you before, and I'm telling you now: he's using you. You're his trophy. After he executed your parents like common criminals, defiling their daughter is the final nail in the coffin of Atherton's respectability. Surely even you can see that."

Miranda shouted again. "Let her go!"

"Keep your voice down, little girl," Drew snarled, "or we'll find out what a traitor looks like on the inside. Are you wondering how I've controlled her mind? After all, I'm not a demon. And she's not wearing a necklace."

Rosalind swallowed hard, finding that her mouth couldn't form words, but even if she wanted to, she couldn't for the life of her think of what she'd want to say. Her own thoughts were buried under the icy rush of his magic.

"Take the knife from me," Drew said. "Hold it against your own throat."

Tendrils of Drew's colored magic clouded inside her head like frozen mist. She couldn't remember what she was supposed to be doing, only that she wanted to take the knife from him.

I'm supposed to lift the knife. Trembling, her hand rose and grasped the hilt. Drew released the weapon, and she felt herself pressing the blade to her own jugular.

Still gripping her waist, Drew stroked the back of her neck. "It's that little scar I gave you," he murmured. "A reminder that you belong to Azezeyl, the One who is All. It lets me control you. And it will never leave your flesh, not as long as you live."

As soon as the words were out of his mouth, the scar on her stomach began to freeze her skin, arctic cold. Her body shook, and cold sweat beaded on her forehead.

Under the icy fog of Drew's magic, one thought thundered through her mind: *Something terrible is about to happen.*

She knew this feeling. She'd been here before.

"Let her go," Miranda whispered, her voice pleading.

Rosalind closed her eyes, trying to clear a space in her mind, free from Drew's aura. Her own thoughts were sluggish and frozen, but they still lurked deep in the hollows of her brain. She needed Caine here; he could manipulate magic without using Angelic. She'd seen him do it. There would be no warning before his aura exploded from his body, no need to move his mouth to launch into a spell. If only she... If only...

What was I thinking about?

All she knew was that she just that she wanted to press herself into Drew, to rub her body against the body behind her. To keep herself warm in this frozen vacuum.

Drew leaned down, his mouth near her ear. "Did you really think you stood a chance, with that broken mind of yours? Half in our world, and half in Cleo's." His hand snaked up her neck, and he gripped her by the hair, pulling her head back. "I wanted to see you struggle. Wanted to watch the sheen of sweat on your throat. It wouldn't be any fun if you didn't put up a fight. And you know what? I'm ready for some real fun."

He kissed her neck, and icy dread spread through Rosalind's chest.

Get away from me.

"Leave her alone!" Miranda shouted.

"I still intend for you to be my wife," he said. "Our children will be powerful, like us. We'll rewrite the world. I'll create a new empire, a new reality." He stroked her ribs just below her breasts. "But you'll need to obey me. And that means I need to teach you a lesson—one you'll never forget. Because you've done something awful, Rosalind. Don't you know that? You've been fucking the man who killed your parents."

"She hasn't," Miranda said. "Not that it's any of your—"

"Silence," he growled, his fingers pressing into Rosalind's ribs.

Involuntarily, Rosalind pushed the blade harder against her throat. Her teeth began to chatter.

He has complete control over me. Why can't I get the auras out?

There was a way—but she couldn't think clearly enough to remember how to do it.

"I know what I know!" Drew yelled, his fingers digging into her sides. "She thinks about Caine, and thinking is just as bad as doing. She wants to be his whore—him, our sworn enemy! But she belongs to me. That's the way it was always supposed to be. And with her at my side, I will rule the world. I just need to tame her first. And then I will control the rocks, the sea, the skies, the night…"

As he spoke, images rose in Rosalind's mind: her own fingertips, raising up mountains, sending storms raging with a flick of her wrist. A cold, raw power thrummed through her body, a glimpse of her future.

Drew pointed to the iron necklace that lay discarded on the bed between two crumpled wildflower wreaths. "Pick up the necklace, Miranda," he said. "Put it on. Or Rosalind cuts her own throat."

Deep under the ice of Drew's magic, Rosalind's mind screamed. *Don't do it, Miranda. Something terrible will happen.*

Miranda stood rigid, glaring at Drew. Her blue aura undulated around her body, like anemones deep underwater. Rosalind could feel it rushing over her skin, cool and wet, yet she couldn't use her magic. Not without getting through an entire Angelic spell first.

Don't do it, Miranda.

Drew flicked his wrist, and glaciers closed over Rosalind's heart. Rosalind slid the blade across her throat, cutting just into the skin, but deep enough to draw blood. Crimson streaked her white nightgown.

"Stop!" Miranda shouted, hurrying to the bed. Visibly shaking, she snatched the necklace from the sheets and fastened it around her neck. As soon as she'd secured it, her dark eyes glazed over and her jaw slackened.

Deep under the fog of Drew's aura, dread knelled in Rosalind's skull. Buried under the layers of his magic lurked the gnawing certainty of impending doom.

Something terrible is going to happen.

Drew stepped away from Rosalind. "Drop the knife, Rosalind. Then I want both of you to walk into the courtyard." His toneless voice echoed off the inside of her skull.

Drop the knife, Rosalind. Her fingers unclenched, and the knife clanged on the stone.

Walk to the courtyard. She felt her legs move, her feet pivoting over the cold floor. Beneath the frozen mists of Drew's magic, panic tore her mind apart. *He's taking us on a death march.*

But despite the protests in the darkest recesses of her mind, she pulled open the door and stepped into the hall.

In the corridor, Miranda walked by her side. Drew's heels clacked behind them, slow and rhythmic like a war drum. The name *Caine* whispered through her mind. Was he supposed to be here? She couldn't keep her thoughts straight.

Caine. He's someone important...

With Miranda by her side, she stalked through the corridor. Frozen to the bone, she stared at the shadows dancing over the floor. *This is the type of cold that seeps into your blood and never leaves. The type of cold that drags you down into the frozen earth, and never lets you out again.*

From behind her, Drew's footsteps echoed off the stones in the stairwell.

At the bottom of the stairs, Rosalind marched into the long hallway, Miranda by her side. *A cold that covers your body like a funeral shroud. The world is cold when it ends.*

In Ninlil's entrance hall, her bare feet padded over the crimson carpet.

This is where the world ends.

She couldn't remember what she was doing, only that she needed to keep walking. She had a vague sense that someone was driving her forward—someone who had completely lost his mind, who wanted to hurt her. But she couldn't grasp the ephemeral wisps of thought long enough to make sense of them.

Her body shook, and she pushed through the front doors into the still-dark esplanade.

"There's a wooden post in the northwest corner of the esplanade. March to it. Both of you."

Icy fear wound through her chest, but her leaden legs carried her forward across the rain-slicked stones.

It shouldn't be so empty here.

Her thoughts moved like glaciers. The heavy silence wasn't quite right. If someone was going to die, the air should be full of screaming, clashing swords, the beating of drums. The army was somewhere else, fighting another battle. But this was where the world would end.

Her fingers tightened. *And this is how the world ends—cold and quiet, thoughts trapped under ice and rock. No one to shout or cry, just a damp death rattle, then silence.*

"Miranda," Drew barked. "Stand with your back to the post. It's time you learned some respect for the One True King."

Rain poured over Rosalind's skin, soaking her thin nightgown. *This is how the world ends, in damp shadows.*

Rosalind stared as her sister, dull-eyed, backed up to the wooden post.

Drew lifted Rosalind's hand and pressed something into it—a thick iron nail. Horror stole her breath. And even beneath the icy fog of his magic, rage ripped her mind apart.

I've been here before. I watched this happen. I saw the monster. And now the monster is me.

Drew traced his fingertips over her wrist. "Do you remember what Caine did to the true king and queen, your parents?"

The image flashed in her mind—rain, just like this. Feet half-sunk in the mud. Miranda's scream. Caine pinning her mother against the stake, driving the nail right under her ribs into her heart. Blood dripping from her mother's pale lips, her brown eyes wide.

Rosalind nodded slowly. *I remember.*

"Good," Drew said. "I want you to drive the nail into Miranda's heart. Just like that."

Rosalind's hand tightened on the nail, and her hand shook violently. Miranda looked so skinny against the post, shivering in her thin nightgown, nearly sheer in the rain. She was going to freeze like that. Someone should get her inside, in the warmth.

But Rosalind had a job to do. First, she had to stick this nail into her sister's heart.

Under the ice of her mind, she had a vague sense that this was all wrong—that she needed to run from here and take Miranda with her—but she couldn't figure out how to do it. The scar on her stomach felt as if it was cutting into her flesh, controlling her thoughts.

Drew pushed her wet hair off her face, a strangely gentle gesture. "You've been disloyal, Rosalind. And you must pay the price. Say it."

Her mouth formed the words. "We've been disloyal. And now we must pay the price."

This is how the world ends.

"Do it, Rosalind," he said. "Pay the price. Kill your sister, just like Caine killed your parents."

Rosalind lifted the nail, taking a step closer to her sister. For just a moment, a flicker of life sparked in Miranda's eyes—a pleading look, her dark pupils glistening.

Deep in Rosalind's chest, a hot rage simmered, burning away some of the ice.

Drew thinks he owns us. We're his playthings.

Fury blazed in her mind, clearing just enough space that she could hear her own thoughts.

It was just like this. Driving rain, clothing drenched. Miranda's scream...

"Do it, Rosalind," Drew shouted.

Rosalind's scar froze her skin, and she gripped the nail tighter. *Blood dripping from Mother's pale lips, brown eyes wide.*

She paused, forcing her hand down. *I won't let it happen again.*

Trapped under all the ice and rock, Cleo's voice whispered along with her own. *Turn, Rosalind. Turn and fight.*

She was stronger than this. With a grunt, she pivoted, forcing herself to face Drew. At the sight of him, nausea turned her gut.

Rain poured down his skin in tiny rivulets. Surprise flickered across his features—just enough of a shock to distract him from the twisted spell he wove. "What are you doing?" he demanded.

Gritting her teeth, she stepped closer to him. Her body still moved glacially slow, but it was her own now. She clutched the nail.

This belongs in your heart, Drew.

Before she could strike, Drew punched her in the jaw. Pain splintered her skull. Staggering back, she lifted the nail into the air. She was going to drive it right into his neck.

But before she could bring down the weapon, Drew caught her hand mid-air. He crushed her wrist in his fingers until she dropped the nail. It bounced off the stones.

Hot wrath flooded her body, and she slammed her forehead into his nose, cracking the bone. Blood poured from his nostrils, and she rammed her knee into his groin. *A wedding gift from your beloved wife.*

Grunting, he doubled over, and Rosalind smashed him hard in the kidneys with her elbow.

She reached down, snatching the nail from the ground. She'd kill him right here.

As she rose, Drew slammed a fist into the side of her skull, knocking her back. When she looked up at him again, his powerful aura filled the air around him.

She lunged.

His colored aura slammed into Rosalind's body. He snatched her wrist in his fingers, squeezing so hard she was sure her bones were turning to dust. She moaned, and he punched her in the throat, stealing her breath.

Fluidly, like a trained dancer, Drew whirled—and drove the nail into Miranda's heart, just below her ribs.

Miranda's eyes opened wide with the shock. Horror ripped Rosalind's mind apart.

It's too late.

Miranda didn't shout or cry; she just let out a damp sigh. A thick drop of blood dripped from her pale lips.

This is how the world ends.

8

Rosalind couldn't lift her eyes to Miranda's face, didn't want to see the slackened jaw or the blood dripping from her sister's lips. She didn't want to see the half-closed eyelids, or the crimson streaking her twin's gown. She didn't want to think about the plans Miranda had made, or their house quiet, smelling of fresh-baked bread.

If she gave in to those thoughts right now, they'd bury her alive and she'd never claw her way out again.

Give in to the rage instead. The rage will save you.

Fury blazed through Rosalind's blood, igniting her veins. She grabbed Drew by the hair, pulling him back. She hooked her arm around his neck, squeezing hard. If he couldn't speak, he couldn't use Angelic, couldn't mold reality to his will with his lips.

Her chest tightened. *But I saw him use magic without speaking in Angelic.* He could tap into nature's power directly, just like Caine. Like a god, as if—

Before she could finish her thought, a staggering blast of magic knocked her off Drew. She slammed back against the rock, and pain splintered her skull.

He killed Miranda, her mind whispered. *It's too late.*

Drew whirled and pressed his foot over her throat. For just a moment, she thought about giving in, letting him press the air out of her. Letting him take her as his mute mountain queen.

But a sharp sound hammered in her head. It was the memory of Miranda's ribs cracking when Drew broke them with the nail. Replaying in her mind, over and over...

Rosalind grabbed his leg and twisted, knocking him down. *I'll hear the crack of his ribs...*

Her body burned with wrath, and she leapt onto Drew, straddling him. He gaped at her—afraid for just a moment—and she gripped his hair, slamming his head into the ground once, twice...

In the next instant, his body disappeared—transported away through his strange magic, smoke on the wind.

It's just me now.

A hollow chill crept under her ribs, eating her from the inside out. She kept her eyes locked on the ground, on the stones and tiny rivers of rain. If she looked up, the sight of her sister's body would devour her whole.

Her knees shook, so hard it seemed the earth itself was moving.

Dead.

Footsteps moved past her on the stones, but she couldn't lift her face.

The hero is supposed to come in before the world ends.

"Rosalind!" It was Caine's voice, but she wasn't looking up. *Look up, Rosalind. Face it.*

Slowly, she lifted her gaze, staring at the deep crimson staining Miranda's gown. Caine stood before her. Gently, he pulled the nail from her heart. Miranda's body collapsed into his arms, lifeless. He laid her on the cold stone ground, tracing his fingertips over her heart.

She's dead. Rosalind was certain of this down to her marrow. One more corpse to feed the soil of her nightmares. *I can't look at her face.*

Caine lifted his gaze to Rosalind.

He didn't get here in time.

Her thoughts and Cleo's scuttled around her mind like beetles, and she couldn't grasp any of them.

In the next moment, Caine was standing before her, his hands warming her arms. Was he just going to leave her sister there?

He lowered his face, staring into her eyes. His pale eyes glistened. "I need you to focus, Rosalind. What happened to Drew?"

She looked into his eyes. What difference did it make now? It was all over.

His fingers tightened on her arms. "What happened to Drew, Rosalind?"

Her teeth chattered; her body shook. "He disappeared. He can do magic like you can. Without Angelic. Not just shadow magic. All kinds, I think." She closed her eyes, feeling the auras washing over her skin—faint tendrils of leafy green and a burning gold.

He was still here.

"I can still feel him in Lilinor. He's not far. He still plans to take me as his wife. He wanted to teach me a lesson first."

"I need you to conduct a spell with me. I've driven most of the alu demons out, but I need you to help me track Drew. We can seal up this city after we rip his spine out of his body and bury him under the earth."

A deep pain gnawed at Rosalind's chest. "What about Miranda?"

"She's gone."

Her sister's voice played around the edges of her mind. There was something she'd said. *The things that are buried rise up again.*

Rosalind grabbed Caine's arms. "You can bring her back."

Caine's face hardened. "No. Listen to me, Rosalind. We need to find Drew."

Right. Aurora had said Caine didn't approve of necromancy.

Fine, then. She'd just have to do it without him. Her fingers curled into fists. *After, all, what's the point of being a powerful mage if I can't raise my sister from the dead?*

A tear slid down her cheek. "Why weren't you here? We needed you."

Caine's face changed, his brow furrowing in an expression she'd never seen on him before: vulnerability. "I was with Ambrose. I thought I was supposed to be with him. I thought he was the target."

Rosalind shook her head. "Drew is obsessed with punishing me."

"For what?"

"He thinks I chose you over him."

Caine brushed his knuckles over her cheek for just a moment, then his features hardened again. "We need to act now. I'm going to use gods-magic. I'll shield us. We'll travel on the wind. I need you to direct me, to help find Drew's aura. Are you ready for this?"

She shot a glance at her sister, whose blood mingled with the rainwater. She looked like she'd be frozen if she woke now...

How long would Rosalind have before Miranda's body was too far gone?

Still, it wasn't like she could ask Caine these questions. "I'm ready to go."

Caine wrapped a hand around her waist, pulling her in close, steadying her shaking body. He arched his neck, and black wings sprouted from his back. "Hold on to me tight," he said.

She wrapped her arms around his neck.

She felt a strange liquid darkness flow from his chest into her own, quelling some of her rage. His magic seemed to make her body weightless. *A taste of the void, gifted from Nyxobas.*

"Hold tighter," he said.

In the next moment, they were in the air below Lilinor's magic-darkened sky. Her dress slid up, and she wrapped her legs around Caine's waist, turning her head to look at the city. They rose high above Ninlil's sharp spires. Caine's powerful arms held her tight, his heart beating against hers.

Craning her neck, Rosalind scanned the city for the tendrils of Drew's magic. And there, she saw what she was looking for—curling from Ambrose's White Tower, whorls of copper, gold and blue.

Drew had a perfect view of the city he planned to conquer.

"There, in the White Tower," she whispered. "I see his magic."

They moved lower, closing in on the tower. Cold air rushed over Rosalind's skin, but at least the spell had been broken. At least the cold no longer iced over her soul.

They landed on Ambrose's marble floor. Rosalind unclasped her arms from Caine's neck, and whirled to face Drew.

He'd hidden himself with magic, but she could see him all the same. He stood by one of the windows, magic curling around him—a broad silhouette in a maelstrom of colored auras.

As she stepped closer, she felt the heat coming off his body. Her fury ignited, and she lunged for him, grabbing him by the throat.

He killed Miranda.

She squeezed her fingers, tightening them around his neck, feeling his body twitch—but before she could finish ripping the life from his body, the air cracked with white heat. Drew's body burned with white light, and he disappeared.

Slippery fucker. How was she supposed to kill him if he wouldn't stay in one place?

Rosalind stepped away from the window, her eyes flicking to the sky. Red tinged the darkness again, and sunlight pierced the storm clouds. But she could no longer feel Drew's magic.

She shivered, glancing at Caine. "I failed."

"Do you think he's still in Lilinor?"

She stared out the window again. With that strange magic gone, she felt a shift in the air. It was like a white noise that you didn't notice until it turned off. "Pretty sure he's gone."

"I need to raise a shield so he doesn't come back for you. We're going to find him, Rosalind. And when we do, the next time... it will be on our terms."

"How did he get here in the first place?"

Caine scrubbed a hand over his mouth. "You said he used magic the way I do? Gods-magic?"

She nodded.

"Then he used Nyxobas's power to create a portal. Only Malphas and I are able to create them, between Lilinor and the rest of the world."

"What if I'm wrong and he's still in Lilinor?"

"I'll make sure he can get out. But he won't be able to get back in."

She felt tears rising to the surface, but she couldn't give in to her sorrow. Not now. She still had to find a way to save Miranda.

Rays of amber sunlight broke through the clouds, bathing Caine's face in gold. "I need to darken the skies. Then I'll work on the shield."

"I'll help with the spell."

He shook his head. "You need to stop using magic for now. It's affecting your mind."

Her nails pierced her palms, and Cleo whispered, *Don't listen to him, Rosalind. He fears your power. All men fear women's power. It's why they call us witches.*

Caine closed his eyes, and she stared as the shadows around him thickened, growing denser. Silvery vines of magic grew from his body, reaching to the reddening sky over Lilinor.

Wracked with fatigue, Rosalind crossed to Ambrose's bed. She threw herself down on the silky sheets, watching as Caine began to work his magic. Under the blood red sky, his strong body glowed like starlight.

If Caine can use the night to cloak a world, she thought, *I can bring life into Miranda's body.*

9

*R*osalind pushed through the door to the Gelal Field, retracing her steps to the last place she'd seen her sister smile: the old temple of Nyxobas.

Everything was in its place again. The moon hanging in the sky, the stars twinkling from a blanket of black.

She'd slept just long enough so she could walk steadily again—enough time for Caine to fully shield the city from any more alu attacks, or from Drew's return—but her legs still quaked. And that sound... the breaking of Miranda's ribs... it replayed in her mind, hammering over and over like a war drum.

Her footsteps crunched over the dirt path. It hadn't been that long ago that she was walking down here to meet Miranda. But now the myrtle and sycamore trees didn't smell quite as sweet. In fact, their scent was overpowering, the sickly perfume of a funeral wreath.

It wouldn't be long before they'd want to bury Miranda's body. The wind rushed over her skin and rustled the leaves. Everything had begun to rot. Miranda was dead. Tammi was gone. Half of Lilinor had been slaughtered. And in the chaotic aftermath of the slaughter, Rosalind still didn't know what had happened to Aurora.

A sharp pain pierced her chest. *So this is what it feels like when your heart breaks.*

A tear rolled down her cheek, and she wiped it off with the back of her hand.

She was supposed to bury Miranda soon, by the old yew tree. She was supposed to tell stories of Miranda's life, to free Miranda's soul. But she hardly knew any.

She just needed some time alone, to think things over. To cleanse her mind of Cleo's thoughts.

The sound of tinkling bells floated on the wind, and Rosalind crossed through the door into the old ruin of a temple. She glanced at the spot where Miranda had woven the wildflower wreaths, then crossed to the tall window. From here, she had a perfect view of the giant yew.

She climbed through the window, landing in the dirt. Hugging herself, she trod the path that meandered down to the yew. Where would they want to bury Miranda? Would she get her own grave, or would they throw her in the whore pit?

Emptiness bloomed in Rosalind's chest. She had no idea what had happened to her parents' bodies. Out there in the wilderness, they'd probably been left on the stakes until they'd rotted off.

And that was what Drew had planned for Miranda—to leave her pinned to the post like an entomologists specimen, after he'd forced Rosalind to kill her.

Bile rose in her throat, and she choked it down.

As she drew closer to the yew, the tinkling of bells floated on the wind. Aurora had said that was the dead speaking... Was Rosalind losing her mind, or could she hear Miranda's voice whispering on the wind?

Sometimes, what's buried doesn't stay underground...

Rosalind's pulse raced, and she hurried under the canopy of the yew boughs. Around her, mementos of the dead sparked in the moonlight—silvery ribbons and lockets. She traced her finger down a sheer streamer, to the tiny glass bottle at the bottom. The keepsakes here were beautiful and delicate—but forgotten. No one came here to remember the dead. How many years until Miranda was completely forgotten, until Rosalind had forgotten the sound of her voice and the briny smell of her magic?

She turned her back on the trunk, sliding down to the ground. A threadbare gold ribbon dangled near her head. She turned and saw the name *Julietta* written in old, faded ink. Who had Julietta been? No one remembered her now.

Another body for the whore pit.

Rosalind wasn't going to let her sister lie here. Miranda deserved a second chance.

Sometimes, what's buried doesn't stay underground...

Bone-conjuring. That's what Aurora had called it. And whether or not Caine approved, Rosalind was going to learn how to do it. She'd get her revenge on Drew. And when she did, her sister would be by her side.

A flicker of movement through the branches caught her eye. From the darkness, a raven fluttered to the ground before her. Rosalind stared, her pulse racing, as the raven began to grow larger. With the sound of a hundred bones cracking, and a low grunt, the raven transformed before her eyes.

In the next moment, Caine stood before her, silver magic curling off his body.

Rosalind's heart thumped. "What the hell was that?"

"What?" He took a step closer.

Her throat had gone dry, and she stood slowly. "Nothing. It's just that I've never seen you transform before." As she spoke she realized her cheeks were wet, and she wiped the tears off with the back of her hand. "How did you know I was here?"

"I could smell you."

She wrinkled her nose. "That's disturbing."

"I like your scent." Caine closed the distance between them. "I needed to find you."

"For what?"

Gently, he wiped a tear from her cheek. "I know what it's like."

She flinched at his touch. She wasn't ready for kindness right now. Rage was the one thing keeping her from collapsing under a wave of grief. "What do you mean? You know what *what's* like?"

His expression darkened. "Never mind. Tell me what happened with Drew."

Not a question, she thought. Even when Caine was comforting someone, he gave orders.

"Is it important now?" she asked.

"I need to understand our enemy." His voice was low but insistent. "If he can truly use gods-magic, I need to know what he wants, how he operates. We need to understand his power."

"Right." She squeezed her eyes shut, trying not to picture the crimson stain on Miranda's gown, the blood pooling in the rainwater. She wrapped the bluebell stem around her finger. *Focus, Rosalind.* What was important here? "For one thing," she began, "Remember that scar that Drew gave me in Maremount?"

"On your stomach, yes."

"It serves a purpose. It wasn't purely sadism. He could control my body, like a demon can."

Caine growled. He, too, had the power to control her mind— but he'd never once used it.

"He uses gods-magic like you do," she continued. "But not just one. All the gods. I saw and felt all their auras."

The shadows around Caine grew heavy, so thick they almost

seemed tangible. His magic crackled the air. "And what did he do to Miranda?"

His voice was low, laced with cold fury. She could feel the rage coming off him, darkening the very light from the stars. No matter how many times Caine saved her life, when he turned primal, the ancient part of her brain told her to run.

She took a small step away from him, backing up to the tree trunk. "Drew thinks you're his nemesis. He thinks my parents were the true king and queen, and that you killed them. He thinks I'm a traitor for sleeping with you."

Caine cocked his head, but didn't respond.

Maybe her grief had made her a little reckless with her words. "I told him it wasn't true," she added. "But he said it was just as bad if I thought about it. He's totally lost his mind."

The temperature dropped in the cemetery, and goosebumps rose on her skin. A cloud of steam rose from her mouth when she exhaled.

"What else did he say?" Caine pressed. "What did he do when he controlled your mind?"

"He put a collar on Miranda. He made us walk outside, into the rain. To the esplanade." She swallowed hard. The sound of Miranda's ribs cracking played again in her skull.

"What happened next?" he asked softly. The air chilled further, and frost spread over the yew leaves.

"He wanted to teach me a lesson. He told Miranda to stand against the stake. He told me to take the iron nail from his hand."

Caine's eyes had turned to pure black, and his body was completely still. When she glanced into his eyes, she felt as though she were looking into the void itself. She had the feeling that he kept his energy coiled tightly inside that lean, muscled body, and if he were ever pushed too far it could burst forth at any moment, leveling the whole city.

"A stake and an iron nail. Recreating your parents' death, what I did to them. He was punishing all three of us at the same time." Icy venom laced his voice. She could feel the shadows seeping off him, cold and empty. "He made you stab her."

Rosalind shook her head. "I was able to stop it; I'm not sure how. But I didn't stab her—Drew did. He's really rotten at his core. I don't know if he was always this way, or if the magic twisted his mind."

"I'm going to slaughter him in the most painful way possible," Caine seethed.

"I almost killed her." Her voice broke. "I really wanted to stab her. I nearly did it."

"But you didn't." A sharp tone undercut his words. "Count yourself lucky."

At his words, hot rage simmered. "Lucky? Are you serious?"

"You didn't kill her. Drew did. It was a lucky escape for you."

"Not so great with your people-skills, are you? Sometimes, it's like you have no humanity. When someone watches their sister murdered, you don't tell them three hours later that they're lucky."

He glared at her, his dark eyes completely demonic.

"Of course, you're not really human," she muttered.

"And I suppose your humanity makes you better than me, right?" Bitterness poisoned his words. In his black eyes, she couldn't find a hint of compassion. "You resisted. A demon would have given in to the lure of the slaughter."

"Yeah, probably," she snapped. "I guess I am lucky, then." *And I'm going to raise Miranda from the dead. Not a damn thing you can do about it.* "I just ask that you don't bury my sister in the whore pit with all the other humans you've discarded in Lilinor."

His silver aura sliced the air around him. "Where the hell did you hear that term?"

"Esmerelda. She quite helpfully pointed out that Miranda and I would end up in the whore-pit. Another body for the mass grave. And since you won't help raise her from the dead, I guess she'll stay there, right?"

"I'm going to murder Esmerelda."

"You can't solve every problem by murdering people, you know." She shook her head to clear her mind. "Do you need anything else from me, or are we done?"

"Ambrose is calling together a small council. Aurora, Malphas, me, and you. He wants a debriefing."

"Aurora and Malphas are okay?" This was the first good news she'd heard.

"They're fine." His eyes had returned to their usual pale gray. "Meet us in the armory as soon as you can."

He turned, walking away. And just as he took his third step away from her, his body darkened, condensing in a burst of silver magic. In his raven form, he took off into the air, leaving Rosalind alone with the faintly tinkling bells.

10

Rosalind stalked through a long stone tunnel, deep in the bowels of Ninlil Castle.

A dark, empty hole burned in her chest. Her whole body felt cold, like she'd died alongside her sister. She certainly didn't feel lucky.

She hugged herself, rubbing her arms. After the chaos of the massacre, at least she'd see a few more familiar faces. Aurora might be her only friend left in the city, since Tammi had been stuck in the Abzu.

And then there was Malphas, Caine's brother. She hadn't seen him since arriving here. The incubus had hardly left his room, from what she could tell.

Would Malphas help her raise Miranda from the dead? Not likely. He probably blindly followed the same rules as his older brother. He'd probably tell her she could count herself lucky since she hadn't delivered the final blow herself, and she should just get on with things without complaining.

That meant there was only one person who could help her: the demented witch who inhabited her body. "Cleo, I need you now. I need to know how to bring the dead back to life."

Cleo's aura washed over her skin. *That magic belongs to Nyxobas, and I belong to Druloch. Why don't you ask your lover?*

A lump rose in her throat. "He won't allow it. Neither will Ambrose."

So how else was she going to figure this out? Maybe Lilinor had a library or something. A collection of forbidden spell books.

And how would she find that? Maybe Aurora knew. Aurora, at least, had known the term *bone-conjuring*.

At the end of the hall, she pushed through the door into Ambrose's armory, a large black dome crammed with weapons. In the center of the room, Malphas leaned against an obsidian altar, its sides hung with ornate silver axes.

She didn't want to meet his pale gray eyes—she wasn't sure what she'd find there. After all, she'd tortured him. Maybe he thought she deserved what had happened today.

Either that, or he'd look at her with sympathy. She wasn't sure she could take that, either.

Instead of meeting his gaze, she surveyed the room, scanning the medieval armor hung from the walls. She crossed to one of the displays, running her fingers over a smooth, silver breastplate. The sharp-peaked silver helmets screamed menace, yet the armor drew her in. How would it feel to live shielded by impenetrable silver, immune to arrows and bullets, to iron nails?

What would it be like to stop feeling pain?

She shoved her hand into her pocket, curling a bluebell's stem around her fingertip, and her chest unclenched just a little. Miranda had been right: the wildflowers did bring peace to her mind.

"Rosalind," Malphas said. He spoke quietly, but his voice echoed off the high ceiling. She turned to look at him, and when she did, she recognized the sadness etched on his beautiful face. "I'm sorry for what happened to your sister."

Rosalind could only nod mutely. She couldn't tell him about her plans, that she'd find a way to bring Miranda back.

"She was always kind to me," he added, "when we were little. She gave me food when I was starving. She gave me a blanket to sleep in when I went to bed at night in the prison cells."

A lump rose in Rosalind's throat. This wasn't what she wanted to hear now. She was holding it together by shoving her grief and fury deep under the surface, like ravenous demons too dangerous to unleash. It would take just a light brush of kindness to unearth them, and who knew what destruction they'd wreak. "Yes," she said. "She was the sweet one."

His brow furrowed for just a moment, as if he was confused. "I loved you both."

A hot tear poured down her cheek, and she wiped it away. She hadn't expected to hear that at all. She blinked away the tears. "Where are the others?"

"Coming," he said.

At just that moment, the door creaked open and Caine stalked into the room. Like her, he was dressed for battle: black leather clothes, laden with silver blades. In contrast to his battle gear, his features were soft when his gaze met hers. As he crossed to her, his aura rolled off his skin in waves of thrilling power.

He stopped mere inches from her. "How are you?" The question sounded almost unnatural for him, like he'd never uttered those words in that sequence before.

"Still alive. I guess I'm lucky." Tears brimmed again, and she blinked hard. *Keep it together, Rosalind.* "But we're not here to talk about me. We're here to talk about what we're going to do next, right? Ambrose must have a plan."

Caine's arctic eyes were fixed on her. She had the uncomfortable feeling that he could read her thoughts, unearthing her darkest secrets. *He can't do that, can he?*

"Ambrose is planning a death feast for all the fallen," Malphas said. "In six hours, after the dead are buried. We will honor Miranda there."

Miranda wasn't going to stay underground, but Rosalind wasn't going to bring that up now. "What's a death feast?"

"It's a ceremony to honor the dead," Malphas said. "It's where people tell stories about someone's life and drape mementos on the yew branches. They offer bread to Nyxobas, and pour libations. It helps to open the gates to the afterworld, and frees the souls from the House of Shades. Miranda's spirit will have an easier time finding its way to the celestial realm."

"We have very little control over what the gods do," Caine said. "Death is their domain. We just do what we can to placate them."

"So it's mostly just for show."

"Not just for show," Caine said. "It helps people accept death." For just a moment, he shared a dark look with his brother, his gray eyes piercing in the low light.

"Something we all need to accept," Malphas said.

"Even those of us with very long lives," Caine said. "We must watch the ones we love grow old and sicken."

Rosalind's fingernails pierced her arms. *Maybe. Maybe not.* She nodded. "And what do I need to do at this death feast?"

"You only need to tell stories about her," Malphas said. "The things you'll remember the most."

She stared at the floor, her chest tight. "I hardly know any, apart from the ones you told me. And the past few weeks, I was only starting to get to know her." She straightened. "Anyway, we have more pressing concerns than symbolic gestures. First and foremost, we have to deal with the delusional maniac who nearly razed the city."

Candlelight wavered over Malphas's porcelain skin. "It's all related. We need your power, and your power is no good if your mind is fractured. The death feast will help you heal."

Cleo's aura roiled in her skull. *Don't listen to them. They want you to bury your twin in the whore pit.*

Rosalind heaved a sigh. "Miranda needs her own grave. I don't want her in the mass grave." She didn't want Miranda walking up surrounded by rotting corpses.

"Of course," Caine said. A lock of hair fell in Rosalind's eyes, and he pushed it away, studying her. "Have you been hearing Cleo's voice?"

She really couldn't keep anything from his gaze. "The iron ring doesn't work anymore. But Miranda told me bluebells would bring me peace, and they work better. I've got wildflowers in my pocket. She made me a wreath..."

"With magic as powerful as yours," Caine said, "you have to take care that it doesn't warp your mind. Especially with everything that Drew did today. He was trying to break you."

Her fingernails dug harder into her skin, and she shook her head. "I'm not broken."

"I know," Caine said. "But you can't use more powerful magic. Understood?"

At the far end of the hall, Aurora pushed through a silver-plated door into the circular room, her normally tidy hair flying around, unkempt. Her bright gold dress was torn and singed. For just a moment, her gaze flicked to Rosalind. "I'm sorry about Miranda." She stalked over to a high-backed chair and sat, her gaze lowered.

91

Rosalind swallowed hard. She wasn't the only person in here who'd lost someone today. Everyone in the room had watched their friends die at the hands of Drew. She turned to Caine, staring at his perfect profile—the thick eyelashes framing his pale eyes. "Did you lose anyone you cared about?" she asked. "Any friends?"

"Soldiers. Not friends."

She was nearly certain she caught a subtle eye roll from Malphas.

The silver door opened again, and Ambrose strode into the room, leveling his emerald gaze on her. His black aura curled from his body in thorny spikes, and an icy breeze whispered over her skin, scented of rowans and cloves.

At the scent of him, Cleo's aura roiled, a vibrant, leafy power. Even now, as Rosalind was dealing with the shockwaves from her sister's murder, Cleo wanted to jump on the vampire lord and rip the clothes off his perfect body.

Down, girl. This is not the time.

"Who can tell me what the fuck happened today?" Ambrose's voice was a low, animalistic growl that seemed to rumble in her gut.

Apparently, vampires weren't into offering condolences or sympathy. Maybe a side effect of watching one generation of humans after another die .

"What happened today," Caine began softly, "is that we lost half our army. And we lost our chance at creating daywalkers, when one of our mages was murdered. By a *human*."

Contempt filled his final word, and she couldn't help but think of what he'd said by the yew tree. *And I suppose your humanity makes you better than me, right?* By his tone, she'd known exactly how he felt about humans.

"How did this happen?" Ambrose asked, his words low and controlled.

"Drew can apparently control the sun. Rosalind says he uses gods-magic. He's protected by the Brotherhood in Boston, and he has the power to control Rosalind's mind."

"In other words," Aurora said, "we're fucked."

11

"*W*hat happens to Miranda's second soul?" Ambrose's gaze slid to Rosalind, as if he was searching for a reaction.

She kept her expression impassive. *This isn't the end for Miranda. Sometimes the things that are buried will rise again.*

Caine crossed his arms. "My best guess is that her second soul is trapped in the house of shades. I can retrieve it."

"That's dangerous," Malphas said. "You know you could get lost there."

Caine shook his head. "I'll be fine. And once I find it, we'll need another human to take it on."

"Or a half-human," Malphas said. "Like you and me."

Caine's expression darkened. "Not you."

Malphas frowned. "Why not?"

"You *know* why not, Malphas," Caine snapped.

Ambrose stalked closer, his gaze fixed on Caine. The vampire lord was nearly as tall as Caine—at least six foot three. "He may be your brother, but this is my kingdom. If Malphas agrees to do it, then so be it. He understands what's at stake."

An electric tension crackled through the room, and goosebumps rose on Rosalind's skin. Dark magic curled off the two men.

Who would win in a fight between these two, if it came down to it? Caine had a broader, more muscled build, but Ambrose had a certain quiet ferocity to him that unnerved her. Caine might be the grandson of a shadow god, but a lethal darkness ran deep in Ambrose. If they ever came to blows, the carnage would be brutal.

Clearly, neither of these men were used to hearing the word *no*.

Ambrose was a king. But when it came down to it, he was just a vampire. Caine was a demigod. He'd been allowing Ambrose to rule the city for centuries, probably because he had no interest in being a king. Rosalind had the sense that Caine felt he owed Ambrose something, though she didn't know what. He seemed to have some deeply ingrained sense of loyalty—but after five centuries, that loyalty might have started to wear thin.

"Relax, brother," Malphas said. "We know the risks now, and we know how to avoid them. It won't be like last time."

The vampire lord narrowed his eyes, studying Caine. "We lost half the city today," he hissed. "Half our army. And we'll continue to lose them, as long as they're vulnerable to sunlight. Malphas is the only answer we have. He's the only human in Lilinor who isn't a courtesan."

"So use a courtesan," Caine snapped, his eyes blazing with a pale light. "The shield I created will hold. Drew, the alu, the hunters—they won't be able to get through."

"And then what?" Aurora asked. "We stay trapped in here until we starve to death? We won't be able to get a fresh supply of courtesans or other humans."

"I'll be able to get to and from the other world. I'll ensure that some of us can come back through the shield," Caine said quietly. Even he seemed to understand this wasn't a long-term solution.

Rosalind's gaze flicked to a row of silver axes lining the sides of the altar. *If the vampires are going to start starving here, maybe I need to upgrade my weapons.*

"Quite the impressive arsenal," she said. "I don't suppose I could get my hands on some of that, considering you all are gonna be pretty hungry within a few days."

Ambrose stared at her. "These weapons are six hundred years old. We captured tens of thousands of humans in Târgovişte. The vampires showed no mercy, and impaled each human on a stake. We created a forest of the dead that the world has never forgotten."

Rosalind's skin went cold, and she swallowed hard. *Not sure how to respond to that.*

His black aura cut the air around him. "I want to recreate the glory of that army. I can't always depend on night attacks, as I did back then. We need the power of daywalkers for true glory."

Rosalind winced. "A forest of dead humans isn't exactly my ideal vision of the world. Nature has its own balance, don't you think?"

Aurora leaned down, pulling an axe from the altar. "We need to be able to defend ourselves from Drew's new empire. Just like you need to defend yourself." She crossed the room, handing Rosalind the heavy silver weapon. "Drew not only has the power of the Brotherhood on his side, keeping him safe, but he can use gods-magic. It's an abomination. And if daywalking vampires are an abomination too, maybe that's what we need to be to fight back."

Rosalind gripped the ax. "What can you tell me about gods-magic?"

Caine raised his hand, and inky shadows curled from his fingers. "As a demigod, I have a direct line to shadow magic."

"Right. And Drew can use magic from all the gods," Rosalind said.

"But Drew wasn't sired by the seven gods," Ambrose said, "so what the fuck is going on?"

Rosalind cocked her head. "Actually, according to Drew, we're both sired by the seven gods. We're direct descendants of Azazeyl. The One Who Is All. The original fallen god. He fragmented into seven broken gods, who slowly went insane from the split."

"Seven tormented gods," Caine said, "desperate to be whole again."

"Ridiculous." Ambrose frowned. "Azayzeyl never existed. He's a myth that only lunatics believe."

"Apparently not," Rosalind countered, "given what we've seen my cousin do. He says that the blood of Blodrial—the seventh god—awakened his powers. Now he drinks it regularly. I've had the ambrosia before, but I was wearing an iron ring, so nothing happened. Except it gave me the ability to see magic."

"It's real," Caine said, so quietly she almost didn't hear him. "When Rosalind's parents called the second souls into our bodies, they used the seal of Azazeyl."

Ambrose's dark aura curled from his body. His green eyes locked on Caine.

Rosalind's throat tightened. "I want to get more ambrosia. If Drew is right, I have the same powers he does. I'll need to leave here long enough to steal some blood from the Chambers. I can be just as strong as he is."

Caine's gaze slid to hers. "You said Drew lost his mind."

Her lip curled. "I'll only use it long enough to murder the bastard."

Aurora shook her head. "You want the power of seven gods at your fingertips? Why do I feel like this won't end well?"

Rosalind sighed. "I get it. Humans weren't meant to have this power. Drew seems far crazier than when I first met him. And given that a bluebell stem is the only thing keeping me from being controlled by the voice in my head, there's a serious risk I could end up completely mental. But like you pointed out, maybe we need to fight Drew with another abomination. You'll just have to help me get back to normal when it's all over."

Deep in her pocket, she wrapped the stem tighter around her fingertip, nearly cutting off the circulation. "Gods-magic is what we need to kill Drew. I'll drink the blood. You all can pay for my therapist when we're done."

"Don't do anything yet," Caine said. "I'm going back to Maremount first."

"Why?" Rosalind asked.

"I'm going to rip Drew's flesh from his bones," he said. "And I'm going to find the seal of Azazeyl while I'm there. If I can get into the House of Shades, I should be able to find Miranda's second soul. I'll trap it in the sigil."

Rosalind bristled. She wanted to be there to watch Drew die, but she couldn't leave Lilinor. She still had to raise Miranda from the grave.

"Good. Find the sigil," Ambrose said. "And how, exactly, do you get into the House of Shades?"

"That's for the gods to know," Caine said.

Rosalind's stomach tightened. What was going on with Caine? That was no way to address a king.

Ambrose tilted his head, his eyes darkening. "Fine." His controlled voice belied an icy rage. "But do not try to hunt down Drew on your own. We will have an army to do that, once you return with the sigil. We will create my daywalkers. That is our priority, and I'm not losing another one of my mages."

Caine's eyes had turned black as coal. "My priority is slaughtering Drew."

"You may be a demigod," Ambrose said, "but if Drew is what you say he is, he has the power of *seven* gods. And I need you to return alive. Do you understand me, incubus?"

Caine simply tilted his head, staring at Ambrose. The air between them seemed to crackle with tension.

Rosalind took a deep breath. "The legend is true. I've seen the magic with my own eyes. If I drink the blood, I could be used as a weapon against Drew."

"This should get interesting," Aurora muttered.

Caine touched her arm. "You don't need to figure this out now. You're still mourning your sister's death. Humans are not meant to wield gods-magic, just like you said."

Ambrose surveyed Caine coolly. "If these legends are as real as you say, she should drink the blood. Maybe we won't even need a third soul to create the daywalkers. Rosalind might be enough. I'll believe it when I see it, but it's worth a shot—unless you're worried that your little girlfriend could become more powerful than the great demigod?"

Caine glared at him. "Has it bothered you all these years, Ambrose, that I'm connected to your god more than you'll ever be?"

An oppressive silence enshrouded the room, and the candles flickered in their sconces.

"Let's stay focused," Malphas said, before his gaze slid to Rosalind. "My brother is right. You should mourn your sister before you make any big decisions."

"No." The word came out of her mouth too quickly, too insistently. But the fact was, she wasn't going to mourn her sister. She was going to bring her back. When she spoke again, she tried to soften her voice. "I mean, we have plenty of other things to worry about. Mourning won't kill Drew. And you know what will make me feel better? Killing Drew."

Burn him, Cleo whispered.

She shook her head, trying to clear her mind. Maybe her own sanity was no longer worth preserving at all costs. "The point is, I think Ambrose is right."

"Of course I am," he said. "If this works, I'll want to see how you fight. I'm not convinced the Brotherhood trained you properly."

Rosalind thought she heard a low growl rise from Caine's throat. The temperature in the room cooled again, and Caine's icy gaze bored into Ambrose. "You don't know how to use gods-magic."

"I want to see how she fights," Ambrose said. "Malphas can teach her the rest. Unless you're worried about another incubus getting his hands on her."

Caine's sharpened silver aura sliced the air around him. "Why does the idea of this turn my stomach?"

Aurora straightened. "Because Ambrose and Malphas are the only men on earth who look as good as you, and you're all thinking with your dicks."

Caine turned to Rosalind, and nodded at the ax in her hand. "I trust you know how to look after yourself."

She frowned. "What, exactly, are you worried about?"

"Just take care of your yourself. And don't let anyone get in your head."

12

*R*osalind stood in in her bedroom, wrapped in blankets. She wore a black gown, and had her hair piled up on her head.

How long would it be before Miranda would rot beyond repair?

Through the open window, the sound of chanting floated on the wind. Beyond the Gelal Field, and past the temple of Nyxobas, the vampires were holding their funeral in the Garden of the Dead.

She'd lasted about thirty minutes at the death feast—just long enough to listen to some of the eulogies and to give her own half-hearted tribute under a yew tree. She'd felt entirely numb as she'd stood by Miranda's corpse, with the eyes of an entire vampire city on her.

She told the one story she knew: that Miranda had never stopped looking for her. It wasn't a brilliant tale, with a beginning and an end, but it was the one thing she knew for certain. As she'd spoken, Caine and Malphas had stood on either side of her. And when Caine leaned in to tell her she could go if she wanted—before they covered Miranda in dirt—she took off up the hill on her own.

Now, from her spot on her bed, she could still hear the mournful songs drifting through the city. She hadn't shed a single tear today—but maybe there was no point in mourning a sister who wasn't going to stay dead.

A knock on her door interrupted her thoughts, and she rose from her bed. She wrapped the sheet tightly around her as she crossed the room to pull open the door.

Aurora stood in the hall, dressed in a long red gown, a red rose tucked behind her ear. All the vampires had been wearing red at the funeral—apparently it was Lilinor's color of death.

"Caine sent me to check on you," Aurora said. "He couldn't leave yet."

"I'm fine. I'm just taking the time alone to think a few things over."

Aurora studied her. "Why do I feel like you're planning something?"

"Maybe I am. Come in." Rosalind turned, stalking back to her bed.

Aurora stepped into the room. "Starting to get a bad feeling about this."

"Miranda's story wasn't finished. No one even knows what it was."

"I'm sorry." Aurora reached into her handbag, pulling out a small, silver flask. She handed it to Rosalind, and when she did, Rosalind noticed the tremor in the vampire's hands.

"Are you okay?" Rosalind asked.

Aurora plopped down on the bed. "I'm sick of watching vampires burn. A couple of months ago, the Brotherhood's Hunters took us to a field in Belmont. They opened the van in the broad daylight. Caine saved me, but I heard the screams as the other vamps died. I still hear them in my dreams. I can still smell their flesh burning. Today, it was worse."

Rosalind's chest ached. "I can see why you'd want the daywalker spell so badly. "

"All I know is, if we don't do something, all of Lilinor will burn. And now we've lost Miranda."

"What if we could get her back?" Rosalind asked.

"What are you going on about?"

"Caine will never let Malphas take on the extra soul. I don't know what happened to Caine after he gained his extra soul, but whatever it was, he won't talk about it. And he doesn't want the same thing to happen to his baby brother. Neither Caine nor Ambrose trust the courtesans enough to allow them to take on this power. Plus, they'd have to be trained to control magic, and we don't have time for that."

"Right. But Miranda's dead."

And if we don't act quickly, we won't be able to get her back. Rosalind's fingers tightened on the bedsheets. "But maybe she doesn't have to stay that way."

Aurora stared at her for a long moment. "I hope you're not talking about bone-conjuring."

"You said it's possible. Isn't there a book somewhere?" She took a deep breath. "The night before she died, she said something to me: 'Sometimes what's buried rises again.' I think it was some sort of message. I heard her voice again, whispering through the bells by the yew."

"No," Aurora said, frowning. "Caine won't allow it."

"Why?"

"Because it's a sacrilege to steal souls from the gods."

"I have no loyalty to the gods," Rosalind said. "Do you? Because they don't give a fuck about us."

"I'm not particularly religious, but Caine's a bit close to Nyxobas. And I'm loyal to Caine."

"You didn't want to see any more vampires burn. This is your way out. Bring Miranda back. We'll get the soul back in her."

"And how do you expect that to work, when we're relying on Caine to complete the spell?"

"He's forbidden people from conjuring the dead—but once it's done, it will be too late. I mean, he's not going to kill her. And surely Ambrose will back us up. He wants his daywalkers more than anyone, and Miranda is the best person to handle the task."

Aurora just stared at her.

Rosalind continued. "We'd have the three mages we needed, too. We could perform the daywalker spell, just like we planned. We'd have to wait for a courtesan to be trained, or wait to see if she lost her mind. Miranda knows how to control the magic already. With the three of us reunited, we could stop the Brotherhood from immolating you all again and again."

"It's tempting. Extremely tempting." Aurora took a deep breath. "But Caine will cast me out of the city if he finds out."

"I'll take full responsibility. I'll never let them know you were involved. I promise."

Aurora stared at Rosalind for so long that Rosalind couldn't quite hold her gaze.

At last, Aurora spoke. "Fine. I'm not promising anything." She took a long swig from her flask. "We can look for the spell. And then I'll decide. Don't tell a single person."

Rosalind stood by Aurora's side on the third story of Ninlil's library, a balcony overlooking the pale stone floor.

Silver moonlight streamed through the tall, arched windows, sparking off glittering silver titles on the books' spines. A portrait of a beautiful dark-haired woman, her skin illuminated by pearly light, hung between the shelves. She held a scroll unraveled in her hand, inscribed with Angelic. Behind her, walls of scrolls burned. *Alexandria.*

Aurora turned, walking to another shelf; her heels clacked over the floor. She ran her fingers over the spines, scanning the titles. "These are the plague and pestilence grimoires."

A flicker of movement caught Rosalind's eye, and she glanced at the stone vaults that arched high above. Bats circled overhead. *Eerie place.*

"Here!" Aurora plucked a black grimoire from a shelf. A silver skull marked its spine. "Necromancy. Death spells. This is the one."

Rosalind's pulse raced. *We have what we need.*

Aurora cracked the book open, flipping through the yellowed pages. "It's here. The song of the Manzazuu." She narrowed her eyes. "We will need to make preparations. We'll need a fire pit under the stars, human blood, and a life to sacrifice to Nyxobas."

"Please don't tell me that has to be human, too."

"Animal is fine. We need to drink some wine and eat some black bread, whatever that is." She glanced at Rosalind. "You'll have to do the eating. I don't eat food."

"What's the purpose of that?"

"Nyxobas wants us to acknowledge death's power. Decay, decomposition, rotting flesh. All that good stuff. When you eat fermenting foods, you acknowledge that you're mortal, that the gods rule your death. You're stuck in a body that's slowly rotting until it gives out and you cease to exist. The gods are quite keen on that idea."

"Well, I feel better already."

"And you're acknowledging that when you bring Miranda back, it won't be forever. She'll be brought back to life, but in a mortal body, slowly dying, as all mortal bodies do."

"Right. Lovely."

"The gods are fucked up. Now you know why Caine has some personality issues." Aurora glanced down at the page. "We need a magic circle. Nyxobas's sigil. We put Miranda's corpse in the center, add in a few of her belongings, and we incant the spell. *Usella Mituti Ikkalu Baltuti.* And that's it. The spirit will be called back from the House of Shades, and will inhabit Miranda's body once more. From what I can tell, anyone can do it." She closed the book, meeting Rosalind's gaze. "But are you sure you *want* to?"

"I have to," Rosalind said. "Miranda went through hell to find me, to reunite us again. I feel certain that if the roles were reversed—if I'd died—she'd do whatever it took to bring me back." She took a deep breath. "But I want to make sure you don't get in trouble for this. Are you sure you want to do the spell with me?"

"You'll only screw it up if I leave you to your own devices. But you can't tell anyone." Aurora slammed the book shut. "I don't suppose you want to do this now?"

Tempting, but... Rosalind shook her head. "I won't be able to. Right after the Feast for the Dead, I'm supposed to meet Caine by the portal. He's going to open the shield for me before he leaves for Maremount. And then I get the gods-blood."

Aurora took a deep breath. "Once you've got gods-magic, you'll owe me one. I'm going to be asking for some favors."

"You trust me with gods-magic?"

Aurora arched an eyebrow. "Not even a little, but I don't get to call the shots here."

13

*R*osalind climbed the pale marble stairs to the White Tower, where Caine and the portal waited for her. Thin rays of moonlight lit her path. She ran her fingers along the cold stone walls as she climbed the steps.

She had a pretty good idea what she'd be getting into when she got to the portal room.: A plunge into freezing water before climbing into a cemetery crypt, just a mile from the Brotherhood's headquarters, the Chambers. Unless things had changed drastically in the past month, the Chambers' halls would be equipped to sense magic. Guards would patrol the halls, and the whole place would be rigged with electronic devices to attack intruders.

Still, she had a good idea how to get to the ambrosia she needed. She just needed to disable all their alarms. And if anyone got in her way, she'd have to do a bit of ass-kicking. Before heading up to the Tower stairs, she'd stopped by her room to change into her fighting gear: leather clothes, boots, and a weapon belt.

There had been a time when she would have found all this intimidating.

At the top of the stairs, she pushed through a set of doors into a marble hall. Her footsteps echoed off the high ceiling as she walked down the hall, her eye on the two guards standing before the door.

The guards pulled open the doors; Rosalind climbed the stairs and crossed the threshold.

Caine stood waiting for her by the placid pool. Moonlight bathed his broad form in frosty light. As she crossed the marble floor, his icy gaze pierced her through the darkness. "Rosalind. Are you ready for this?"

"Of course."

"I don't think this is a good idea."

"Why?"

"You told me that Drew is insane. You have enough mental demons to contend with."

She heaved a sigh. "I know. I haven't decided for certain yet, but I'm going to get the blood all the same. Then I'll make up my mind. There are bigger factors at play than just my own mental state—like that whole thing about how Drew and the Brotherhood want to enslave the human race."

"And you're the sacrificial lamb."

"You're taking a risk, too," she pointed out. "You're going into Maremount on your own." She ran her fingertips over the hilt of one of the knives in her belt.

"Fine." He nodded at the pool. "And you know what to do when you get there?"

"I know exactly where the ambrosia is kept. I know how the building operates. I'm going to cut the power before going in. The magic sensors will be disabled, and I'll use an invisibility spell to get around the building."

Plus, she probably had more weapons on her than the entire vampire army.

He studied her closely, the moonlight sparking in his eyes.

Cleo's vernal aura flared at the sight of his beauty. *It all started with him,* Cleo whispered. *He slaughtered your parents, and now you've paid the price with Miranda's death.*

He's a god. Rosalind's fingers tightened.

Cleo's voice rang in her skull. *Don't you know that gods are meant to be killed?*

"What's she saying to you?" Caine asked. "Your second soul? She's speaking to you, isn't she?"

Rosalind took a deep breath. Pain gnawed at her chest. "She thinks Miranda's death is your fault, since you killed my parents in the first place. She suggests that I should kill you."

Caine stood perfectly still, but for the wisps of his dark hair caught in the wind, and the silver aura snapping the air around him. "And what do you think?"

"It's Drew's fault." But she still had so many unanswered questions. "I just need to understand. Why did you kill my parents? Was it revenge?" She crossed her arms. "Why did you have to do it in front of us?"

He stared at her for so long that she thought he'd never answer the question. She considered just turning and jumping through the portal, but he finally spoke. "I wasn't fully in my right mind."

She turned to face him head on. "What happened when you lost your mind?"

He nodded at the pool of water. "It's time for you to go, Rosalind."

She took another step closer to him, so close she could feel his warmth. There were so many things he wasn't telling her. "Miranda said you were tortured in the town square—that it was a punishment. But that was before you killed my parents. So what were you punished *for*?" Even as the words were out of her mouth, she knew she was touching a raw nerve.

Shadows whorled around him, cloaking his body, and his eyes flashed with an eerie silver light. "It's buried history." The coldness in his voice slid through her bones. "And it's time for you to go."

"Right. I know. You've got to get back to Maremount."

"Yes." He nodded at the pool. "You can come back through this portal. Only you, Ambrose, and I will be able to get through the shield for now."

"Be careful in Maremount. I want to see you back here soon."

"You will." He leaned in closer. "And like I said, don't let anyone get inside your head. Understood?"

"You mean, apart from the dead witch who controls my thoughts?"

"Apart from her, yes."

"I'll do my best." She turned to the pool, momentarily entranced by the moonlight glinting off its surface. *Here I go.*

She jumped into the icy water, plunging deep under the surface. Frigid water enveloped her body, dragging her under. The silver weapons weighed her down.

As she sank deeper, her lungs burned. When she saw a faint sheen of greenish light streaming through the water, she kicked her legs, pushing her way toward the air. Gasping, she breached the surface, pulling her way to the side of the pool.

She'd emerged in one of the crypts in Mount Auburn cemetery. The air hung heavy with the smell of moss and mildew, and silvery light streamed in through latticework in the stone doors.

She grunted, pulling herself out. Murky crypt water soaked her clothes and hair, and her teeth chattered. Her body still ached from the battle with Drew. She stood, wringing out her hair, then peered through the door into the old Victorian cemetery. No one lingered on the hawthorn- and maple-lined paths at this hour.

I'll need Cleo for this. She was getting a little tired of having to negotiate with her second soul for everything, but until she memorized an entire library's worth of spells, this was the best she could do. Shivering, she hugged herself. "Cleo," she whispered. "I need you to show me the spell for invisibility."

Cleo's leafy aura curled in Rosalind's mind, and she tried to envision forcing it lower, into her chest. Cleo was easier to control there.

And what will you do for me, pet?

Rosalind sighed. "I know what you want. We'll see Ambrose when I return to Lilinor."

And will you run your hands over his perfect porcelain skin? Will you kiss his neck, listen to his breath catch in his throat? He likes it when a woman strips completely—

"Seven hells, woman," Rosalind snapped. "No. I'll hold his hand or something."

The vernal aura churned in her chest. *I want you to kiss his neck.*

"Fine. I'll kiss his neck." She would do no such thing, but she'd have to deal with the fallout another time.

As soon as the words were out of Rosalind's mouth, Cleo offered up the spell, graven in white light. Rosalind read the words out loud and felt the magic whisper over her skin, hiding her body from the rest of the world.

The spell completed, she pushed through the cemetery door. Stone scraped against stone. Outside, the air was clear, heavy with magnolias. She broke into a fast sprint along the path, her feet pounding on the pavement of the winding cemetery paths.

At the entrance, she scaled the wrought-iron cemetery gate and leapt over the top to the sidewalk below. She pumped her arms, running hard toward the Chambers by Harvard Yard.

As she ran, her eyes flicked to Drew's house, the yellow mansion on Brattle. She halted her sprint for a moment, sniffing the air for the scent of his aura, and held out her arms, waiting for the powerful tingle of his unmistakable magic. *Nothing.*

Of course. Even he wasn't stupid enough to come back here. It hadn't been long ago that she'd stood in his entryway, letting him heal her flesh with a potion of his own making. How stupid she'd been then, drinking from the devil.

Her stomach clenched at the thought of him.

She pushed her disgust to the back of her skull and broke into a run, heading once more toward the Chambers. Hardly anyone walked the streets, which meant it must be well after midnight. Without regular daylight in Lilinor, it had become impossible to keep track of the time.

As she sped through Harvard Square, her eyes trailed over the empty streets. *This is where the keres attacked, where they ripped into human flesh.* At the time, they'd seemed like pure monsters. She'd had no clue that they were actually humans under the alabaster flesh and black eyes—or something in between, at least. Just like Tammi.

Rosalind crossed into Harvard Yard, the night air rushing over her skin. As she sprinted closer to the Chambers, she pulled a long, silver blade from her pocket. Before she went in the building, she was going to make sure she'd disabled all the electronic weapons. The hawthorn stakes rigged to shoot from the ceiling. The aura-burning dust.

And now that she had the power of Cleo's magic at her fingertips, she didn't need to hack into their system.

Just outside the Chambers, she stopped, catching her breath below the yellow glow of a streetlamp. Through the Chambers' glass windows, she could see pale light illuminating the marble floors, and tiny red lights glowing from the network of alarms and weapons in the stone walls.

Most of that was familiar, yet the Chambers had changed. It hadn't been long since she and Caine had rampaged through the building, shooting through windows, lighting the walls on fire and freeing prisoners—yet the building now stood in a pristine state. What was more, an entire new wing had appeared near Oxford Street. the architecture there—a classical stone façade adorned with Greek columns—stood out in stark contrast to the Victorian brick.

Where the hell did that come from?

There was no way all this could have been built in a month. Not without the use of magic.

The Brotherhood—the ancient organization of soldiers who existed solely to rid the world of magic—had thrown themselves wholeheartedly into Drew's thrall. All it took to turn them, apparently, was for their favorite witch to drink blood from their god. But who was really in control—Drew, or the Brotherhood?

There's time to figure that out later. Now, she had to get some blood of her own. She closed her eyes, trying to ignore the fatigue burning through her body. "Cleo," she whispered. "I need a spell for…" She swallowed hard. It had only just occurred to her that a sixteenth century spirit would have no clue what she was talking about. "I don't suppose you know what an electromagnetic pulse is?"

Cleo's aura roiled. *Speak in English, girl.*

She folded her arms. Electricity wasn't discovered until the seventeenth century, but she could work with this. "You know lightning?"

Cleo's aura sparked green in her chest. *I'm not a complete fool.*

"I need to mix that power with magnetism. The technology that powers compasses, or that draws metal to rocks. I need to send out a shockwave of that power."

A vernal aura licked at her ribs. *For magic such as this, I'll need you to seduce Ambrose. Walk into his bedchamber, and take off your clothes so he can see your body. Then let me take over.*

Rosalind hoped Cleo didn't pick up on her eye roll. "Sure. I'll get naked." She was making all sorts of sordid Faustian bargains tonight. "Can you help me with the spell now?"

Magic simmered over her skin, and from the depths of her mind, a spell rose, blazing in white light. She spoke the words, and a powerful flare of hot, electric magic burst from her body, rippling over the horizon. A low rumble filled the air, and she opened her eyes. As the magic spread from her body, the street lamps flickered and snuffed out. In front of her, in the Chambers entry hall, the red lights dimmed to black. Pure, thick darkness enveloped the campus.

Nice work, Cleo.

Rosalind prowled to the front doors. At the glass doors, she peered inside. Nothing moved. She narrowed her eyes. All was quiet inside—but it didn't seem quite right. A faint hum of magic vibrated over her skin.

Magic. In the Chambers. Was Drew here?

She pulled open the front door, stepping into the hall. Part of her wanted to hunt through the Chambers for Drew, but she wasn't strong enough to fight him yet. When they came face to face, she'd be the one in control. She'd see the fear in his eyes as he trembled before his angel of death.

And for that, she'd need the ambrosia.

Luckily, she knew exactly where to find it. She tiptoed through a set of doors toward the Great Hall, straining her eyes to see in the dark. A shiver rippled over her skin as she took in the chalice carvings on the hall's oak door. This was where Miranda had nearly killed her; in the dark hall beyond this door, she'd nearly burned to death. Both she and her sister had had their minds broken and twisted by Blodrial's followers.

She checked over her shoulder, making sure the hall was empty, then pulled open the door. As soon as she did, a deep crimson aura curled through the air—and with it, the sound of a blaring siren. So they were using magic now.

Heart racing, Rosalind closed her eyes. *Cleo. I need some help now, or your little vessel won't live long enough to seduce Ambrose.*

In an instant, shining Angelic words blazed in her mind; she incanted them, letting the magic ignite her body with power. As she chanted, the alarm faded.

Still, the damage had been done. A banging noise made her turn her head, and she glimpsed two men running down the hall—Hunters, gripping canisters of dust. A tall, wiry man and a stocky blond. She didn't recognize either of them.

Good. That'll make this easier.

Her pulse raced. *Kill or be killed.* She drew her knives. If she let them spray her with that dust, she'd be helpless here—visible, magic-free, and in extreme pain.

She threw the first knife, and it arced through the air, finding its mark in the wiry Hunter's heart. The blond's eyes widened, in too much shock to act quickly. She threw the second knife, and it buried in his chest—a few inches to the right of his heart.

Shit. She'd missed the mark.

117

He fell to the ground, dropping the canister and gasping. Her heart thundering against her ribs, she ran to him. As she stood over him, he stared into the air, unable to see his executioner. A gurgling rose from his throat. A drop of blood slid from his lip, and his eyes blazed with fear. He was going to die, and he knew it.

Rosalind's throat tightened. It was a lot easier to kill a guy from far away. Still, she had to act fast; more Hunters would follow. She pulled the misericord from her belt, crouching down. She plunged the thin blade into his ear, watching his eyelids flutter.

There wasn't time for guilt now. She stood, rushing for the door. Adrenalin surged in her veins. *Where the hell is the magic coming from?* She pushed through the door. Moonlight streamed through the oculus, casting a circle of light on the floor. Just outside the pale sphere stood a stone lectern with an iron compartment, locked by an electronic keypad.

The Hunters were still using human technology, but it wouldn't be long before they evolved.

Luckily, she didn't need to know the code—not after Cleo's electromagnetic pulse. Her hands shook, and she hurried to the lectern, yanking opening the compartment. An iron flask stood in the center. She snatched it, shoving it into her belt.

But as she rose, a familiar aura seeped into her nostrils: moldering hemlock, the color of dried blood. Fetid magic crawled over her flesh like spider legs, erasing the cloaking spell. She glanced down at herself. she was completely visible now.

Slowly, Rosalind turned. Stepping into the light was a behemoth of a demon with bone-colored skin and cheekbones sharp as knives. Horns grew from his forehead, and sharp tattoos marked his bare chest. He glared at her with empty, ivory orbs.

Bileth.

14

*R*osalind's heart climbed up her throat. "What are you doing here?"

"I was going to ask you the same, my little beauty." His voice rumbled through the hall. "And then I saw you take the ambrosia."

If there was ever a time to have a direct line into magic, it was now. She was trapped in a standoff—unable to chant an Angelic spell without Bileth snapping her neck with his mind.

He took a step closer, a grin curling his lips. "I do remember with fondness the time you impaled me with a silver spear. In fact, it fuels my most depraved fantasies. I trust the memory is fresh in your mind as well?"

Her throat went dry. She'd always wondered what had happened to Bileth—he'd been full of fury, desperate for revenge. And then he'd simply given up.

Still, she couldn't quite get her mind around what he was doing in the Chambers. Drew was one thing. Drew, at least drank Blodrial's ambrosia. But Bileth was pure, muscled shadow demon. An ancient acolyte of Nyxobas, forged in the shadow void.

"What are you doing with Randolph and the Hunters?" she asked in desperation. "Why have they allowed you in here?"

He clenched his meaty fingers and took another step closer. "The enemy of my enemy is my friend." His deep red aura curled off him, and he glided closer. "Accomplice. Close enough."

She didn't understand. "You mean me?"

A low growl rumbled through the room. "You really think you're that important, little girl? You think *you're* my enemy?"

She needed to get out of here. Any second, a phalanx of Hunters could appear. At least with Bileth, she could figure out a way to distract him long enough for her to launch into a teleportation spell.

"Okay, so I don't know who your enemy is." She took a step closer to him, and surprise flickered in his eyes. "But you still think fondly of the time I stabbed you. What do you mean it fuels your most depraved fantasies?"

If she could pull a knife from her belt, she could stab him a second time. It wouldn't kill him, but it would stun him just long enough that she could get out of here.

He glided another inch closer, and her fingers twitched at her belt. Before she could grip a knife's hilt, Bileth's powerful hand was around her throat. With one hand, he lifted her from the ground, crushing her neck. She kicked at him, but the demon simply reached down, ripping the blades from her weapon belt and flinging each one across the room. Her lungs burned as he squeezed her throat.

He pulled the flask from her belt, looking it over. "Poison," he snarled.

He dropped her, and she fell to the ground, gasping. She touched her bruised throat. *Shit. So much for the knife plan.*

"What do I mean about my depraved fantasies?" Bileth reached down, pulling her up by the hair. "When I think of your impertinence, your stunning human arrogance, it makes it all the more exciting when I think of all the ways I will punish you. You thought you'd escaped, didn't you? You thought I'd forget?"

His fetid aura slithered under her skin, and her heart hammered. He was going to try to control her mind.

And maybe she'd play along, just long enough to figure out how to get out of here.

She focused on forcing the maroon tendrils out of her body. *If I can see magic, I can control it.*

"Take off all your weapons," Bileth growled.

Rosalind widened her eyes, giving her best impression of a compliant little victim.

Bileth shifted closer, stroking his thumb up her cheek. The demon's touch was cold and damp, and she tried not to shudder. Still gripping her hair, he trailed his thumb over her lips, then shoved it in her mouth. His waxy skin tasted of stale milk, and she tried not to gag.

Her stomach turned. *Okay. I don't want to play along anymore.*

He released his grip on her hair. "Take off your clothes."

Rosalind's heart pounded. *Cleo, I want the spell now.*

Cleo's aura roiled. *Not yet, Rosalind. Wait until he can't see your mouth moving.*

Swallowing her disgust, Rosalind reached down, unbuttoning her shirt. Bileth let out a low growl, staring at her. He reached out, stroking her collarbone. Then he pinched her skin between his fingers, twisting it hard.

Her breath caught in her throat, and she tried not to shout. She needed to act compliant.

Bileth pulled his hand away. "The rest. Now."

She bent down, unzipping her boots and sliding them off. *Any time now, Cleo.* She slid her hands down to her pants, unbuttoning them. *Fucking hell. This was a bad idea. I should have kept the weapons on me.*

Revulsion twisted her gut as she slid out of her pants. *Cleo, I need to get out of here.*

No spell rose in her mind as she straightened, staring straight into his blazing ivory eyes.

The door slammed open, and from the corner of her eye she saw a line of Hunters burst into the room, guns drawn.

Her cheeks burned. *And here I am, standing in my sheer black underwear.*

Cleo's aura blazed. *It's your body, you fool. Don't be ashamed of it, and they have no power over you.*

Her mage friend had a point.

"Lie on the ground and put your hands behind your head," shouted one of the Hunters.

Bileth held up a hand. "She's mine right now. You can watch."

So they knew he was here, and they allowed it.

"But, you..." one of the Hunters stammered. "We need to arrest her."

You. Hunters addressed their officers as *Sir*. Rosalind had the sense that the Hunter didn't know how to address Bileth. He was stronger than they were, completely lethal, and to some degree the Brotherhood had opened the doors to him.

But they didn't accept him. He terrified and revolted them. *As he should.*

Bileth gripped the back of her hair again, pulling her head back. Her heart tightened.

I need two spells. One for the flask, and one to leave. Two spells, Cleo.

The Hunters looked on as Bileth slid his other hand around her waist. He pulled her closer.

Two spells, Cleo.

Bile climbed up her throat as the demon opened his mouth. Her stomach clenched as she waited for a slimy tongue or cold lips on her neck.

But Bileth had another idea. He opened his mouth and bit down hard on her shoulder, tearing at her flesh.

Pain ripped her apart, and she clenched her teeth, trying not to cry out. *Two spells, Cleo.* She tilted her face away from the Hunters just slightly. She didn't want them to see her grimace, to see her lips move.

Letters blazed in her mind, an angelic word for magnetic rock. Rosalind whispered it, holding out her left hand out of the Hunters' view. The iron flask flew into her grip.

Bileth bit deeper, and the pain nearly blinded her.

Cleo offered up the second spell, the one for teleportation, and Rosalind whispered the words, keeping her head slightly turned. The pain was excruciating, but after one last rip of Bileth's sharp teeth, she was free, her body teleporting away.

At the edge of the dank crypt, she fell to her knees, clutching the flask. "I'm free," she whispered to herself. She touched her ravaged shoulder, wincing at the deep wound. Her body trembled, and nausea flooded her.

She needed to get back to Lilinor *now*. Bileth knew how to find the portal to Lilinor. In fact, Bileth could probably come into Lilinor whenever he wanted—his ugly portrait hung over the damn entrance to the castle.

Shit shit shit.

Flask in hand, she stood and leapt into the pool of freezing water. The cold shocked the pain from her body, and she sank deep under the water. When her lungs burned, she glanced up, glimpsing the rays of moonlight streaming into the water. She kicked her legs, fighting her way up.

Her arms breached the surface, and she pulled her way out of the pool. The pain from her shoulder stole her breath, and she watched the blood pour from her wound, pooling in red rivulets on the tile.

It was only a moment before strong hands were lifting her up. Ambrose's green eyes widened, and he slid a hand around her waist. He pulled her closer, his touch like silk on her skin. Moonlight streamed in from the open ceiling, washing his skin in silver. He wasn't wearing a shirt.

In the next moment, his mouth hovered over her neck, his fingers clamping on her waist in a vice-like grip. He emitted a low groan.

Rosalind's heart pounded against her ribs. *Shit. I've just presented a bleeding neck to a vampire.* She slid her hands up his chest, hard as marble, and tried to push him away. "Ambrose. Stop."

He growled, gripping her tightly. A full head taller than her, he stared down. Fury blazed in his eyes. "Don't ever come to see me like this again—half naked and covered in blood."

Cleo's aura swirled off her body, stroking Ambrose's skin, and her voice rang in Rosalind's skull. *Why don't you give him what he wants?*

Rosalind ignored her, trying to gather her thoughts. Her body burned from the exertion of the teleportation spell, and it was hard to concentrate with Ambrose's iron grip around her. "Ambrose. I need you to listen to me. Can Bileth get through Caine's shield?"

Ambrose's entire body went rigid. "Why are you asking about Bileth?" he growled.

"He's the one who took my clothes and the chunk of flesh from my shoulder." A cool breeze whispered over her back.

Almost imperceptibly, Ambrose's fingers tightened on her waist. Dark rage crossed his features, nearly distracting her from the searing pain in her shoulder. "Bileth did this? How? Why?"

"He was in the Chambers. He seems to be working with the Brotherhood. He mentioned that old adage about 'the enemy of my enemy is my friend.' But I have no idea who he's talking about."

Ambrose loosened his grip on her, forcing himself to step away.

Her gaze flicked to the bed, where two nubile blonde courtesans pulled up sheets to cover their naked bodies. Blood dripped from their necks. Apparently, she'd interrupted a little vamp-on-human menage.

A drop of blood glistened on Ambrose's lip, and he licked it off. "Bileth can't get in here with the shield Caine put in place."

"What did he mean about his enemies? Why is he working with the demon hunters?"

"He's talking about me."

Pain still screamed through her shoulder, but his eyes transfixed her. Her pulse raced, and Cleo's voice rose in her mind. *You should feel his kiss.* "Why would Bileth consider you his enemy? I thought you worked together. His picture hangs in the castle."

He lowered his mouth to her neck. Without thinking, she tilted back her head, exposing her throat. *So that's how vampires control their victims.*

Before his fangs reached her throat, he abruptly dropped his grip on her. His body buzzed with dark magic. "I can't think straight around you." His gaze slid down her body, taking in her bare skin. "I need to heal your shoulder. Now."

Ambrose, Cleo whispered. *Come closer.*

He bit into his wrist, letting his own blood pool, and held it to her mouth. "Drink." Blood dripped from his wrist.

You'll like this, said Cleo.

"What will happen if I drink your blood?"

"You'll heal. Drink."

"If I drink your blood, won't it change my thoughts and make me one of your mindless followers?"

"Drink."

Her lip curled. "I like the way Caine heals me better."

Ambrose inched closer, and an impulse from the ancient recesses of her brain compelled her to tilt back her head again. He pressed his bleeding wrist to her mouth, and as soon as the first salty drop hit her tongue, she began to suck.

A dark heat flooded her body, a primal power. As she drank from Ambrose's wrist, the pain in her shoulder melted away. She drank deeper, letting it drip down the back of her throat. Deep in her core, a slow fire simmered.

Ambrose gripped her hair, pulling her mouth away from his wrist. "That's enough, Rosalind."

Raw power blazed through her veins, and she stared at the vampire lord. His pupils had turned blood red.

"You got the ambrosia," Ambrose said, slowly pulling his gaze away from her. He stared at the night sky, obviously trying to avoid eye contact. "Good work."

Cleo's aura lit her body on fire. *Now, Rosalind. It's time to make good on our bargain.* With Cleo's iron will urging her on, and the intoxicating rush of Ambrose's blood burning through her veins, she couldn't resist taking another step, running a hand up his chest...

A sly smile curled his lips, and his fingers found their way around her waist again. His gaze trailed over her neck. "I thought you belonged to Caine."

"I don't belong to anyone." *Except Cleo, apparently. Sweet earthly gods, I can't do this.* "Cleo demands things from me," she blurted. "Every time I want a spell from her, I have to strike a bargain."

He froze. "What sort of bargain?"

"I know you have a history with her. She *knows* you. And you know her, too, don't you?"

Ambrose's muscles tensed, and he pulled his hands away from her waist, grabbing her chin. "I could smell her on you the first time we met." He stared into Rosalind's eyes, and her pulse raced. Ambrose was every bit as unnerving as the first day she met him. "And I think I know what she wants from me." He dropped his hand.

Rosalind tightened her fists to keep herself from touching him. *She wants to bang you, and then murder you.*

"She wants my death," he said.

"That's part of it." Rosalind wiped her chin, glancing down at the smear of blood on the back of her hand. "Who is she? What happened between you?"

Ambrose stared down at her. "Here's the part you need to know. I want you to drink that gods-blood. Now. You need to tap into the gods-magic. You can't strike a bargain with Cleo every time you need to use a spell. You can't let her control you. You will use her only when it's time to make the daywalkers."

I just love how these vampires speak in commands. "I need a little more time."

"For what?" he barked.

"Just give me an hour to do a little research first." What she really wanted to do was to dig Miranda up from the earth and try the spell for Nyxobas, but Ambrose seemed to be pushing her along at a breakneck speed to develop the gods' powers.

"And how do you intend to do research?"

"I'm going down to the dungeons. I'm going to talk to your wife."

"Whatever you need to do, Rosalind, do it fast. We have work to do."

15

$\mathcal{R}$osalind stalked down the narrow stairwell, clutching a flask.

She tugged up the front of her dress—a delicate gown of sea-foam green, flecked with gold threads that curled down to the hem like vines. Not exactly standard dungeon-attire, but it would do the job for meeting with Erish. Ambrose had quite helpfully called for a servant to bring her a dress, so she wasn't forced to climb down to the dungeon half naked.

And on her way down she 'd stopped by her room for a few crucial items—namely, the weapons she now had discreetly strapped to her thighs below the tulle.

Apart from her blades and stakes, she carried only one thing: a flask of ambrosia. The blood of a god, right at her fingertips—a potential bargaining chip for her meeting with Erish.

At the end of the stairwell, she pushed through a misshapen oak door into a dank, earthen hall. The old dungeons had been crushed by a giant, but Ambrose had ordered his men to work day and night to build a new one. It now held a single prisoner: Ambrose's wife.

From silver lanterns, warm light danced over the hall. It smelled like a grave down here.

A sharp pain pierced her chest. Was this what Miranda felt, buried under all that dirt? Suffocating under the earth, trapped in darkness? Her fingers curled into fists, and she shook her head. *No. Miranda doesn't feel anything.*

Tears stung her eyes, and she blinked them away. As soon as she was done with her little interview, she and Aurora would try to raise Miranda.

She ran her hand along the earthen walls as she walked toward the dungeons. A single lantern lit the space, casting wavering light on an iron-barred cell at the end of the hall. As she moved further into the hall, her chest tightened. Crumpled in a heap on the stone floor lay a bag of bones, dressed in rags.

Erish. The stunning succubus queen.

Rosalind swallowed hard, crossing to the iron cage. Erish's black hair, once lush, lay snarled over her emaciated arms. Iron chains bound her neck, wrists, and ankles.

Rosalind crept up to the cage.

Is she even alive?

"Erish?" she said softly.

The queen lay still. *Sweet earthly gods.* Erish was a traitor and a terrible person, but her husband could have at least given her some food and a blanket.

Standing just outside the cell bars, Rosalind crouched down. "Erish?"

In the next instant, the queen lunged, her hand flying for Rosalind's head. Rosalind dropped the flask, trying to dodge backward, but the queen had her by the hair. Erish snarled, and Rosalind caught a glimpse of a savage red scar on the queen's neck.

"Rosalind," Erish spat. "The special little human." Her eyes were wide, her grip on Rosalind iron-clad. "Did you think you could decapitate a succubus and live?"

Rosalind's heart raced. Gripping the bars, she kicked between them, her foot connecting with Erish's face—but quick as a flash, Erish grabbed her foot, twisting it. Rosalind slammed forehead-first onto the stone.

She yanked her foot out of Erish's grasp, recoiling. When she touched her forehead, her fingertips came away coated in blood. Thick red drops stained her green gown, now smudged with dirt.

"Great to see you, Erish," she said from the floor. "I'm so pleased captivity hasn't dampened your spirits."

Erish leaned back on her haunches, her snarl more animal than human. "You're the reason I'm here, filthy human wench. And now you've come to gloat, dressed like a queen. If I could, I'd eviscerate you slowly and drape your entrails over my shoulders like a shawl."

Shuddering, Rosalind brushed the dirt off her bodice. "I'm not here to gloat. I just came to ask you a question."

"Do you remember that time you cut my head off?" Erish pulled down the iron collar just an inch, exposing the angry red scar on her neck. "I'm not clear why you think I would help you."

Because I'm reasonably sure you're an addict. "I'll give you a taste of ambrosia."

Erish's eyes widened, and her body went completely still.

Now I have your attention. Rosalind would give her just a drop—enough to tempt her. Not enough to imbue her with fresh powers.

"What do you want to know?" Erish asked in a low voice.

"If I drink the ambrosia, what will happen to me? I've had it before, but only when wearing iron. I've never used the gods-magic the way Drew has."

Erish's lip curled. "What are you afraid of? Are you scared some little human tart will sever your head from your body, and you'll wake up in a dank sewer, chained with the rats? That your husband and king will bury you under the earth, that he'll let you starve? I can't imagine where you'd get that idea."

Rosalind crossed her arms. "Lay off the guilt trip, Erish. You were kidnapping humans to turn them into mindless, flesh-eating demons—including my best friend. You caused hundreds of deaths."

"I was revered as a goddess in the ancient world," Erish hissed. "I deserve an army to defend me. And now you find me sitting in my own filth. That is your fault."

"If you tell me what I want to know, I'll have a word with Ambrose about your living conditions. I'll make sure you're sent food, and something to wash with."

"And why would he listen to you?" Erish lunged forward, gripping the bars. "You think you'll be his new queen? You think your pretty face is enough for him?"

Rosalind frowned. She was growing impatient—she had a sister to raise from the dead, and Erish was stalling. "What? No. I'm not going to become his queen."

"That's right, you won't. You spend enough time with Ambrose, and he'll rip through that delicate human neck. And if somehow you managed to survive his rapacious blood hunger, he'd have to watch you growing old and wrinkled. Rotten with cancer. He'd be repulsed at your sagging skin, your creaking knees, your bladder giving out. That is your fate, after all. Another body for the whore pit."

Suddenly, Rosalind wanted to be anywhere but here. "I have no desire to become queen."

Erish's grip tightened on the bars. "Turning humans into demons—is it really so terrible? I gave them eternal life. Without me, they'd be cursed with corrupted, rotting bodies. Just like yours." Her mouth twisted in a bitter smile. "What a choice for a sanctimonious cunt like you—become a demon, or die. You do realize those are your only options?"

Rosalind shrugged. "I guess I could live forever and watch myself abandoned one by one by everyone who ever loved me, until there was nothing left but my narcissistic rage. But somehow, that doesn't seem appealing."

"Do you know what will happen when you die, Rosalind? Will you be trapped in a void, with nothing but your sad little memories?" Erish licked her lips. "You'd best figure it out fast. You're dying right now."

"And you're stalling. Why do I get the feeling you're trying to keep me here as long as possible? Getting a bit bored of hearing your own bitter thoughts? Even you're growing sick of yourself." Rosalind rose to her full height, brushing off the back of her dress. She was quickly losing control of this conversation. "I'm here to ask about the blood. The ambrosia. Did it drive Drew insane?"

Erish sneered. "Have you seen him lately?"

"Yes. He paid us a visit. I guess you missed all the excitement down here."

"Did he seem sane?"

"No."

Erish tilted her head. "You already know the answer. You're just not willing to admit it to yourself. You've already lost half your mind anyway. What difference does it make if you lose the rest?"

"You didn't lose your mind though, did you?"

"Like I said, I'm practically a goddess. Don't expect the same rules to apply to me." She frowned. "Do you ever wonder what your corpse will look like?"

Rosalind's stomach tightened. "I don't have to wonder anymore." Not since she'd seen her identical twin's graying corpse.

"Now that's intriguing."

"Will I become addicted to the ambrosia, like you are?" Rosalind asked. "I mean, I've had it before. But I've never used the gods-magic. Is that what's addictive?"

"I don't expect that you'll be any stronger than I am. You can hardly deal with your second soul. Honestly, you should just give up and let her take over." She licked her lips. "I can see her in your eyes now. Look at your reflection."

She knew that Erish was playing mind-games with her, but curiosity compelled Rosalind to lift the metal flask, gazing at her own face. Her breath froze in her lungs. She stared at a stranger: long, platinum hair, pale skin, and green eyes. She blinked hard, and her dark hair returned once more. *What the hell was that?*

She glared at Erish. "Did you create that illusion?"

The succubus lifted her chains. "I can't do any magic with this iron all over me. I can see Cleo—that's her name, isn't it?—taking over. She's really quite beautiful. I see why Ambrose would have given in to his carnal desires all those centuries ago."

Rosalind's fingers curled. "What happened between them?"

Erish arched an eyebrow. "Are you jealous of your second soul? Tell me, which demon do you want more: the incubus who killed your parents, or the vampire who wants to fuck you and kill you?"

"Neither," Rosalind grumbled. She unscrewed the cap on the flask, poured a few drops into the cap, then handed it over. "I have to go. Here's your payment."

To her surprise, Erish didn't complain about the tiny pour. She simply glared at Rosalind and sipped it, before handing

Rosalind the cap and wiping the back of her hand across her mouth. "Maybe someday I'll tell you what Ambrose did to Cleo. Then we'll see how much you like him."

Rosalind screwed the top back on the flask. "I'll ask Ambrose to send down some food and blankets."

"Where is it you have to run off to so quickly, little tart?"

"I have to go visit my sister."

Erish only grunted as Rosalind turned, stalking through the dirt tunnel again.

Her stomach churned. Her worst fears could be true. Drew had probably been driven insane by using the gods-magic.

Maybe human bodies weren't meant for such power. And as much as she hated to admit it, Erish was right. She didn't have much of her mind left to lose. Not with Cleo taking over, one brain cell after another.

Rosalind rubbed a knot in her forehead. She didn't want to lose what was left of her sanity, but she was running out of options. And if they needed an abomination to fight Drew, maybe she'd have to fill the role. She pulled open the door and began climbing the stairwell.

Despite Erish's claims of addiction to ambrosia, she'd spent the entire conversation stalling, trying to prod at sensitive topics. She hadn't really *seemed* like an addict. Maybe Erish was desperate, but it wasn't blood she craved. She was starved for attention, desperate for conversation—even if it meant talking with her worst enemy. Maybe isolation was the worst punishment of all.

Do you know what will happen when you die Rosalind? Will you be trapped in a void, with nothing but your sad little memories?

At the top of the stairwell, Rosalind pulled open the misshapen door.

Suddenly, nothing seemed more important than raising her sister from the grave.

16

*R*osalind pulled a shawl tight around her shoulders as she walked down the winding path to the yew. She could already see Aurora standing near a fire pit. By the tree, cedar smoke curled into the air, and the flames cast a glowing light over her sister's corpse. The sound of tinkling bells filled the air.

Thank the gods for Aurora. The vampire had volunteered to arrive early for the necromantic spell, so Rosalind wouldn't have to face digging her own sister out.

As Rosalind drew closer, she could see a thin layer of dirt covering Miranda's skin and her white gown. She took her place next to Aurora. "I can't tell you how much I appreciate this."

The vampire wore a long, black gown and held two silver cups. "Are you sure you're up for this?"

"We have to try," Rosalind said quietly.

Aurora handed her a silver cup. "Here. Wine."

"Is wine the first step?"

Aurora took a sip. "Wine is always the first step. Especially when you're standing over your sister's corpse."

"Good point." Rosalind sipped the fruity wine—the same wine she'd had at her picnic days ago.

But for this picnic, Aurora had brought a macabre feast: black bread, a necromancy book, goat blood, and a caged raven. Aurora bent down, snatched the spell book from a wicker basket, and flipped through the pages.

Against her will, Rosalind's gaze slid to her sister's body. Miranda's face had taken on a greenish tinge; her lips were a deep blue.

Rosalind couldn't breathe. She felt as if she was staring at her own corpse, glimpsing her own future. A hollow opened up in the pit of her stomach. *It's not me. It's Miranda.*

"Rosalind?" Aurora said. "Are you with me?"

She tore her gaze away. "Yes. I'm here."

Aurora held out a piece of black bread. "Eat this. Food doesn't agree with me. I had Caine's fae chef bake it for us."

Rosalind took it from her, and her stomach rumbled. *When was the last time I ate?* She took a bite, chewing into the rye bread, delicately sweetened with molasses. "Now what?"

"Now you throw the bread into the fire."

Rosalind took one more bite and tossed the rest into the bonfire, to a burst of flame. Black smoke curled into the air.

Aurora stepped closer to the fire, opening a silver flask. She took a sip, then poured a thin stream of blood onto the fire; it hissed as the flask emptied. "Now all we have to do is drink more wine, and sacrifice the bird."

Rosalind took a sip of her drink. "Would Caine be upset about the raven? What if she's a friend of Lilu? His familiar?"

Aurora glared at her, picking up the birdcage. "I told you, Caine would be upset about all of this. Anyway, Nyxobas likes ravens."

Snatching the spellbook from the ground, Rosalind shivered. *Right. Well, good thing he's not here.*

The raven flapped its wings, squawking, and Aurora cooed gently, stroking its head. In a split second, she flung open the birdcage and with a soft crack, she snapped the creature's neck.

Brutal.

Aurora tossed the bird's limp body onto the fire and glanced at Rosalind. "And now, all we need is the spell."

Rosalind propped the book on her hip, holding it open with one hand. Hand-drawn skulls, ravens and waning moons decorated the spell's page. She scanned for the spell, then chanted: "*Usella Mituti Ikkalu Baltuti.*"

Aurora joined in. Their voices mingled with the tinkling of the bells. The wind picked up, toying with Rosalind's hair.

Usella Mituti Ikkalu Baltuti.

Rosalind's veins flooded with a strange power, dark and ancient. She closed her eyes, her vision swirling glimmers of stars. And with the piercing glow of starlight in her mind, she thought of Caine's eyes. Caine was the closest thing she knew to the god of night. She tried to imagine how he conducted the magic—his body blazing with pale light, shadows moving around him, his movements predatory and precise.

A scent wafted past her, electric and earthy at the same time. The whorls of stars gave way to an earthly vision: a room with dark wood, dirty ivory sheets. Sunlight streaming through a warped window. A shapely woman dressed in a ragged nightgown, brushing her blond hair.

Where am I?

A wail pierced the air. She glanced down and saw that it was a baby crying in a basket on the floor. She reached down to pick the child up. It looked at her with gray eyes. Cradling the infant in her arms, she soothed the baby, and a protective warmth enveloped her.

She glanced up at the crooked bedside table. A hairpin lay on the surface—a sharp spike of silver, with a thorny design decorating the top.

Recognition hit her like a fist. *Caine.*

The night sky swirled again, enveloping her, and a sharp hollow rose in her chest, eating at her ribs. The image was replaced with a thick forest, gleaming with daylight. Pines towered over her, and she gripped a sword. She glanced down at her arm, taking in the thickly corded muscle and golden skin. *Caine.*

He slid his fingers into the V of his shirt, feeling the small divot over his heart. The scar that Rosalind had given him. The sunlight seemed to darken, and through Caine's eyes she looked up at the sky. A legion of shrieking valkyries were coming for him, and he tightened his grip on the sword.

White light burst in her vision, and she gasped, opening her eyes.

She stood before the yew, and the night breeze whispered over her skin. Her body shook from her visions. Had they been real, or some sort of hallucination?

Aurora touched her arm. "I think I felt the shadow magic."

All around them, deep, silvery magic whirled through the air— but when Rosalind glanced down at her sisters body, Miranda lay still. None of the magic had actually been directed *into* her body, and it was already disappearing like smoke.

Rosalind's stomach dropped. Maybe it had worked? Her legs shook, and she rushed to her sister's body. She traced her fingertips over Miranda's skin. *Cold.* She stared at her sister's chest, willing her lungs to swell with air.

Aurora, her brow furrowed, pressed a hand over Miranda's chest. "There's no heartbeat."

Rosalind lifted her fingers to her sister's throat, feeling for a pulse. She felt only cold, dead flesh. "Nothing." Sadness tightened its grip on her heart, and she pulled her hand away. "I felt the shadow magic. I think I even got some mental images from Caine. But the magic didn't go where it was supposed to."

"What mental images?"

Grief ate at Rosalind's chest, sharp and hollow. A tear streamed down her face, and she wiped it away. This had been the best plan she had.

"I think it was an image from Caine's life. That tattoo on his arm that looks like a knife? It's not; it's a woman's hairpin." Her chest tightened. "But that's not the concerning vision. I saw a legion of valkyries coming for him. It could be a vision of where he is now, because he already had the scar I gave him, but I sure as hell hope not. It wasn't looking good for him."

Aurora shook her head slowly. "Maybe it was just a hallucination. Just nonsense."

Rosalind rose on shaking legs. "Why do you think the spell didn't work the way it should have?"

"I have no idea. Apparently, Nyxobas doesn't want to give your sister back."

17

*D*ressed in her battle gear, Rosalind stalked down the hall to the armory, choking down her bitter disappointment. She was supposed to meet Ambrose; he'd said he wanted to see how she handled herself in a fight.

She shuddered. It would be hard to focus on Ambrose when she could still feel the shadows of Nyxobas whispering through her blood, tempting her to the cold, clean void.

As she walked, her footsteps echoed off the ceiling. Nyxobas had dominion over the dead, and she'd toyed directly with his power. They'd tried the spell three more times, and each time she'd thought of Caine, and felt the power of the night god flowing through her. She'd seen the visions from his memories: the woman with blond hair, the child with gray eyes. She'd watched the valkyries attack Caine, closing in on him in the forest, had recoiled as he'd cut into their flesh.

But each time the visions cleared, the magic simply wafted uselessly in the air above her sister's corpse before disappearing into the night sky.

Why the hell didn't it work? Maybe we baked the bread wrong. Maybe the ancient alchemists weren't big on the specifics of spell mechanics.

And by the final try, the spell hadn't worked at all. No visions from Caine, no rush of shadow magic. Nyxobas hadn't granted her permission, and Miranda still lay dead in her grave.

Almost as bad was the nagging worry that she might have seen a vision of Caine in some serious trouble, plagued by a horde of valkyries. She was pretty sure he'd been in a forest in Maremount.

Or maybe Aurora had been right, and it was nothing but a hallucination.

The cut on her forehead, from where Erish had knocked her into the floor, still stung. She reached up to touch it, and a smudge of blood came off on her finger. She hadn't had time to clean up properly—it had been a mad dash from Erish, to the yew tree, back to her room to change, and now down to the armory.

She approached the armory, wiped the blood off on her pants, then pulled open the door. As soon as she stepped into the room, her pulse sped up.

Ambrose stood in the center of the room, dressed in black. He stood rigid with that eerie, preternatural stillness that raised the hair on the back of her neck. Shadows licked the air around him.

"Close the door," he snarled.

His steely tone unnerved her, and she swallowed hard, pulling the door closed behind her. She was suddenly acutely aware that she was alone in a room with a predator. One who—right now— seemed more demon than human, who seemed to be staring at her from the depths of hell itself.

Silently, he cocked his head, the movement oddly reptilian.

She wanted to break the tension, to draw a spark of humanity from him. "I went to see Erish," she ventured. "To find out about the ambrosia. She confirmed it would make me lose my mind."

"A small sacrifice."

"She's very skinny, and cold. And she's filthy. I told her I would speak to you about—"

His eyes flashed with white light. "Lock the door."

So much for that. Her heart thudded, and she turned to the door, sliding the bolt to lock it. When she faced forward again, her heart leapt into her throat.

Ambrose had crossed the room in that fraction of a second, and was standing within inches of her. His hands shot out, and he gripped her wrists, pinning them to the wall. He stood a head taller than her, his body made of pure muscle. His eyes—two dark abysses—stared down at her, and her stomach flipped.

Why do I get the feeling that I screwed up, big time?

His sharp incisors glinted. "You've done three things wrong. Can you tell me what they are?"

Rosalind pressed herself flat against the wall, desperate to get away from that dark, penetrating stare.

She had a guess about one of those infractions. She hadn't been willing to leave Miranda, so she was probably a minute or so late. *Is he really that particular about lateness? Seven hells.*

Still, with her arms pinned to the door, this didn't seem like the time to argue. "Why don't you tell me?"

"One, you showed up late."

Okay. So he is a stickler for punctuality.

"You won't waste my time again." His lip curled in a sneer. "Two. You won't show mercy for our enemies. Not Erish. Not Drew. Not anyone who has tried to kill us. Mercy will be your death."

"Right now I feel like *you'll* be my death."

Lantern light contoured his sharp cheekbones, like a perfect marble sculpture. "That brings me to my third point. I told you not to come to me when you were bleeding." His gaze lowered to her neck.

Her pulse raced. He had her pinned in a vice-like grip, and there wasn't a damn thing she could do if he wanted to tear out her throat. Cleo's aura whorled through her belly, warming her body. *He's beautiful, isn't he? Now is the time. I told you to take off your clothes and show him your body. Kiss his neck.*

Part of her was deeply, seriously pissed off at this flagrant display of vamp testosterone, yet Cleo wanted her to give in to it. Wanted his mouth on her neck, his teeth in her throat.

Somehow, she no longer felt complete control over herself. She felt her head tilting back, exposing her throat to him. Heat warmed her chest. Her heartbeat pounded in her ears.

Ambrose let out a low growl—softer than she'd expected. The tips of his fangs grazed her skin.

But this wasn't why she'd come here. She hadn't come to give Ambrose her blood.

She was here to fight.

With Ambrose's spicy scent in her nostrils, Cleo's magic curled around her spine. *Touch his powerful body,* Cleo whispered.

"Shut up Cleo," Rosalind said through clenched teeth.

Immediately, Ambrose dropped her hands and jumped away from her, a horrified look on his face. "What did you say?"

She rubbed her wrists where he'd been gripping them. "Nothing. I was just telling Cleo to shut up."

"Cleo," he said. His skin had gone a shade paler than normal.

"Right." The name *Cleo* seemed to agitate him. She swallowed hard. "My extra soul."

For now, maybe best to leave out the part where she wants to bang him and then light him on fire.

A muscle worked in his jaw. "Sorry about the blood hunger. That's why you mustn't come here with blood on your body." He looked away from her, staring at the wall. "There's water for you on the altar. I know humans require it when you exert yourselves."

She crossed to the altar, picking up a small pitcher. "What, exactly, are we doing here?"

"I want to see how you fight."

"I can fight fine. But if I drink the ambrosia, I'll need magic training." She poured a few drops of water onto her hand to wash off the blood on her fingertips. "I'll need help controlling the gods' power. And I need Malphas for that."

"I didn't ask for your opinion." He ran his tongue over his sharpened incisors. "Apparently you don't know the true place of humans here in Lilinor."

A shiver ran up her spine. *What the hell is his problem?* "Oh, I've met one of your courtesans," she said, glaring at him. "but I'm not here as one of your human slaves. You need me—that's clear enough. Maybe you're forgetting *your* place."

She didn't know Ambrose well, but she didn't think Caine would let her stay here under the protection of a complete psychopath—and with that thought, a strange revelation bubbled in the back of her mind: *Apparently, I actually trust Caine.*

Ambrose took a step closer, letting his eyes rake over her body. "I'm going to enjoy punishing you."

Her anger simmered. "What is *wrong* with you?"

In the next moment, his hand was around her throat. "I've added a fourth rule to my list: Don't speak until I've asked you a question. And don't presume to look me in the eye."

A hundred retorts blared through her mind, like *Take your hands off my throat, you alpha dickhole.* But she choked down every one of them, because the fact was she couldn't take Ambrose in a fight. She knew better than to argue with a vampire lord in the thrall of blood-hunger.

But her anger simmered, and Cleo's rage was only adding fuel to the fire. In the darkest recesses of her mind, Cleo's melodic voice sang, *Fuck him to oblivion. Then kill him.* Cleo's song drowned out Rosalind's own thoughts, until she could think of nothing else. Angry heat warmed her cheeks, and her body began to shake. Her teeth chattered as molten anger flooded her veins. *I know what's coming next. I know what it feels like when battle fury claims my body.*

Surging with adrenalin, she slammed her forearms into Ambrose's wrists, kicking him in the groin at the same time. He dropped his grip, and she punched him hard in the carotid artery.

His eyes bulged, then his hands flew out, gripping her wrists again. With stunningly swift power, he pinned them to her side. He stared down at her again, his lip curling in a terrifying smile.

He thinks he owns you, Cleo whispered. *Punish him now. Kiss him later—when you've tamed him.*

Anger flooded her, and she headbutted him. His head whipped back, but he only held tighter to her wrists. She brought her knee up into his groin a second time; when it connected, his grip loosened just a little. She yanked one hand free, slipping it into his hair to pull back his head.

I have you in my thrall now.

Cleo's aura surged, claiming Rosalind's mind. She was no longer in the armory, but standing in the center of the rowan grove, in a silky dress that caressed her thighs. *Stars engrave the night sky. When Ambrose comes, he'll run his fingers over my hips, over my belly, gentle as a flower petal... He'll bed me in the wildflowers. He says he'll always keep me safe...*

Rosalind's vision cleared, and she was in the armory again—pressed between the altar and Ambrose's strong body. He pinned both wrists behind her back, gripping them tightly in one of his hands. Inky shadows curled from his cold body, and a low growl rose from his throat as he glared down at her.

Her stomach lurched. "What the hell are you doing, Ambrose?"

Cleo's aura caressed her ribs. *He's doing what's in his nature. Taking what he wants. Using you, like he did to me.*

Damn it, Cleo. That was the worst possible time to hit me with one of your visions.

What exactly was Ambrose doing here? Caine had told her not to let anyone mess with her mind, and she was pretty sure Ambrose was doing exactly that.

And there it was again: She actually trusted Caine.

Cleo's aura stroked her skin, raising goosebumps. *You have more than one way to disarm him, Rosalind.*

Rosalind tilted her head back, exposing her neck. Cleo purred in the back of her mind, and the filthy scent of blooming rowans enveloped her. *Now I remember how sweet you were, Ambrose. Don't you remember how sweet I could be, before you destroyed me?*

Rosalind pulled Ambrose closer, and his beautiful lips hovered just over hers. "You said you'd always keep me safe," she whispered, leaning in to kiss him.

Ambrose pulled away. "What did you say?"

Rosalind blinked, shaking her head. "That wasn't me. That was Cleo."

Ambrose's eyes widened. Hands shaking, he smoothed his shirt.

Rosalind frowned. "Can you explain to me what's going on? Or am I not allowed to speak unless I'm spoken to?"

He straightened. "Now you understand why you must never come to see me while you're bleeding. If I see your vulnerability, I won't be able to control myself. It's part of the curse of the vampire."

"Complete domination of anyone you perceive as weak."

"That is the heart of any demon. If you want to survive among the monsters, you must remember our nature."

This was the first time she'd heard a demon admit that. "Surely not all demons have the same nature."

"Some want blood; some are driven to rule your mind. We all want sex. And an incubus in particular... well, I'm sure you understand."

She knew how incubi were supposed to work. But Caine had never lost control around her, had never tried to control her mind or force her to do anything she didn't want. He'd been completely in control of himself, even when she'd stripped off in front of him. "I haven't seen that side of him."

Ambrose arched an eyebrow. "Apparently he has more restraint than I do."

She crossed her arms. "Honestly, he's always been a perfect gentleman around me."

Ambrose smirked. "Then I would assume he has no interest in you. He has been with many beautiful women before."

His words stung, and suddenly she wanted to change the subject. "Why am I here? What were we *supposed* to do before you went psycho-vamp?"

"I need to teach you to fight. *Real* fighting, not what you've learned among the humans. I know how you practice at the Brotherhood. You have rules—no gouging out eyes, no tearing out flesh with your teeth. You'll have to abandon those trappings of civility."

"I see. You're accusing me of being civilized."

"You fight more viciously than I would have expected. Was that you, or Cleo?"

"At least some of it was me," she said. "I'm no stranger to fighting after the past month, and I've been training in combat fighting. I just need to learn magic. Do I really need to learn how to gouge out eyes, or can we get on with figuring out how to take on Drew?"

Ambrose cocked his head. "If you let that sort of savagery out when you fight Drew and the Brotherhood, perhaps you don't need me. Maybe you need to let Cleo do the fighting."

Rosalind bit her lip. "What did she look like? Blonde hair, pale skin, hazel eyes?"

He narrowed his eyes. "How did you know?"

"I saw her reflection. Erish saw her too, a glimpse of her when she looked at me." She frowned. "What happened with you and Cleo?"

Ambrose's eyes darkened. "It's none of your concern. I need to know if you're going to drink the blood."

Rosalind stepped closer to Ambrose, grabbing him by the wrists. "This is how you like to have conversations, isn't? And my answer is... I'll tell you when I'm ready."

18

Rosalind strode down the dank, earthen hall, on her way to see Erish a second time. According to Ambrose, she wasn't supposed to show mercy to her enemies. But Ambrose had a little preoccupation for total domination that she didn't share. She could think for herself, and her own thoughts highlighted two things.

One—there was no benefit in making a captive suffer. Erish needed to be caged, sure, but they gained nothing by freezing and starving her.

And two—maybe Erish could be useful. Erish knew how to use gods-magic, and she knew how Drew operated. And she wasn't likely to give up her secrets when resentment boiled her blood.

Rosalind carried a basket full of fresh bread and cheese, some freshly cleaned and folded clothes, water and washing cloths. Tucked under her arm were a wool blanket and a small pillow.

Dim candlelight danced over Erish's barren cage, and the succubus sat rigid in her cell. She looked more skeleton than human. Only her dark eyes swiveled to Rosalind, glinting with anger. "Ah. You've come to gloat again."

"I told you I'd speak to Ambrose about your conditions." This wasn't the time to ask for a bargain. If she wanted to get Erish on her side, she'd have to be patient.

"And now you're sneaking down here on your own. Looks like he takes your opinion very seriously."

"He's got a bit of a god complex."

"So you've noticed."

Rosalind sat on the dirty floor, lowering herself to the same level as Erish. She handed Erish the bread and cheese. The succubus snatched them, ripping into the bread with stunning ferocity.

As she chewed, she fixed her eyes on Rosalind. "You're not gloating, are you?" she said between bites. "You're miserable." She swallowed hard. "What do you have to be so miserable about? Apart from the fact that you're dying, you have everything you need. Beauty. Food. The attentions of gorgeous men who want to fuck you."

"When we were in Maremount, you said that your sisters were killed."

"By humans," Erish snarled.

Rosalind had seen one of their heads—now petrified—adorning the city's drinking fountain. "Well, now we have something in common."

"Your twin?" Erish ripped off another hunk of bread. "What happened to her?"

"Drew killed her. Right in front of me."

Erish swallowed a bite of bread. "He is a bit twisted, isn't he?"

You don't know the half of it. As she sat across from the ancient demon, an idea sparked in her mind. "I don't suppose you know how to raise a body from the grave?"

"Is that why you've come here with this bread and those clothes?" Erish snarled. "I was wondering what you wanted."

Rosalind shook her head. "Never mind." She pushed the blankets and fresh clothes through the bars, glancing at Erish's chains. "Do you need help washing and changing your clothes?"

Erish stared at her. "I'll manage."

Rosalind stood, brushing off her pants. "I'll come back with more food tomorrow." She turned, but as she began to walk away, Erish's voice stopped her.

"Rosalind. Wait."

Rosalind stopped walking.

"Drink the ambrosia," Erish continued. "Use Nyxobas's shadow magic to raise your sister."

The ambrosia. Rosalind turned back to Erish.

"I wish I'd had the gods-magic when my sisters died," the succubus muttered softly.

"When I saw you in Maremount, after you drank the ambrosia—"

"I lost my wits." Erish cocked her head. "But they've returned. I can't promise the same will be true of a human. You must decide if it's worth the risk."

"I don't yet know how to use gods-magic. Malphas is supposed to teach me, after I drink the blood."

"It's shadow magic. Just think of your lover, and he'll find a way to help you."

"What lover?"

"Don't play coy. I've told you everything you need to know."

Rosalind nodded, gripping the empty basket. "Thank you."

She turned again, hurrying down the earthen hall. *Gods-magic.* She had a choice to make, but it wasn't much of a choice at all. She could abandon her sister to the afterworld. She could let Drew take over Boston and Cambridge, burn all the vampires, destroy Caine, and force her to be his mindless, brainwashed wife. A dead-eyed vessel for his progeny.

Or she could drink the ambrosia.

What did she have to lose? *Her mind.* And what good was that anyway, with a dead witch taking control?

Climbing the stairs, she pulled the flask from her pocket. *If Caine were here, he could tell me what gods-magic feels like. How to use it.*

How was he doing, anyway? She couldn't tell day from night here in Lilinor, but it must have been two days at least since Caine had left. Loneliness pressed on her like a hundred rocks.

At the top of the stairwell, she pushed through a tall oak door into a dark stone hall. Moonlight streamed through the windows, but shadows crept over the hall like long fingers. A chill rippled over her skin.

Maybe it was time to pay Miranda's grave a visit again. Maybe it was time to drink from Blodrial's veins.

Drink, child, said Cleo. *Let the gods-magic flow through your veins.*

Rosalind stalked through the dark halls, the candlelight dancing over the stone floor. As she walked, the hair rose on the back of her neck. She shivered. *Why do I have the feeling that I'm not alone?*

A scraping noise turned her head, and she caught a flicker of liquid movement in the shadows. She reached down to her waist, pulling a hawthorn stake from a holster. "Who's there?"

"Easy there, Hunter." Frowning, Tammi stepped from the shadows, dressed in white.

Rosalind heaved a sigh of relief. "Tammi? What are you doing in here? I thought you were supposed to be stuck in the Abzu."

Tammi crossed to Rosalind, wrapping her arms around her. "I knew something was wrong. No one would tell me what had happened." She squeezed Rosalind tight, and Rosalind hugged her back. "I just snuck out to find you."

Gods, it was a relief to have Tammi back. Rosalind sucked in a deep breath. "Something terrible happened."

"I knew it. What was it?"

"Miranda is dead." Rosalind's eyes filled with tears.

"*What?*"

"Drew found his way into our city, with an army of demons. He's turned into a complete psychopath. He burned dozens of vampires." A tear rolled down her cheek. "He stabbed Miranda. He tried to make me do it, but I didn't. So he killed her."

Tammi's jaw dropped, and her eyes filled with tears. "No."

"I'm going to try to bring her back."

Tammi wrapped her arms around her in a tight embrace. "And how do you plan to do that?" she asked, her voice muffled by Rosalind's neck.

"Ambrosia. The starved succubus in the basement tells me it will work."

Tammi pulled away. "You can't possibly trust her. Won't the ambrosia make you mental?"

"I'm already mental."

"You seem fine to me."

Rosalind shrugged. "Well, I guess I have practice wrestling with the voices in my head. So maybe I'll deal better with madness than Drew has."

Tammi narrowed her silver eyes. "I'm not sure about your reasoning."

Rosalind clutched the flask—her new salvation. "It's not just to raise my sister. We need it to stop Drew. He can wield a new kind of magic that's nearly impossible to fight. And since I'm from the same blood line, apparently I can too. I need to fight fire with fire. Otherwise I'll end up as his slave, and he'll turn half the country into mind-controlled demons."

"There's got to be another way."

Rosalind waved a dismissive hand. She didn't want anyone dissuading her, now that she'd made up her mind. "It'll be fine. How did you find me here, anyway?"

"I smelled you."

Rosalind wrinkled her nose. "Seriously?"

"Your blood smells amazing." Tammi took a step back. "I probably shouldn't hug you again."

"Right." She lifted her flask, whispering, "Speaking of blood, it's time for my medicine."

Tammi narrowed her frosty eyes. "You want to do this now?"

"Yes. We need to get Aurora, and then we're heading right for the Garden of the Dead. I don't know a lot about necromancy, but I'm pretty sure it can't be a good thing to let the body rot for weeks." She lifted the flask. "So are you going to help me, or are you going back to the Abzu?"

Flanked by Aurora and Tammi, Rosalind stood before the yew, covering her nose and mouth with her hands. Aurora had unearthed Miranda again, and this time the smell of death was overpowering. Her skin had turned even more greenish, and dark blood dripped from her nose and mouth.

"I'm not sure about this," Tammi said, coughing into her hands. "She seems a bit... putrified."

Rosalind swallowed hard, trying to steel her resolve. "There must be some healing process as part of Nyxobas's resurrection magic."

"There are two options," Aurora said. "Either you get Miranda back, or you get Zombie-Miranda back. If she's all rotten, we'll have to put her down. Then she'll be dead, which is no worse than she is now. So, two options: life or death. That's all there is."

"Right. We have nothing to lose by trying." Rosalind's fingers tightened into fists. "I'm ready."

She unscrewed her flask, taking a sniff. She hadn't tasted this since she'd been in the Brotherhood's chambers. Now, the smell turned her stomach. Would this really work? Or would it merely drive her mad?

Only one way to find out. Grimacing at the taste, she took a swig of the blood. She wiped a hand across the back of her mouth. Nothing but the cold trickle of salty blood down her throat. *Gods damn you, Drew.*

But just as she began screwing the cap on, a burst of power flooded her body, rushing over her skin and through her bones. Wet marine magic, rough coppery auras... electric silver and spicy gold. Her knees trembled at the rush, and she opened her eyes again. Whorls of colorful magic snaked around her body.

Tammi was staring at her wide-eyed. "Is it working?"

Rosalind nodded. "It's definitely working."

She closed her eyes, feeling the breeze rush over her skin, whipping her hair around her face. She'd watched Caine use this magic. He'd simply held out his hands, and let the gods-magic flow through him. But then—he was part god himself. It must come naturally to him. Right now, she felt such a stunning rush of power she hardly knew where to begin.

At last, the tendrils of magic rushed into her body—filling her bones and blood—almost as if they were becoming part of her. She rolled her neck.

"So what do you need to do?" Aurora asked.

"I need to figure out how to use shadow magic."

Think of your lover. Erish must have meant Caine—not exactly Rosalind's lover, but he *was* the last man she'd kissed.

He was the closest thing she knew to Nyxobas, so close that when she'd used the power of the night god, he gave her a glimpse of the incubus's life. And while he wasn't her lover now, she was lying to herself if she didn't admit that she wanted him.

Caine was her closest connection to Nyxobas. She'd been there when he'd used his gods-magic. She knew how it felt when his electric power rushed over her skin, how the air looked as the silver tendrils whipped out of his body. She just needed to tap into those memories.

Closing her eyes, she called up an image of Caine in her mind. His golden skin. Those glacial eyes. Warm and cold, sun and ice. The shadows curling around his powerful body, the black tattoos marking his chest. She could almost feel him wrapping his strong arms around her, lighting her body on fire with his touch.

Not my lover... yet.

Dark magic coursed through her veins, and Caine's smell, loamy and electric, enveloped her. In the next moment, she found herself in that wooden room again. Sitting in a chair, facing a dark wood wall, a blonde woman brushed her hair. A baby's cry pierced the air, and Rosalind watched herself pick up the gray-eyed child, cradling him in her arms.

Shadows crept over her vision, and an empty ache rose in her chest. She wanted to see that child again, but darkness stole him from her. Her stomach lurched as she reached out, trying to grasp something tangible and finding only wisps of shadow.

Where am I?

Now, she walked through a dark stone hall, surrounding by whispering voices. Shadows climbed the walls like fingers. A deep voice rumbled from the emptiness. *What are you doing here?*

What *was* she doing here? She could hardly remember her name. Right now, she wasn't even sure she'd ever existed.

What are you doing here? the voice demanded again.

She had a purpose. She just needed to remember what it was. A sister, one with brown eyes who smelled of the sea.

"Miranda!" she screamed, suddenly finding her voice. "I want to fix her. To bring her back."

An electrifying power flooded her, rooting her feet on the earth once more. She opened her eyes, watching the silver magic flow from her fingertips. It rushed over Miranda's body, washing her in moonlight.

This time, the magic found its target.

Miranda's skin warmed, her cheeks reddening. At the sight of her sister's fluttering eyelids, Rosalind's breath caught in her throat. Miranda's back arched, and the blood disappeared from her face. Rosalind's pulse raced.

It's working. Nyxobas's will is my own.

Miranda gasped, sitting up straight, her eyes wide. Blood pounded in Rosalind's ears, and she lowered her hands, her body drained. Miranda looked up at her and screamed; the sound pierced the air, and Rosalind's knees nearly gave way.

Something is wrong.

Tammi rushed to Miranda, wrapping her arms around her. "Shhhhh, girl. It's okay."

Rosalind stared wide-eyed at her sister, who pulled away from Tammi, crawling on her hands and knees. She vomited dark bile onto the grass.

"Are you okay?" Tammi asked.

Miranda sat back on her knees, wiping the back of her hand across her mouth. "What's going on?" she asked, her voice husky. "I don't feel so well."

Rosalind took a breath for the first time since Miranda had opened her eyes. She ran to her sister, hugging her.

Miranda's body felt warm through her thin dress, and she hugged Rosalind back.

And once again, she smelled like the sea.

19

As she waited for Malphas, Rosalind stood at the shore of the Astarte Sea. Waves gently lapped at the rocks, and moonlight flecked the water with silver sparks.

She'd spent a long night, watching over Miranda as she'd slept. So after just an hour of sleep, she'd rushed off to find Malphas. Today he was supposed to teach her how to use Borgerith's magic—the coppery, mountain aura that Drew had used the first day she'd met him.

But that was just the beginning. Tonight, she'd also learn to harness Dagon's power. Yet she wasn't sure she was up for meeting the god of the depths. Tiredness had claimed her mind, and she swayed on her feet.

When was the last time she'd slept for more than six hours? It was nearly impossible to keep track of normal sleeping hours in a city with no daylight.

Last night, after some tea and a warm bath, Miranda had seemed almost normal again. Exhausted, but speaking in full sentences. Except she didn't seem to remember having died, or anything about Drew's invasion of Lilinor.

And how, exactly, did one broach that subject delicately? "Remember that time you died? No? Well, you did. Want another muffin?"

Rosalind didn't want to break it to her just yet. Whatever death did to a body, it had to be a shock to the system. She saw no reason to add another shock just yet. What if Miranda's newly pumping heart just stopped again? So during the quiet hours when she'd normally have been sleeping, she'd watched over her newly-living sister, listening to her deep breaths. She'd watched the blood pump through the veins in Miranda's neck, and marveled at her own creation.

Now, on the Astarte shore, Rosalind blinked hard, fighting fatigue. A briny wind rushed off the waves, and she pulled her cashmere shawl tighter around her shoulders. She wouldn't be fighting today, and she'd worn a long dress, the color of sea-foam.

When she looked at the dome of stars above the sea, she could see a faint shimmering of Caine's silver magic. *The shield.* If she let her eyes go out of focus long enough, his magic became clearer—the stunning sterling gleam rippling over the sky.

Cold magic thrummed over Rosalind's skin, scented of lilies. *Malphas.* She turned.

He stalked toward her, the wind ruffling his brown hair. Moonlight washed his milky skin in silver, and he carried a faded maroon tome under his arm. The sight of him tightened her chest. Sharp cheekbones, porcelain skin, cold eyes and dark lashes. She couldn't help but think about her own hands, drowning that delicate beauty in the Brotherhood's dungeons.

Whenever she looked at him, the memories hit her like fist. The nail, driven into his chest. The chains. The water poured on his face, his legs kicking as he drowned. Hard to forget what she'd done, when it was staring her right in the face with those pale eyes.

And yet, she reminded herself, his fragility was an illusion. As an incubus, steely strength coursed through his muscles.

"Thanks for meeting me." She glanced at the dark sea. She wanted to ask about Caine and the valkyries, but that particular vision was hard to explain without delving into the whole necromancy subject. "Do you think Caine will be home soon?"

"That's the thing." Malphas's aura snapped the air around him. "He should have returned already."

A sharp tendril of dread coiled through her chest. "You think something happened to him?"

"I don't know. I haven't been able to see anything through scrying, because of the shield Caine created. That's why I want to make sure we get this right. We might need to get him back. Are you willing to do whatever it takes to win this war?"

No pressure. "Of course. I'll do whatever I need to."

Malphas closed the distance between them, and she could feel the warmth coming off his skin. In the V of his shirt collar, pearly light illuminated the top of his scarred chest—marks left by Rosalind. A chill crawled up her neck, and she tried not to stare at the slashes of raised skin.

"From what I've seen," he said, "you are the type of soldier who will do whatever it takes to get the job done. Even if it involves pain."

Her body went cold. *Okay. He's still thinking about the torture thing, too.* "What sort of pain are we talking about?"

He leaned down, smelling the air near her neck. So close to him, his aura crackled over her skin—a sharp, electric thrill that made her lean in closer.

"Oh, Rosalind," he said. "I know the smell of Nyxobas's magic. The smell of damp earth and the air after a rainstorm. So why would you smell like the gods-magic, if you haven't used it yet?"

Her stomach tightened. *Guess the secret is coming out anyway.* Maybe it was for the best. She was desperate to come clean about what she'd seen in her vision, and to ask Malphas what he thought.

"After I drank the ambrosia," she said, "I tried a little spell. I tried it several times before I drank the ambrosia, and something happened—almost like I was channeling Caine's magic—but I had no way to direct the power. It wasn't until I drank the blood that it worked effectively."

Malphas stared down at her, and the hair raised on the back of her neck. No matter how much time she spent around demons, their preternatural stillness and penetrating eyes still made her want to run far in the other direction. It was an intent focus, like a coiled snake about to strike.

Still, she held her ground. After all—she had gods-magic now, too. Maybe she didn't need to be scared of demons anymore.

Malphas's dark power thrummed over her skin. "What sort of spell?" he asked.

"Just a little one," she lied. "I snuffed out the candles and extinguished the flames in the fireplace, like Caine does when he's angry."

Shit. I hope incubi can't tell when you're lying.

"You're lying."

Of course they can. "Let me guess. You heard my heart rate speed up?"

"And your pupils dilated. Your skin warmed. A thin sheen of sweat rose on your forehead. Incubi are skilled at noticing these hallmarks of arousal. Either you're extremely turned on by talking about fireplaces, or your pulse is racing at the lies tumbling from your lips."

She frowned. "I don't suppose I can convince you I have a thing for fireplaces?"

He cocked his head, ivory light glinting in his pale eyes. "What kind of spell did you conduct, Rosalind?"

Rosalind waved a dismissive hand. "It's not important. The important part is..." She cleared her throat. *I can't talk about this.* She needed to change the subject. "I think it was connected to Caine's magic somehow. And I think I saw visions of his life. Maybe visions of him now."

A heavy wave crashed over the rocks, and briny spume misted the air.

"What did you see?" Malphas asked.

"I saw a woman with long blond hair. And a baby with grey eyes, the exact same color as yours. On a table by a bed lay a hairpin." She held out her arm, running her fingers from her wrist to the hollow of her elbow. "It was the same as that tattoo Caine has here."

Malphas seemed entranced by her fingertips. "You've stolen a glimpse into my brother's life."

Ocean spray dampened her skin, and she licked the salt off her lips. "But then I think I saw him in Maremount, surrounded by valkyries. They were closing in on him."

The air seemed to thin around Malphas. Had he blinked once this entire time she'd been speaking to him? She was sure he was searching her for signs of lying again. "And then what?"

"In the final vision, he was walking in a dark stone hall, surrounded by whispers and shadows."

Malphas's body glowed with a deep silver light. "It sounds like the House of Shades, where spirits go after death. Perhaps that's where Caine is now. Looking for Miranda's second soul."

"Is it dangerous?"

"Only if he stays too long, and gets lost among the dead."

She shivered.

Caine had once said to her, *You have no idea how dark hell is.*

20

*R*osalind frowned. "How did I end up with those visions?"

"I think you borrowed power from Caine, not Nyxobas. Caine must have allowed it. You wouldn't have been able to use his magic unless he'd granted you permission. It's good news. It means he's still alive."

"Would he know what sort of spell I'd conducted?"

Malphas arched an eyebrow. "What *exactly* did you do, Rosalind?"

"Would he know?" she repeated.

"No, only that you used it. And I do hope it was important. You might have weakened him, and he may need strength to free himself from the House of Shades."

A chill washed over her skin. *Please be okay, Caine.* "He'll come back soon. And if not, I'll find him with the gods-magic you're going to teach me." She rubbed her arms. "Where do we start?"

He opened the book, thumbing through the pages. "You're lucky I found this book in the library." He met her gaze. "Or perhaps unlucky. From what I read earlier, in order to use the gods-magic, you'll need to go into many hells. They will be painful, and agonizing, and you'll want to die. I've been to one only—the shadow void. But you'll go into all of them."

Her heart skipped a beat. "Was there not a better way you could have phrased that?"

"There's no point sugar-coating it. You'll learn soon enough." He narrowed his eyes. "You know, I remember quite vividly the feeling of iron nails driven into my chest, and the water you poured into my lungs. Perhaps that will help me put some of my sympathy aside so we can get on with things." He ran his fingers over the jagged scars on his chest. "But the real question, Rosalind, is do *you* have the stomach for it?"

"I'll do what I need to. We have to stop Drew somehow."

"Good. I know you can take orders—I saw you follow Josiah's. And now you have to be prepared to follow mine. You'll have to trust me."

She nodded. "I'm ready."

"You'll have to keep your second soul in check. It's easy to let someone else take over when your mind is ripped apart by terror and agony."

Rosalind's pulse raced, and Cleo's aura curled around her lungs. *Let me come out to play. I can take it,* the mage whispered. Rosalind schooled her face into calm. "Where do we begin?"

"Tonight, we begin where life began, on the sludgy rocks and in the sea. I'm glad you asked about Borgerith first. It's a good place to start."

"Why is that?"

"She will grant physical strength and help stabilize your magic. Ambrose tells me that when you fought in the armory, he was able to overpower you easily. The only reason he didn't rip your throat out was that some part of him exercised extreme restraint. So you've learned to fight, but you still need strength on your side."

"And when I have this power," she ventured, "I won't need to use a spell to conduct magic. Physical power will just flow through my body. Like yours."

"Exactly. Once you're finished visiting all the hells, you'll be able to defend yourself against anyone. Vampires. Demons. Even me, should we ever find ourselves on the opposite side of a war again."

"I hope we don't."

"But most importantly, you'll be able to fight Drew." He nodded at the ground. "Take off your shoes. I want to see what you can do before you experience Borgerith's hell."

She slipped off her thin flats, stepping onto the damp, jagged rocks. The marine wind kissed her skin through her dress.

"Close your eyes," he said. "Tell me what you feel."

She cleared her throat. "Wind. Seawater. Slimy rocks and sand. Jagged stones and pebbles."

Malphas stepped behind her, his aura tingling over her skin. Heat radiated from his body. "I want you to feel Borgerith's power through the rock. Bend her will to your own."

Rosalind arched her back, opening herself up to the power of the mountain goddess. A rough aura brushed over the skin of her ankles, and the smell of a craggy breeze surrounded her. When she opened her eyes, she caught a glimpse of a coppery magic, curling around her ankles and up into her dress. The magic snaked around her waist, and buzzed over her ribs.

"I feel it," she said.

Malphas ran his fingers down her arm, sending shivers over her skin. He let his fingertips rest at the end of hers. "Do you feel the power flowing through your arms, into your hands? Call the pebbles into your fists. Use a magnetic charge. Borgerith has the power of magnetism."

Rosalind looked down at her fingertips, which brushed lightly against Malphas's. A coppery aura played about their hands. *Right. I just need to lure the rocks to my hands, with the power of my mind.*

Borgerith's power flowed around her, along with Malphas's magic, a stunning vortex of silver and copper.

What would Caine do if he discovered she'd raised her sister? He wouldn't kill Miranda—would he?

Malphas leaned down, whispering in her ear, "You're not focusing."

She closed her eyes, imagining the pebbles on the ground. She tried to picture them flying through the air into her palms.

Malphas's fingertips continued to brush hers, but her palms remained empty. He exhaled. "I was hoping to avoid the hells, but it's not working." He stepped in front of her, scrubbing a hand over his chin.

"So, now it's time for Borgerith's hell?"

"Yes. You'll need to lie back on the rocks."

Her pulse raced. "Of course."

Seawater misted the air as she lowered herself to the rocky ground. She lay back, her head resting on the cold, damp stone. Sharp rocks bit into her skin through her dress.

Malphas stood above her, the moon forming a silvery halo around his head. "Spread out your arms and legs. Press your fingers to the rocks." He spoke in a low, soothing voice. "Root yourself to the earth."

She flattened her palms against the damp, sandy rock, and spread out her legs. The wind flowed over her skin.

Malphas knelt down. "Let her power flow into your body through your skin. Feel her immense strength, rooting you to the ground."

She closed her eyes. A wave crashed on the shore, splashing over her feet. Rough magic brushed over her legs, faintly scented of pine.

His fingertips traced over her arms. There was no way around it. Incubi were extremely tactile.

"Let her magic flow into your body," he said. "You must let the ancient part of your brain take over."

Power thrummed over Rosalind's skin, and she breathed in the scent of mountain air. Another wave rushed over her, misting her dress with cool water.

"Feel the weight of Borgerith's strength," Malphas said.

As he spoke the words, Rosalind felt an immense pressure on her chest, crushing her ribs. She gasped, her eyes snapping open.

"Don't resist it," Malphas said. "Let her strength become part of you."

Gods, the weight was grinding her ribs into dust. She struggled for breath. "Malphas." She choked out the word. Agony crushed her like a boulder on her chest, stealing her breath. Any minute, her ribs would crack and pierce her lungs, her heart. She squeezed her eyes shut, trying to block out the pain.

"Take the power into your body," he said.

Another ton of rocks pressed her into the hard earth, ready to break her body. She opened her eyes, nearly ready to cry uncle, but a coffin of rock surrounded her.

She hated being trapped more than anything. Panic blazed through her mind.

I'm going to die here, ground into dust.

The weight of a mountain crushed the breath out of her, and pain tore through her body. Deep within her rocky coffin, an image began to play before her eyes: Smooth stone walls. Another buried room. Malphas, chained to a chair, his porcelain chest bleeding.

173

And there was Rosalind, standing before him, gripping a jagged iron shard in her fist.

Raw fear shone in his pale eyes.

But as Rosalind rammed the nail into his chest, a very different emotion glinted in her eyes: pleasure. A dark thrill. As the vision disappeared, the word *monster* roared in the back of her mind.

Monster. Monster. Monster.

And what happened to monsters? They needed to be locked up, to be buried deep within the earth's core.

Grinding pain cut her to the marrow. This was her punishment. The rocks would rip her body apart, would bury her under the earth.

I have to get out of here, before the weight of this destroys me.

21

She looked down at the copper magic whirling over her chest. *Let it in.* Right. That was what Malphas had said, right? It was so hard to think straight when the pain was ripping her mind apart.

Even as her chest felt like it would cave below the weight, she concentrated on forcing the magic further into her own ribs. A scream tore from her throat as the aura plunged into her body, cracking her bones. Yet, as it flowed into her, power surged through her muscles. The weight on her chest lifted, and her back arched with a blazing power, healing her body.

A cool mountain wind rushed over her skin, and her coffin of stone thinned, giving way to a canopy of stars. She sucked in a deep breath. *I can breathe.*

Slowly, some of the agonizing pain left her body. A cool wave washed over her legs. She grabbed her ribs, her eyes flicking to Malphas, who knelt over her.

Malphas touched her cheek. "You made it." He let out a long breath. "I wasn't sure what would happen."

Magic ignited her nerve endings, but so did pain. Flinching, she rose, her limbs shaking. She couldn't stand straight. She was lucky her ribs hadn't punctured anything. "I think something's broken."

"Come here."

She stepped closer to him, suppressing a groan of pain.

Frowning, he brushed his fingertips over her ribs. "Broken in three places. After tonight, you won't break so easily." He closed his eyes, whispering a spell. His aura caressed her skin, soothing her body.

As the pain left her ribs, she sighed. She had to admit, incubus magic felt amazing.

He dropped his hand, eyeing her carefully. "What did you see?"

A wave lapped at her feet. "Me. And you. In the Brotherhood's prisons." She hugged herself. "I was hurting you."

"I see. And how did you feel when you were doing it?"

She let out a slow breath, her gaze trailing over the brutal scars on his chest. She couldn't exactly tell him she'd looked like she was having a great time. "What difference does it make?"

"Did you enjoy hurting me?"

"Of course not."

In a blur of silver movement, Malphas lunged closer to her, pinning her arms with one hand, and grabbing her throat with the other.

She struggled against him. "What are you doing?"

"You're lying to me."

Her heart raced, hammering against her ribs. "Malphas! Stop!"

"Do you know the natural instincts of a demon?" he snarled. "To take what's ours. To fuck and kill. To rip out the throats of our enemies and leave twitching carcasses in our wake. And when you stabbed me and left me for dead, you marked yourself as my natural enemy."

She stared up at his pale eyes—no longer sad, but full of icy rage. Still, he was Caine's brother. He wouldn't kill her. Would he? "Can we talk about this inside?"

His large fingers tightened around her neck.

Anger simmered in her chest, and she glared at him. "I thought we were moving beyond the past," she choked out.

"I was. I'm not sure that you did. And maybe the vampires are right. Maybe you need to be put in your place."

The raw power of Borgerith burned through her muscles, and fury ignited her veins. She'd have to fight back if she wanted to get out of this intact. Malphas's demonic instincts had been inflamed, which meant she was in some serious danger if she didn't break free.

She slammed her forehead into Malphas's nose. He dropped his grip, and she followed with a hard punch to his jaw. Malphas staggered, his head swiveling with the blow. When he turned back to her, blood dripped from his lip. His eyes had turned completely black. In a whirl of silver magic, he rushed to her, spinning her around and pinning her arms to her side.

He's lost his fucking mind. She struggled him, but he'd been too fast, and his steely body pressed against hers, trapping her.

"What the hell, Malphas?" she shouted.

And yet, somewhere, deep in the hollows of her mind, Cleo was enjoying this. She relished the fighting, the adrenalin, the feel of Malphas's powerful body against her own.

Malphas leaned down, whispering into her ear. "It's okay, Rosalind. I needed to see if it worked."

"What?"

"I needed to how you'd handle it when you had to fight for your life."

"You could have warned me." Raw power coursed through her muscles.

"Then you wouldn't have really fought."

She leaned back, turning her head to look at him. "If I'm so strong, why are you the one pinning me?"

"You don't have speed, and you haven't been trained. Yet." He loosened his grip and stepped away from her. "And when you have both speed and training on your side, you'll be terrifying. I've probably seen more of your vicious side than I need for an eternal lifetime."

Her body burned with a strange mixture of energy and fatigue. "One hell down, five more to go. That's right, isn't it?"

"Yes." He pulled the book from under his arm, flipping through. He landed on a page with a drawing of tentacled appendages gripping a galley ship. Muttering to himself, Malphas dragged his finger down the spidery text. "It says you must return to the place where life itself began."

The black sea churned, and marine air rushed over her skin. *Time to meet Miranda's god.* "What can I expect from this hell?"

"According to this text, the sea teams with life, but it's not always beautiful. It can be ancient, brutal and ravenous." He met her gaze. "If you want Dagon's power, you must keep swimming under the water until you find him. Don't come up for air until you feel the gods' arms around you, and he embraces you with his magic."

She shivered. "So I just swim into the sea?"

"Seems that way."

She stared at the churning black water, and the chilly moonlight glinting off the waves. "You think I'll make it through this?"

Malphas closed the book, his expression softening. "I know you'll face whatever challenge you must. I remember when you were a little girl. You led the way through the Tuckomock Forest when we explored. You were first into the dark caves. You were fearless."

"Sounds vaguely familiar."

"You were attacked by a wolf. The thing ripped right into your leg. And the next time we went into the woods, you were first in the cave again. Like you had no sense of self preservation. I don't think you'll come up for air until you meet Dagon." He stepped back into the shadows, leaving her alone on the shore.

A faint memory sparked in the back of her mind. *The boy with gray eyes, bandaging her bleeding leg.*

On the dark Astarte shore, cold wind rushed off the sea, chilling her body. As she walked over the rocks, icy water rushed across her toes.

The sea's dark, oily sheen warned her away, but she had to go through with this. It might be the only way to free herself from the One True King. She needed the pure, intense power of gods. She took a deep breath, her body buzzing with adrenalin. A waved rushed over her legs, cold as a grave.

Deep below the waves lurked one of the dark gods.

22

$\mathcal{R}$osalind stepped deeper into the water, her muscles bracing at the cold. Her teeth chattered as the water reached above her belly button.

A strange baptism, Cleo whispered. *Are you sure you can handle the gods-power without losing your mind, little blossom?*

Rosalind tried to block out Cleo's voice, focusing only on the feel of the icy water swarming around her ribs and the algae-slicked rocks below her feet. She really didn't need Cleo's doubts adding to her own apprehension.

A wave rushed over her skin, shocking her with cold.

Time to make the plunge.

With a deep breath, she dove under the chilly water, kicking her legs to take her deeper under the waves. With the power of Borgerith still pulsing through her limbs, she was moving at a fast clip, plunging deeper into the sea.

After what seemed an eternity, her lungs began to burn, and the waters grew darker.

Where the hell is this god?

She was desperate for air. Pain ripped through her lungs, and seaweed brushed over her legs. She turned her body, glancing up at the water's surface. Faint shards of moonlight streamed through the dark water.

Air. I need air now.

She kicked her feet, turning for the surface. But before she could get anywhere, a slick limb wrapped around her leg. Her heart thudded hard against her ribs, and a cold dread bloomed in her chest.

Dagon.

His presence alone filled her a terror that pierced her to the bone.

A long, slimy appendage slipped up her dress, climbing up her leg and pulling her deeper under the water. Another curled around her waist. She kicked her limbs, flailing in the water.

I need air.

Dagon's limbs gripped her tight, pulling her deeper. Pain blazed through her lungs, and a vision rose in her mind. She was standing by the shore of Maremount's river, rain hammering her body. Miranda stood by her side. Four rotten stakes jutted from the ground, skeletal fingers clawing out of the earth. In a blur of silver, Caine dragged Rosalind's mother through the mud. Her mom kicked helplessly, eyes wide.

Caine's magic chilled the air as he slammed her mother against one of the stakes, pinning her arms.

Icy terror trickled into Rosalind's lungs. *I know how this ends, but I don't want to see it.* She wanted to tear her eyes away, but there was no escaping the vision.

It took only a fraction of a second for Caine to ram the nail through her mom's ribs. The crack of breaking bone sent a shudder up Rosalind's spine, and she gaped as her mom's eyes snapped open.

When Caine turned to look at Rosalind, his eyes had turned black as the void. Here he was, the angel of death, come to wreak his vengeance.

He disappeared in a blur of silver, but she knew he was coming back.

Why had her parents thought they could defeat a god? What kind of insane hubris had led them to that conclusion?

While Miranda screamed, Caine returned with their father, throwing him with brutal force against the second stake. Rosalind had forgotten what her own father looked like—those narrow hazel eyes, the full beard. A strange familiarity surged in her chest.

Her father tilted back his head, screaming, "I am the One True King! I am—"

The thrust of Caine's second nail cut him short. Her father's eyes bulged, and a low moan rose from his throat. Blood dripped from his lips, and his head slumped. The life left his eyes.

Miranda wouldn't stop screaming—or was that herself?

Caine turned to her again. Black wings rose from his back. His eyes were deep and dark as the opening of a cave. Her stomach curdled.

Here he was—her executioner. She took a step back, slipping over a rain-slicked rock and falling to her back. The fall knocked the wind out of her. When she pushed herself up again, Caine was gone.

Sobbing, Rosalind glanced at her twin. Her shoulders shaking, Miranda looked so small. Rosalind watched as her sister turned, running back for the city.

Her father's head lolled. The One True King, pinned to a rotting piece of wood like a butterfly specimen.

She stood on the river's shore, her clothing soaked. Completely alone. A bitter loneliness pierced her to the core. Rain poured down her skin, and emptiness welled in her chest. A gnawing, ravenous emptiness, like she was drowning here in the dark, under the waves. Dread trickled down her throat, filling her lungs.

Not dread. Water.

She was drowning—deep under the black sea, enveloped by the slimy limbs of a sea god.

Dagon, please.

Slick flesh wrapped around her head, covering her mouth. All the air had left her lungs, and death beckoned her closer. It would be so easy just to give in...

As Dagon tightened his grip, she bucked and flailed in his grasp. *I must get back. I must return to Miranda—to Caine.* Adrenalin surged, and she fought against his grasp. She couldn't die here below the waves, in the cold and the dark. *Sometimes the buried things claw their way out again.*

Her throat began to convulse. This was what Malphas had felt when she drowned him.

Let the magic in. Don't fight the gods.

As water poured into her lungs, she opened her eyes. A deep, blue magic undulated around them, like sea anemones caught in a current. She let her body go limp, imagining the blue magic filling her body. It flowed into her chest, mingling with the copper and vernal magic in a vortex of power.

Her lungs still burned, but as she let the magic in, the feel of Dagon's limbs around her changed; they were no longer slimy and alien. His monstrous body had been replaced by a man's. His smooth, strong arms embraced her for just a moment before releasing her into the water.

She turned to see him, but the god had disappeared. Around her, the ocean teemed with life, and shimmering moonlight poured through sapphire water. On the seafloor, amber and crimson urchins nestled among the undulating seagrasses. The sudden flash of beauty was so overwhelming she nearly forgot the water filling her lungs.

She kicked her way toward the moonlight, swimming between seahorses and colorful fish. Fatigue tore her body apart. This had been too much at once.

When her head breached the surface, she coughed and spluttered.

I'm not even sure I can make it to the shore.

As she pushed herself on, her mind churned. Deep in her chest, Cleo's aura was roiling.

Malphas nearly killed you, Cleo whispered. *Are you quite sure he's not after revenge? He was right about what he said. Demons are made for one thing—fucking and killing.*

Malphas had been right. With her mind ripped apart by terror and pain, it was hard to keep her second soul quiet. She gasped for air. *Shut up, Cleo.* She kicked her feet, fighting her way to shore.

He is using you, Cleo whispered. *The demons let Miranda die. And if you die, they'll only find another vessel for their dark desires. They use people, then discard them. Don't think you're special.*

As she swam, her body drained of energy, Cleo's aura began to rage like a tempest.

They'll let you die when you no longer serve their purpose. Ask Ambrose what he did to me.

Rosalind's muscles throbbed. Just when she thought she could no longer continue, her feet brushed against the seafloor, and she stood. She trudged through the waves, falling to her hands and knees in the shallow water. Sharp rocks bit into her palms, and she coughed, spitting up salt water onto the rocks.

This is how the demons want you, Cleo whispered. *On your knees. Knowing your place.*

"What happened?" Malphas asked.

Get up, Rosalind.

The rocks scraped her knees, but she couldn't make herself stand yet. She heaved another lungful of saltwater onto the rocks.

Malphas kneeled. "It doesn't look like it went well."

Another series of coughs racked her body.

Get up, Rosalind. It's humiliating to be on your hands and knees before the shadow demons.

She coughed up a final mouthful of seawater before pushing back to sit on her knees.

Cleo's aura roared through her. *He's trying to kill you.*

With shaking legs, she rose, trying to steady herself. She gripped Malphas's collar. "I nearly drowned before I succeeded. You're sending me to my death."

Were these her thoughts, or Cleo's?

Malphas's eyes darkened, his fingers tightening around hers on his collar. "Did you want sympathy for the water in your lungs? I'm fresh out."

Cleo's vivid memories whirled in Rosalind's mind: the night she'd met Ambrose, and the gold rings on his fingers. He'd worn an embroidered shirt, and he'd looked at her like he'd wanted to devour her.

"No man should be that beautiful," Rosalind said, the words tumbling from her mouth. "I should have known he'd be my ruin." She blinked hard, trying to clear her mind. "Stop it, Cleo."

Malphas pulled Rosalind's hands from his shoulders, and looked into her eyes. "I can see that we went too far. Next time, we do one hell at a time. You need to rest in between."

"No," she said, shaking her head. Her mind still flashed with images of gold rings and piercing green eyes. "What if Caine needs us?"

"You won't be much good to him when you're hallucinating. Next time you're starting to lose control, tell me. Go home and sleep."

He turned, walking off into the night.

As Malphas stalked off into the shadows, Rosalind glanced at the sky. She could still see the faint shimmer of Caine's shadow magic rippling over the sky.

Was it just her imagination, or did it seem less powerful than it once had?

She shivered, suddenly feeling very alone.

23

*D*renched with seawater, Rosalind pulled open the door to her cavernous room. Her body trembled from both cold and fatigue. A breeze filtered into the warmly lit room, toying with the silver curtains and nearly snuffing out the candles.

Miranda sat nestled into the corner of the bed, cloaked in shadow. She was so still that Rosalind nearly missed her. She'd wrapped a star-flecked blue sheet around herself, and her shoulders shook.

Rosalind's heart tightened. "Miranda?"

"Where am I?" Her teeth chattered. "What happened to me? I feel sick."

Rosalind crossed to the bed, crawling closer to her sister. She wrapped her arms around Miranda, pulling her close. Miranda's body felt warm—definitely alive. "How sick do you feel?"

"Not so sick you need to smother me with your damp arms. You're getting the bed all wet."

A smile curled Rosalind's lips. "You're awake."

Miranda pulled away from Rosalind, her teeth still chattering. "Yeah but... I'm confused. Where are we? The last thing I remember is being in Maremount. Drew had put a necklace on me, and... I think Caine was there. My mind is cloudy."

Rosalind's chest tightened. *She really has no idea what's going on.* She couldn't hide this from Miranda forever, but she wanted to wait until she seemed a bit stronger before she broke this news. "We're safe now. We're in Lilinor, protected by the vampire lord—sort of. No one knows you're here. I snuck you in, so you must stay in my room for now. You need rest. You had a... an accident, and now you're recovering."

Miranda frowned. "An accident? Like a head injury?" She touched her temples. "I feel really dizzy. I think I'm dehydrated."

Rosalind stood, crossing to an oak table that stood below the window. "I can get you some water." She paused. *She doesn't want blood, does she?* "You *do* want water, right?"

"I wouldn't say no to wine, but water's probably healthier." Miranda frowned. "I don't understand. How did the accident happen?"

Good. Seems normal. No requests for human flesh. "You don't remember anything?"

"Nothing since Maremount."

Rosalind filled a glass of water for her sister. "Drew came into the city. You fought, and he injured you."

"Injured how?"

Too early to tell her—but she'd have to do it soon. "We'll talk about it later. We both need food, and sleep." Someone had left a basket of fresh cranberry bread, curling with steam, on the table next to the water. At the sight of it, Rosalind's stomach rumbled. "Are you hungry?" she asked.

"Starving, now that you mention it. It smells delicious."

Rosalind grabbed the whole bread basket along with the glass of water, and brought them to her sister. "Ambrose still sends me fresh food every day. The other vampires resent it like you wouldn't believe. They feel like they've been made into my servants."

Miranda shrugged. "Sounds like Ambrose wants you."

"What? No, he doesn't." Rosalind sat on the bed, sliding the basket over to her sister. "He hardly knows me."

Miranda arched an eyebrow. "What does that have to do with anything? He *is* gorgeous. Haven't you noticed? I suppose maybe you wouldn't have. You're more focused on Caine."

Rosalind bit her lip. *Maybe I should revisit that death-conversation idea.* "You know our history with Caine. It's all a bit twisted."

Miranda grabbed a piece of bread. "It was horrible when it happened. But maybe he did us a favor. I think Father was like Drew. And face it, most demigods would have killed *us*, along with our parents, for what they'd done to him." She drained the glass of water, then wiped the back of her hand across her mouth. "Is he in Lilinor?"

Rosalind shook her head. "He's on a mission. He's looking for Drew in Maremount." *And with any luck, he won't end up lost in the House of Shades.*

"I can see by your face that you're worried about him," Miranda said, "but I'm sure he'll be fine. Last I remember, we were on a cliffside, and Caine was flying through the air like an angel."

"True. But Drew is powerful, too. He uses gods-magic."

"Right. Drew told me all about that in Maremount—Descendants of Azezeyl. So what's the plan to fight him? Am I involved?"

Rosalind grabbed a warm slice of cranberry bread and shook her head. "No. Like I said, no one knows you're here."

"I don't understand why."

"I'll fill you in later. You've just woken up."

Miranda flexed her neck. "I can't feel my magic." She frowned. "I can't feel Dagon. Or my second soul." She took a shuddering breath, her eyes glistening. "What *happened* to me?"

"The accident... It sort of knocked the extra soul out you."

"What the hell does that mean? What aren't you telling me, Rosalind?"

"You're alive and healthy, and that's all you need to know for now. I'm sure we can get the soul back if you want it."

Miranda took a hungry bite of bread, eyeing Rosalind. "*You* smell like Dagon."

"I went for a swim. I'm training for a fight with Drew."

"Training how?"

Rosalind let the tangy bread melt in her mouth. For a moment, her eyes fluttered closed, and Cleo assaulted her with an image: powerful hands bedecked with golden rings, sliding up a golden silk gown. Rosalind forced her eyes to open again, shoving the unwelcome images to the back of her mind. It wasn't the time to let Cleo take over. She'd just gotten her sister back, and this was the chance to learn Miranda's stories.

She rubbed her eyes. "I want to know about our past. I still don't remember anything from Maremount, apart from the thing with Caine, and a few flickers of Malphas as a little boy. I want to remember the *good* things. I want to know about you."

"You look like you want to fall asleep. You look half-dead."

Rosalind's shoulders stiffened. *An awkward word choice, given one of us is literally half-dead.* "I'm fine. Just a little tired from my swim." She'd just gotten Miranda back. She didn't want to sleep just yet, not when she still had so much to learn. "Tell me something fun. I want happy memories. What games did we play?"

"You liked the water back then." Crumbs rained from Miranda's mouth as she ate. "Our parents should have given *you* Dagon's magic instead of me. You liked to build little ships out of wood, and then we'd go to Athanor Pond to sail them in the water."

The image licked at the corners of Rosalind's memory. "It sounds familiar."

"I had a pet bird. A meadowlark named Poppet. When she died, we had a Viking funeral for her. We put her tiny body on one of the boats and set it alight. We let it drift into the pond, and you made up Viking prayers."

Miranda's voice soothed Rosalind, and the rich cranberry bread filled her belly. She leaned back on the pillow, not caring that her sodden dress dampened the blankets, or that crumbs stuck to the sheets. It was so much nicer to be here with her sister than out in the cold, being crushed with rocks. She rested her head against the stacked pillows. "What else do you remember?"

Miranda lay next to her. "You and me and Malphas, we used to sneak out sometimes at night. We'd lay in the dandelion beds and watch shooting stars. You always wished for the same thing."

"What?"

"Indian pudding. You were simple that way. I always wished that we could live on our own, away from our parents. You, and me, and Malphas, in our own little house."

Rosalind smiled, her eyes drifting closed. "What would you wish for now?"

"The same thing. Or maybe we could stay here in Lilinor," Miranda mused. "Except we need daylight here. And the vampires would have to stop drinking blood."

"And we'd free the courtesans." Rosalind's eyes began to slowly drift closed. "I need more stories."

Miranda pulled a blanket over her. "When we were little, you loved the wildflowers. We both did. We threaded them into wreaths."

As sleep beckoned her closer, Rosalind could nearly see the stars graven in the sky, and feel the dandelions beneath her back. Her arms stretched out over the grasses.

Not Maremount, Cleo whispered in her skull. *Fife. Scotland. We wait here for Ambrose.*

Rosalind's eyes snapped open. *Damn you, Cleo. You're taking up all the space in my head.*

24

*R*osalind sat in an armchair, taking a final bite of her cheese croissant. She didn't have long to linger over breakfast today—not with her next appointment with Malphas looming over her.

Sitting on the floor, Miranda chomped into a sugar cake, white powder dusting her lips. Warm candlelight danced over her pink cheeks, and she looked healthy as ever. Her appetite seemed particularly thriving. In fact, they'd only been awake for ten minutes, and Miranda had already chowed through three miniature sugar cakes.

"Ambrose is wonderful," Miranda said, "sending us all this food."

"It is honestly my favorite thing about him," Rosalind said. "And at some point I need to meet Caine's chef."

"When does Caine return? And what, exactly, is he doing?"

"He's supposed to find a seal of Azezeyl."

"For what?"

Rosalind swallowed her bite of sandwich. "So we can get your extra soul back to you." At least, that was Rosalind's part of the plan, even if Caine didn't know about it yet. "First, he has to find the soul in the House of Shades. And when you get the soul back, then we make the daywalkers."

"Right. Since the accident knocked my soul out of me." She frowned. "That doesn't make sense, you know."

Okay. I'm going to have to tell her soon. "I'm learning a new kind of magic with Malphas. And when I used it, I saw a glimpse of where Caine is—in the House of Shades, looking for the soul. Now we just have to hope he doesn't get lost there."

Miranda lowered the sugar cake from her mouth. "And you're training with Malphas to use this gods-magic?"

"I've drunk the ambrosia, like Drew has. Last night I was learning to use Dagon's magic, and Borgerith's."

Miranda frowned. "Why didn't you ask me for help with Dagon?"

"It's different from the magic you use. It doesn't require Angelic. I had to travel into Dagon's hell, and anyway, you can't leave the room."

"Shouldn't I have the ambrosia as well? If you can do gods-magic, I can too. We're both descended from Azezeyl."

Miranda had a point—and yet, death was just another unpredictable variable in this equation. Rosalind wasn't quite sure what would happen with this gods' blood in her system. "I need one of us to stay sane for now, plus you're still recovering from the accident. The power will drain your resources as you recover. And anyway, Malphas doesn't know you're here."

"I feel fine." Her forehead crinkled. "Explain to me again why no one is allowed to know I'm here?"

Rosalind swallowed hard. *Okay. It's time.* "The accident—"

"The one that knocked the soul out of my body."

"It wasn't really an accident."

"What do you mean?"

Rosalind bit her lip. "I thought you needed a night to recover; that's why I didn't tell you right away."

"Will you just spit it out?"

"Drew killed you. You were dead."

Miranda's jaw dropped. "I was *what?*"

"Drew murdered you. And then I used shadow magic to bring you back to life. It's just that no one knows I did that, except Tammi and Aurora, because it's against the law."

Miranda was staring at her own fingers in shock, as if searching for decay. "How?"

Rosalind touched Miranda's arm. She had a feeling that recounting the details would mean opening a mental wound she wasn't capable of closing. "The important part is, you seem fully recovered. The magic worked. I just had to commit a bit of sacrilege."

Miranda stared at her, her eyes brimming with tears. "Are you sure this was a good idea?"

"What else was I supposed to do? I wanted to get you back. It wasn't fair."

"I don't know." Her lip curled. "I just feel tainted. How long was I dead for?"

Rosalind shook her head. "A couple of days. It's hard to keep track of time here. But you're healed now. You're not tainted."

"Then why is it against the law?"

"Caine has prohibited necromancy. Aurora said it's considered a heresy to steal from Nyxobas. But I don't really give a crap about Nyxobas."

Miranda dropped the remains of her cake in the basket again. "I think I've lost my appetite."

"It'll just take some getting used to. And when Caine returns... I'm hoping we can convince him to give you the second soul back."

"So, I'm a serious abomination now."

Rosalind forced a smile. "I thought we established that we were already abominations. You, me, and Tammi. The land of Abominatonia. Might as well embrace it."

"You were never a corpse with putrefying organs."

Rosalind cocked her head. "No, but I've been drinking ambrosia, like Drew. I've been told by several demons that a human using a gods-power is an affront against nature with potentially monstrous consequences, and if I start to go power-mad, I need you to put me down."

"I'll do no such thing." Miranda raised a sugar-cake again, as if making a toast. "To the abominations, I guess."

Rosalind raised her water glass. "To us."

"And what do you plan to do with this gods-power?"

"First, I need to make sure the shield is functioning. Then, I'm gonna work on my ability to take down Drew in a fight."

She glanced at the old silver clock on the wall. 7:00. *Time to go.* She stood. As she crossed to the wardrobe, she stretched her arms over her head.

"Right," Miranda said. "So I'll just wait in here eating cake while you save the world. On balance, I guess I'm kind of okay with that."

"I don't think you'll be getting out of the fight that easily. You still need to help us make the daywalkers." Rosalind pulled off her nightgown, then bent down to pull a knife and holster from the wardrobe. "You know how to handle a second soul already. You're the best choice for the role. No point dragging Malphas into it."

She strapped the holster to her naked thigh. She wouldn't need weapons for training with Malphas, but she didn't like to walk the halls unprotected. She pulled a black cotton gown from the closet and slipped it over her head. Under a shawl, the long sleeves would keep her warm out in the fields of Enlil.

Rosalind pulled a silver shawl from the closet, wrapping it around herself. As she crossed to the door, she cast one last glance back at her sister. "Will you be okay?"

Miranda frowned. "I'm feeling quite violent toward him right now. Do you think that's a side effect of death?"

"No. I feel the same way. Completely normal." She flashed a faint smile. "I'll see you in a few hours—or however long it takes to master the power of Nyxobas."

"Sounds simple enough," Miranda said, her mouth full of croissant.

Rosalind pulled open the door, stepping into the hall. Her muscles ached and shook from the rush of magic the night before.

She walked through the stone corridor, half-entranced by the candlelight dancing over the stone floor. When she tried using shadow magic, would she get a glimpse of Caine's life again? It was hard not to think of him, getting lost in the House of Shades. It seemed such a dark and lonely place.

As she walked down the hall, she thought of that amazing kiss that had knocked the world out from under her feet. She could almost feel the soft brush of his lips against hers, or the electric touch of his fingertips down her arm...

She didn't really know what he'd thought of it. Maybe it hadn't meant anything to him, yet she was desperate to kiss him again.

She pushed through the door into the stairwell, lifting her skirt to hurry down the stairs. At the end of the hall, she pushed through an oak door that led out of the fortress. The breeze caressed her skin. The waning moon loomed over the gently rolling fields. It bathed the fields of blue flax and calendula in silver light— the color of Caine's eyes.

She strained her eyes in the dim light, picking out a bare sycamore tree that stood in the field of Enlil. As she walked, a damp, floral breeze toyed with her hair. She pulled her hair high above her head, securing it with an elastic.

Last night, after visiting Dagon's hell, she'd nearly lost her mind—yet today she felt no more insane than usual. It seemed that some good sleep and good food went a long way.

At last, she stopped by the sycamore, pulling her shawl tighter. It felt painfully lonely out here on her own. When she glanced up at the sky, she could see the shield's silvery shimmer, thinning just by the moon. This time, she was certain: the shield was falling apart.

Footsteps made her turn her head, and she saw a dark form moving closer—tall, broad shoulders, just like Caine. If it weren't for his pale skin gleaming in the moonlight, she'd hardly be able to tell them apart.

"Rosalind," Malphas said.

"Thanks for meeting me here." She pointed at the sky. "We have a little problem."

As he drew, closer, he gazed up at the stars. "What?"

"The shield is thinning. I wasn't sure last night, but now I can see that it's disappeared in some places."

He arched an eyebrow. "You can see that?"

"Of course. One of my abomination powers. What will happen if the shield doesn't hold?"

"If it doesn't hold, Drew could create new portals into the city using his shadow magic." He stood by her side, the wind ruffling his hair. "Looks like it's a perfect time for you to test out your shadow magic."

"What if I used Caine's magic again?"

"Why?" he asked.

"Because then we'd get another glimpse of him. We'd know if he's made it out of the House of Shades."

Malphas cocked his head contemplatively. "You're quite concerned about him, aren't you?"

"I just want to know he's okay." She glanced at the sky, eyeing the shimmer that thinned just to the west.

His silver eyes blazed from the darkness like stars. "You're hoping to see glimpses of his life again."

She frowned. "Not to spy on him. It's just the only way we have to check on him."

"Why do I have the feeling that you're hiding something? Are you going to tell me what spell you did the last time?"

"Am I not allowed to keep secrets? Ambrose won't tell me what happened with him and Cleo. Caine has a million buried secrets: his tattoo, the blond woman and the baby, what happened when he lost his mind, why he killed the king and queen of Maremount centuries ago... And I don't know any of your secrets, but I know you help bury Caine's."

"The thing about secrets," Malphas said. "Is that they have a way of finding their way into the light."

"I guess we can both look forward to learning about each other when that happens." She tightened her fingers on the shawl. "So, what do you think of my plan?"

"It could weaken him, potentially."

Rosalind glanced at the sky, and the silver aura now seemed dangerously thin. "I think we need to act—"

Before she could finish her thought, a sharp crack sounded across the horizon.

"The shield," she whispered.

The ground began to rumble, and a geyser of water spurted from the ground of Enlil field.

"What's happening?" Rosalind asked.

"Drew is creating a portal," Malphas said. "I think his Hunters are about to enter Lilinor."

25

*M*alphas grabbed her arm. "Do the spell. Now. Use Caine's magic. And while you're sealing it, I'll fight whatever comes through."

Her heart galloped in her chest, and she closed her eyes, listening to sound of distant water gushing from the ground. With the adrenalin blazing through her nerves, it was hard to think straight, hard to think of Caine.

"Hurry up!" Malphas snapped.

"Fine." She closed her eyes, imagining the feel of Caine's lips on her neck. Instantly, she could picture him vividly, as if he stood before her in the hallway. She could imagine that sharp, hot pain of standing so close to him without touching him. His stunning contrasts of sun-kissed skin and icy eyes, the gentle curve of his full lips. She could imagine him moving closer to her, so close that the heat from his body warmed her skin.

He leaned down, his breath hot on her neck. *Are you looking for something from me?* He stroked his fingertips over her hips, sending heat racing through her body.

"Magic," she said.

His fingers slid around the small of her back. "What sort of magic?"

"The shield," she breathed. "I need to strengthen it. They're coming."

His powerful aura rushed over her body, thrumming up her legs and curling around her body. The vision changed, darkening and rippling before her eyes. Whorls of dark silver and black magic gave way to stone walls—powerful, masculine hands, grabbing a woman's throat. She wore a diamond tiara, crooked on her mussed blond hair—blue eyes wild with terror.

Fury exploded. *So easy to snap her little neck. But perhaps that's too easy.*

In a blur of silver magic, those powerful hands threw the queen through a closed window. Her white gown fluttered in the black night like a surrender flag. *Goodbye, queen.* She landed with a *crack* on the hard ground below Throcknell Fortress. *Maremount.*

The vision rippled—and Rosalind was no longer in the castle. She was outside, looking up at it. Rain poured, and lightning speared the dark sky. She'd seen this view before—in fact, she'd seen it in a portrait on Caine's wall.

As she stared up at the fortress, she became aware of a new sensation—pain, searing deep in her gut. She looked down at her body.

No, Caine's body.

A wave of horror slammed into her. Iron nails impaled him—pinning him to a wooden post. Now she felt his pain, and it ripped her mind apart. This was his punishment.

She felt Caine's lips move, and he uttered one word: *Stolas...*

In the next moment, the vision had shifted. Now he walked through Cambridge, but the city had changed. Where squat buildings had once stood around Harvard Square, now stood a labyrinth of towering stone temples and palaces.

A burst of Caine's silver magic flashed around her, and the vision cleared, but the agony still pierced her gut. She clutched her stomach, staring up at the sky over Lilinor. As the magic poured from her body, she lost track of time, lost in a vortex of magic. Some of the thrill of Caine's magic faded, and a cold void bloomed in her ribs.

Nyxobas's power.

The word *Stolas* haunted her mind like a curse.

Powerful shadow magic flowed from her body, spiraling up to the starry sky. It spread over the thinned gaps in a stunning web of silver magic. As the magic moved through her, some of the pain began to slowly ebb, healed by Caine's soothing magic.

At last, a sterling sheen covered the sky once more.

She whirled, searching for Malphas. There, in the distance, he fought a team of muddy Hunters. She lifted her dress, pulling a knife from her holster, then took off across the field. Malphas seemed to be holding his own—in fact, he'd snapped through two necks already. But there were still four of them and one of him.

As she ran, the wind rushed over her skin. A now-familiar ferocity spurred her on, and she felt a battle fury ignite her body. She wouldn't let these bastards get close to anyone she loved ever again, or find their way to Miranda's room. Not while she had breath in her body.

Burn them, Cleo whispered. *I want to hear their screams. It's what they deserve.*

Borgerith's power burned through Rosalind's muscles. Within an instant, she was standing behind a hunter, pulling the man's head back by his hair. She sliced her knife through his neck, slitting his throat. She heard a gun cock behind her, and she whirled, hurling her knife into the man's chest. But as she did, the Hunter unleashed a bullet into her gut. She fell back, hitting the ground.

Two Hunters remained.

Despite her wounds, magic coursed through her body, dulling the pain. From the ground, she kicked the legs out from under another. He slammed against the ground and reached for his gun. She kicked it out of his hands, and her next kick connected with his skull.

With the power of Borgerith's strength, her kick to his head completely shattered his skull, and his head lolled.

She glanced at Malphas, her body shaking.

He nodded. "I guess the magic is working out well for you." His eyes narrowed. "You're hurt."

She rested her hands on her knees, hunching over. As the rush of battle left her body, agony from her wound began to pierce her gut. The magic was flowing from her system again, leaving her shaking with pain. She suppressed the vomit threatening to crawl up her throat.

Malphas rushed to her. "Let me see."

Trembling, she straightened. As soon as Malphas touched her shoulder, his magic tingled over her skin, drawing the pain from her.

"This will hurt for a second," he said, examining the wound. "I'm going to get the bullet out."

She clamped her eyes shut and held her breath. For just a moment, pain pierced her gut. But within the next few moments, as his fingers traced the outside of the wound, his soothing aura washed over her. When she opened her eyes again, she looked to the sky, taking in the deep sterling gleam.

"How does the shield look?" he asked.

"Fixed. For now." She shot a glance at the portal, but it had been sealed over now with an oily mud. "But we'll need to keep an eye on it."

Malphas nodded. "Next time, you need to work your own magic. You can't keep borrowing from Caine."

For just a moment, the memory of Caine's torment burned fresh in her mind, and she pressed on her chest. What was it that he'd said? "Stolas," she whispered.

Malphas touched her arm. His pale eyes darkened. "What did you say?"

"What does *Stolas* mean?"

The air seemed to cool around them. "It means you should never use his magic again."

"Why?"

Black swirled in his eyes. "And more than that—never mention to Caine what you saw. Understood?"

Apparently, she'd stumbled upon another one of Caine's darkest memories.

"The thing about secrets," she said, running her finger over her new scar. "Is that they have a way of finding their way into the light."

26

$\mathcal{M}$alphas stared at her. Nearby, the crickets started to chirp again, as if coming back to life. Six Hunter bodies littered the ground near their feet. Rosalind tried not to look at them.

"I suppose that's true about secrets," Malphas said, "but you'll need to develop shadow magic on your own anyway. You won't need Caine's."

He had a point. And, moreover, she wanted to try out her own shadow magic *now*. Yes, they'd just encountered an unexpected battle, and their bodies weren't yet cold. But she'd come out here to journey into the shadow hell, and already she needed to feel the rush of a new type of magic. She wanted to feel the power coursing through her veins.

"So let's do it," she said.

"Now?"

"That's why we're here, right?"

It felt delicious to kill, Cleo whispered. *Didn't it?*

Malphas frowned. "Are you sure you're up for it? You've just been shot."

"Yes!" she shouted, maybe a little too loud. "I'm fine. You healed me. And when I get back from the shadow void, you can teach me to move like the god of night—like Caine and you do. I want to feel that speed. I want to move like the night wind."

She'd seen Caine in battle, the blur of silver and shadow. If she could combine strength with that speed, she'd be a formidable force. Even among demigods.

"Fine." Malphas pointed to the moon. "This time, think about the jewel of Nyxobas, instead of my brother."

"Any tips for me to survive the shadow hell intact?"

"It's just like the mountain magic you used before. You'll need to let Nyxobas's power into your body without letting it overwhelm you."

"Of course." Her legs still shook from the magic she'd conducted earlier, and she needed to feel that raw thrill of gods-magic.

Malphas moved in closer and his aura curled around her body, whispering over her skin and sending shudders through her body. It smelled like moonflowers.

Caine's not around, Cleo whispered. *Why not take his brother for a ride instead? Believe me, when you're dead you'll regret wasting your time.*

"Shut it, Cleo," Rosalind snarled.

Malphas took a deep breath, and his eyes returned to their usual pale gray. "I'm not sure that you're ready for this power. I wouldn't have started with magic this intense if we'd had any choice. Flickering candles would have made more sense as a starting point."

"But like you said, we don't have a lot of time. So how does this work? Before, I lay on the rocks and then swam into the sea. But the night isn't a physical place."

"That's why it's a good thing you have me here, to lead you into the void."

She still sensed tension in his powerful body. Whatever *Stolas* meant, she'd touched a raw nerve. She stared up at the moon. "Lead away, Malphas."

As soon as the words left her mouth, silvery shadows thickened around them, enveloping Rosalind's body. Electric power crackled over her skin. Malphas's body seemed to fall away from hers, and his warmth disappeared.

And then there was nothing but the dark. No up, no down. No sound, nor comfort. Just a sharp emptiness that bloomed in her chest, and grew until it seemed like it would eat her from the inside out.

Dread took hold of her heart, and a loneliness so thorough she couldn't hear her own thoughts. All she knew was that she'd always been here. And she always would be. Rosalind had never existed at all...

The realization tore her mind apart, until she could no longer remember who she was, her name, or anything she loved at all. For what seemed an eternity, she drifted in the void, consumed by emptiness.

At last the darkness thinned, and she found herself on solid ground. She sat in an empty house—a room with glass windows that overlooked a dusty, gray landscape. When she glanced down at the chair in which she sat, she saw it was more of a throne, made of onyx. The cold marble chilled her skin. But at least she could feel again.

She took a deep breath.

I'm alive. I'm here.

Where, exactly, was she?

A cold room, built of white and black marble. Windows looming over a desolate landscape.

From the corner of her eye, she caught a flicker of movement. A figure loomed by one of the windows, but she didn't want to look. *I don't want to see...*

A deep voice, like thunder, rumbled over the horizon.

Look up, Rosalind. See your future.

Terror stole her breath.

I don't want to look.

And yet, she seemed to have no control over her body. She felt her head turn, her eyes swivel toward the window...

There, through the glass, her own face gaped, open-mouthed like a dying fish. Horror slammed into her. Somehow, she was in two places at once, and the world no longer made sense. And worst of all: the Rosalind who stood on the other side of the window didn't look right. Her eyes were empty and lifeless, her skin gray, her body unmoving.

The Rosalind on the other side of the glass—the second Rosalind—was already dead.

See your future.

Bile climbed up her throat.

I need to get out of here.

With shaking legs, she stood. She ran for a black door, pushing through it into a gray, marbled hall. It seemed to stretch on for miles, and her footsteps echoed off the ceiling. She didn't know where she was running to, just that she was desperate to get away from her doppelgänger.

But as she ran, an aura filled the hall—tendrils of black, scented of the grave. From out of nowhere, a powerful hand gripped her by the hair, yanking her head back.

In the next second, someone was slamming her against the wall with a painful *crack*. Her heart thudded against her ribs, and she stared into the pale, waxy face of Bileth.

He was bare-chested, a sword slung around his waist. The stench of decay filled her nose, and a low growl rose from the demon's throat. He snarled, exposing his long teeth, and gripped her wrists hard; his nails pierced her skin. "My little Hunter. What has brought you here? To my home?"

This can't be happening.

Was she really here, or was this some sort of vision? It certain didn't feel like a vision. Not from the nails digging into her skin, or his fetid aura crawling over her body.

"Is this the shadow hell, then?" she asked.

"No." He leaned in closer to her neck. "But you smell like you've come from there. I can smell the dread on you. And now you're here, in my manor. What have I done to deserve this pleasure?"

His hot tongue licked her neck, and disgust rose in her gut. As he touched her—without her permission—she could feel Borgerith's power flooding her body. It gave her a strange sense of certainty that she could fight him, an uncanny strength that blazed through her muscles.

And *speed*. Now, she had speed. Her power could match his. And he had no idea.

"Open your legs," he said.

"I have a better idea." She slammed her knee into his groin.

He grunted and dropped her wrists, his eyes widening with shock. Clearly, he hadn't expected her new power.

While he was dazed, she took the chance to punch him hard in the side of the head.

He staggered back, howling with pain. She followed up with a kick to his chin. His neck snapped back with the blow.

She had him where she wanted him. And yet... where the hell was she supposed to go? Somehow, she'd ended up in his manor. Where was this magic from Nyxobas she was supposed to let in?

213

She kicked him again, this time in the chest. The blow knocked him back into a window, shattering the glass. Broken shards rained over him, slicing into his skin. Then, in a blur of shadows, he pulled the sword from his sheath.

He swung for her, and she leapt back. But not fast enough. The blow cut into her gut, and she screamed. Bileth's dark magic whorled around her in a cyclone of shadows, wild wraiths that tore at her hair. As the world around her darkened, she found herself floating in the void once more. The painful emptiness gnawed at her.

But this time she was going to let it in.

She took a deep breath, letting the shadows fill her blood, until nothing remained but the dark. She fell to the ground—the wildflower and grass. She clutched her stomach, and in the next moment Malphas was leaning over her, gently touching her arm.

"Seven hells, Rosalind. What happened?"

Pain speared her gut. "I ended up at Bileth's house, I think."

Malphas shook his head. "That's not possible. You were here the whole time."

Blood soaked her fingers. "Then how do you explain what's going on with my stomach?"

"I'll explain in a minute. Right now, I need to heal you, okay?" Deftly, he ripped open the tear in her gown. His fingertips brushed over the skin around her wound, and she felt his magic thrum over her body for the second time, in waves of electrical power.

As his magic worked its way over her skin, the pain left her stomach, replaced instead by a soothing warmth.

She looked up into his silver eyes.

"What happened? he asked. "For fuck's sake. I just fixed the last one."

When she remembered that empty room—the sight of her own dead face—the agonizing emptiness still cut through her heart, so raw she could hardly remember how to speak.

"Rosalind?" Gently, he touched her forehead.

She swallowed hard, sitting up. "I definitely went to the void. Just at the start." She shook her head. "And then, somehow... I was in Bileth's mansion. We fought."

He nodded slowly. "You had a vision in the void."

"A vision?" She frowned. "Is that what it was? How does that explain the giant slash in my stomach, then?"

"Sometimes, your own mind has control over your body. If you believe it's real, then it's real."

Her body shook with fatigue. Images whirled in her mind: the dead Rosalind, staring at her through the window; the nails, piercing Caine's gut to the post; the fields of wildflowers, where Cleo waited for Ambrose...

The queen's murder. The hairpin on the wood table. The word *Stolas* falling from Caine's lips.

She shook her head, trying to think clearly. "No. I was in a lot of places. I was in Maremount, and Bileth's mansion. I've been with Ambrose, in the sycamore grove."

"Rosalind," Malphas said. "You're losing focus."

"I'm the collector of too many people's memories now— Caine's and Cleo's and my own, clamoring for attention in my skull. Trying to outdo each other."

"You need rest."

"I'm fine. I just..." She trailed off. She wanted more of that rush again. How would she convince this man to do what she needed him to do?

"You need rest, Rosalind. I'm not going to be responsible for your insanity."

"We need to keep going. I'm fine now." She clamped her eyes shut.

Think, Rosalind. Convince him.

She couldn't quite keep her thoughts from drifting away, couldn't remember how to speak clearly. But maybe Cleo could.

She let Cleo's aura bubble in her chest. "You know," she said, her voice clear as a bell. She sat up straight, smoothing out her hair. "I feel fine now. I just had some aftereffects from the shadow hell, but my mind is clear as day now."

Malphas narrowed his eyes. "What's the rush?"

"Caine seemed like he could be in trouble." She heard the words tumbling from her lips as Cleo took over. "And Drew could break through that shield at any moment. We don't have time to waste."

"You nearly died. Twice."

"I'm fine," she heard herself say, with a hint of growl. "Let's go. You said I needed to be prepared to go as far as it takes, and I am. Are you?"

There was no way around it. She was going to lose her mind. Might as well try to save the world while she was at it.

27

They trudged into the Edin Woods, and Rosalind tried to ignore the gaping tear in her gown. Her mind was a whirlpool of images. Golden rings and bluebells. Blonde queens falling from towers, their gowns fluttering in the wind. Someone seemed to whisper the name *Stolas...*

Her head whipped at the sound, then she blinked her eyes. *Stay focused.* She was in a forest, and she had some more powerful magic to acquire.

The wind rustled through the ash trees towering above them, and faint streams of moonlight pierced the leafy canopy. In the distance, a nightingale trilled. The air smelled heavy here, like damp moss, like the undersides of rocks.

"Druloch is already your god," Malphas said. "You should be familiar with him."

"He's Cleo's god."

"Let Cleo lead you, then. Druloch's hell will be unpleasant, but I'm sure you can handle it."

"You think so?" She just need to feel that raw thrill of magic once more. The godlike power. Already, her body was buzzing in anticipation.

He paused by a towering oak, and leveled his gaze on her. That silver, god-like gaze. "Back up. Against the tree."

She stepped back against the bark. "What will this sort of magic feel like?"

"Power over plants and the life of the forest. Power over death and decay. The power of a mob's fury, desperate to hang the latest scapegoat from the branches of an elm. The brutal strength of a primitive human mind, and the power to give in to divine, liberating frenzy."

"Plants?" She couldn't hide the disappointment in her voice. She'd been hoping for an earth-shattering power.

He shrugged. "Obviously you've never been in a famine, or near death from starvation."

Cleo's aura whirled, slamming Rosalind's mind with a vision of a dingy prison cell. She watched Cleo's emaciated hand, reaching for a half-dead rat.

"Oh, I've starved nearly to death," Rosalind said, with a ferocity that cut through the air. "I've eaten vermin from the filthy floor to stop myself from dying."

Malphas's eyes widened. "When you lived with the man who adopted you? I knew he was brutal to you. But I didn't realize how brutal."

Rosalind shook her head, dropping eye contact. It had been Cleo's memory, not her own. But she couldn't tell Malphas that. He wouldn't let her practice more magic if she was losing her mind, and she was already jonesing for more power. "Let's not talk about the past. What do I need to do for this magic?"

"You can start by feeling the trunk behind you."

She pressed her fingertips against the rough bark, and it scratched her skin through her dress.

Malphas took a step closer to her, and as he did, his eyes slid down to the tear in her gown.

Okay. Maybe he *had* noticed the rip.

She felt Cleo stir. The old witch seemed to like the way Malphas was looking at her.

"Close your eyes," he said, meeting her gaze again. The heat from his body warmed hers, and his silver magic curled around her protectively.

As if responding to Malphas's aura, Cleo's magic came alive, wrapping around her body in green tendrils. *Look at the beautiful incubus,* she whispered. *Until you finally make good on our bargain and throw yourself at Ambrose, I guess one of these demigods will have to do.*

Rosalind gritted her teeth, trying to marshal some control over her mind. She'd wanted Cleo to take over—but not so much that she was going to jump on any shadow demon in her path.

"You okay?" Malphas asked.

"I'm good," she said.

He nodded. "Cleo's aura should respond to Druloch's power. Do you feel it?"

She inhaled the deep scent of pines and oaks, feeling the leafy magic stroke her skin.

I feel Cleo.

"Close your eyes," Malphas whispered.

She did as instructed, letting her eyes drift close, and her entire body buzzed with anticipation. As she lost herself in the vernal magic, vines slithered up her legs, wrapping around her thighs, pinning her arms to the tree. Her eyes snapped open at the sensation, and she stared at Malphas.

His eyes gleamed like icy beacons in the darkness, not a spark of humanity in them.

C. N. CRAWFORD

"What happens now?" she asked in a raspy voice.

"Now, you learn what it feels like to be on the wrong side of mob justice. Something you've only seen from the other side. You will learn what it feels like to be at the mercy of those who fear not only death, but life itself."

Her stomach dropped. "What?"

Shadows enveloped Malphas, and a low rumble filled the air. The vines tightened around her, pulling her back against the tree bark until she thought her ribs would crush. Slowly, the tree bark gave way, sucking Rosalind inside its soft wood.

The trunk molded around her, scented of decay. Bugs scuttled over her skin, up her legs.

So this was Druloch's hell.

From within her own mind, Cleo's voice answered, *No, Rosalind. Not even close.*

From within the tree, a chorus of voices began to chant:

We wait beneath corrupted frozen ground.
Unconsecrated, tangled roots enshroud
our crumpled necks and long-smothered embers,
where the hours fly, and death is remembered.

Her mind whirled. She didn't understand exactly what they were saying, but she thought she understood who they were. The voices of those killed unjustly—the witches, the outcasts, the scapegoats.

They'd come for a reckoning.

From the soft wood, hands clasped at her body, tearing at her skin. As the tree seemed to close in, bugs scuttled over her body—up her dress, into her mouth. She opened her mouth to scream, but a filthy hand clamped over her mouth.

A deep voice intoned in her ear: "The unlamented will claw back their fates from those who fanned the flames with pious breath."

220

Rosalind couldn't breathe. There was no air in here, and the tree was crushing her. Another bug scuttled into her mouth, climbing down her throat, and she gagged. The tree's walls pressed in closer, crushing the hands against her, and screams rose in her mind—the screams of the fallen, the unjustly slaughtered. The women whose feet danced over Salem's grass, and the men who dangled from elm branches.

The tree closed in, slowly crushing her bones for what seemed like an eternity.

Let the power in, Cleo whispered.

Rosalind closed her eyes, envisioning the vernal magic entering her body. Bony hands clawed into her flesh, ripping her open, letting the bugs in. She shrieked in agony, until at last, a vernal magic filled her.

The pain began to subside, and Druloch's power washed through her.

She opened her eyes once more. She stood beside the tree, looking into Malphas's deep, silver eyes. Her body trembled, and she looked down at herself. This time, she hadn't come back with a wound.

"It's okay, Rosalind. You're back now."

Her entire body shook, but ancient power now coursed through her veins. And it felt amazing. She wanted to sew a forest of yews, and bend the elms to her will. She wanted to wrap this shadow demon in vines, and keep him as a toy...

He touched her shoulder, moonlight dancing over his pale skin. "You've had enough for one day."

"No." Her legs were ready to give way. But she wasn't done yet--two more gods to go. She trembled with the power at her fingertips, and Cleo's aura roiled in her chest. Images flashed in her mind: Cleo's emaciated hands picking up a rat; Ambrose's pale skin, glowing like a beacon in the night. Gold rings around his fingers.

"We keep going," she said.

He narrowed his eyes. "But how is your mind?"

Cleo purred. *Why not let me take over again, little thing? It's time for you to rest and let the real warrior take control.*

Rosalind plastered a smile on her face. "No worse than usual. Let's go on."

28

Surrounded by towering elms, they walked through the forest. Here, the air felt damp and salty, and she could hear the distant crashing of waves.

Somewhere, under Cleo's visions, the mystery of Caine nagged at the back of Rosalind's mind. What did *Stolas* mean? And what had he been punished for so viciously in Maremount?

But she could hardly keep her thoughts straight with Cleo taking over.

She found herself staring at Malphas—and when she spoke, the words that came from her mouth were not her own. "You act kind. But surely it's an act. I believe that demons are driven to totally dominate anyone who is weak. For some it's through violence. For some, it's mind control. For incubi, sex. Am I wrong?"

"I suppose it's part of our nature."

Her lips formed Cleo's thoughts. "A demon can never truly love."

"Is that what you believe?"

She could feel Cleo's will urging her to say *yes*, but a little bit of her own remaining resolve stopped her mouth from moving.

Malphas took a deep breath. "We are driven by the instinct

to dominate. If an incubus is injured, he will do anything he can to heal himself. If our lives our threatened, we'll do whatever it takes to survive. Incubi are born to seduce, I'll admit. But I know of only one incubi who takes women by force, and he's a deeply twisted soul."

The wind rustled the leaves, distracting her for a moment. Pale moonlight illuminated the leaves, and a sparrow fluttered from one tree to another. Had she never noticed before how truly *alive* the forest could be? "What were you saying?"

"I was talking about my father. And Caine's. Anyway, we're not just driven by lust and rage. We want to protect, too. To guard what's ours, what we love."

The certainty in his voice angered Cleo. If a demon could actually love, then why had Ambrose abandoned her?

Rosalind turned, clasping his arm. "Can demons love humans?"

His eyes widened. "Of course. But which demon in particular were you curious about?"

Cleo's magic snaked up her spine. *Take it from me, little girl. He's lying.*

"Never mind." She dropped the grip on his arm.

"Anyway, we're not that different from you. Demons are driven by lust and violence, fucking and killing. But so are humans." His eyes slid to hers. "Even you, Lady Rosalind."

A moth circled the air above her. "Don't be ridiculous."

"And now that you have become one with Druloch's magic, maybe you'll find out just how wild you can get in a divine frenzy. For a mortal like you, it lets you forget the greatest mortal curse."

For a moment, Cleo slammed Rosalind with an image of a charred body, tied to a stake. "Death," she said, her voice nearly a whisper.

He shook his head. "Your knowledge of your death—the anticipation. *That* is the real curse. A divine frenzy frees you, just for a while."

"And there we have the stories of witches dancing naked in the woods," she said bitterly. "And the Puritans afraid of life itself."

"Dancing naked in the woods. Is that something you're hoping to try today? I suppose I could accommodate."

Pale hands on my body, stroking my skin... "What?"

His eyes slid down her body, then slowly up again. "Frankly, I'm surprised my brother hasn't seduced you by now. You look amazing. And you smell amazing."

"I do?"

"Like Hawthorn wood, and lindens in full bloom."

Her footsteps crunched through the deadfall. Somewhere, under Cleo's thoughts, a painful thought nagged at the back of her mind. What was it she needed to remember now, while she was out here building her power?

Miranda. We'd lay together in the grasses, making wreaths of dandelions.

Rosalind fought to clear her mind from the webs of green magic. She'd been out here for a while, hoarding magical powers. But how was her sister doing right now?

This whole charade of pretending she didn't exist was getting ridiculous.

She blinked, trying to clear her mind. Recklessly, she asked, "What do you think Caine would say about raising Miranda from the grave, to get her soul back—"

He whirled, gripping her arm. His pale eyes burned into her. "Don't even think about it, Ros. Nyxobas doesn't do favors like that without a price."

A tendril of dread curled in her chest. "And what's the price?"

He turned, walking on again. "You must understand that death is the domain of the gods. It's not for you to toy with. And when we get Caine back, you must not speak to him about this. Don't even let him hear you contemplating it."

Cleo whispered, *If a demon could truly love, he'd entertain the idea. Caine can never love you, Rosalind.*

"Time to change the subject," she snapped.

Malphas shot her a sharp look.

She schooled her expression. "I mean, it's obviously a touchy subject, so we might as well move on." Power. She was here for the power. "What can I expect from the storm god?"

"I will tell you this much," he said. "You ever met a valkyrie?"

"Yes."

"Did she fill you with wrath?"

"Yes." *And you need to feel that thrill again.* "In fact, the last time a valkyrie touched me with her rage, I nearly murdered your brother."

He smirked, like this was a ridiculous concept. "Is that so?"

"I put a stake in his heart."

He arched an eyebrow. "If you got that close to his heart, I'm sure he allowed it."

"Why would he do that?"

"You know how incubi heal. Maybe his well had run dry."

She narrowed her eyes. "Maybe I'm a better fighter than you imagine."

At last, the woods thinned, opening to a rocky cliff that overlooked the star-flecked sea.

This is where I gain the power of the storm god.

Malphas opened his arms. "The realm of Mishett-Ash is in the skies. Stand at the edge of the cliff."

Deep in her chest, Cleo's aura stirred. *This power belongs to me. Give in to me, Rosalind.*

Rosalind trod over the jagged rock to the cliff's edge, and the sea wind whipped at her skin, biting her stomach through the tear in her dress. From here, she had a stunning view of the Astarte sea.

Malphas stood behind her, as he had on the sea shore. "Drop your shawl, and hold out your arms to the side."

Rosalind let her shawl drop to the rocks, and held out her hands to either side. Far below, waves crashed agains the rocks. From behind her, Malphas's powerful body warmed her skin. Just being in the presence of an incubus filled her with a strange mixture of emotions—thrilled and soothed at the same time.

His silver aura, scented of lilies, curled around her body. His fingertips skimmed over her hips.

Incubi can't help themselves, Cleo whispered. *They just need to touch.*

Malphas leaned down, whispering into her ear. "Feel the wind skimming over your body."

Gusts of marine air raised goose bumps on her skin.

"Now," he continued. "Let the wind flow into your chest."

The wind howled around her, and she arched her back, opening herself to the sky. Nearby, thunder rumbled across the sea. Clouds gathered in the distance, rolling over the horizon.

As she stood on the cliff's edge, raw power flowed into her, spiraling inside her ribs.

This is what I need.

Another clap of thunder boomed. Rain began to hammer her skin, soaking her hair and dress. She could feel Malphas's warmth moving away from her.

Then, her shoulder blades cracked, and agony ripped through her back. With a sound like the tearing of tendons and bone, she felt wings sprout from her back. She arched her spine, reaching behind her. Her fingertips skimmed over feathers. Her wings felt as if they reached nearly to the ground.

Now the wind and driving rain sent a delicious chill over her body. As if driven by some ancient instinct, she walked to the very edge of the cliff, and lifted off the ground. She soared into the stormy air, the wind and rain whipping through her hair. Gray magic whirled around her, imbuing her muscles with strength. She soared higher into the storm clouds, above the churning sea, thrilling at the speed of her flight. Power surged through her veins.

This is what I need.

In the distance, she heard the cry of the valkyries. A white streak of lightning speared the sky.

She wasn't Rosalind anymore. She was an angel of death, and this didn't feel like hell at all. This felt glorious.

She circled slowly over the sea, but as she did a new feeling gripped her heart—a slowly building battle fury, so powerful her limbs began to tremble. As gray magic surged, her anger was nearly as blinding. She needed to rip into flesh, to tear through bone. She needed to slaughter, wanted to rip Drew's head off his neck. Her face grew hot, body shaking.

Why did she have the feeling that Drew was here, nearby?

She sniffed the air, scenting mountain air and pine. *He's nearby.* She knew he'd be here, that it was time to rip his ribs out of his back...

She turned, heading back for the cliff. Wind rushed over her skin as she dove lower. She'd find him.

There. He stood just before the forest's edge, his colored magic whirling around his body. His green eyes pierced the darkness, and one clear thought sang in her mind: *Kill.*

She swooped lower and picked up an intense speed, ready for battle.

I am the bringer of death, and I will crush your bones.

29

She slammed into Drew with the force of a hurricane wind, knocking him back into the stones. His head cracked against a rock.

That should have knocked him out, but the man was practically immortal. He hurled her off of him, and she landed hard on a jagged rock. Fury surged, and she jumped up again.

She couldn't remember how to speak. She could only remember how to hurt.

Wrath consumed her, eating her up with a hunger she could never quench.

Drew stood, circling her. He wouldn't go down easily.

Let's try a little of Druloch's magic, shall we?

She didn't know if that was Cleo's voice or her own, only that fury commanded her.

She flicked her hand, and ropes of thorny plants spun from her fingers and coiled around Drew. With another flick of her wrist, she wrapped them tighter, watching his eyes bulge—but before she could split the bastard in two, he flexed his muscles, breaking through the vines.

Gods, he was strong.

"Rosalind!" he shouted.

"Don't you use my name," she snarled. "You murdered my sister."

Blood poured down Drew's skin where the thorns had stabbed him, and the beautiful red streaks entranced her. He stalked toward her, a wild animal ready to pounce.

Bring him down, Rosalind, Cleo whispered. *And this time, don't let him get out.*

Rosalind let Druloch's magic sing: blackbirds trilling, wind through the leaves.

The scent of death coiled around her.

"Rosalind," Drew strode closer, confident as a god.

The deep timbre of his voice made her falter. Was there a reason she shouldn't hurt him?

Kill him, Cleo chanted. *Kill him.*

As he closed in on her, she swung for him, landing a hard punch on his jaw. Her returned the blow, and she staggered back, pain splintering her skull. His strength was otherworldly.

People must pay for their betrayals, Cleo sang.

With a roundhouse kick, Rosalind slammed her foot into Drew's head, reveling in the sharp crack of foot against bone. He grabbed his skull.

Time to finish your work, Cleo trilled.

Drew stumbled back, dazed. His vulnerability fully enraged her. Cold wrath erupted, and she charged for him, knocking him flat onto the rock. She straddled him, raining down one punch after another onto his face.

"You killed my sister, you sick fuck!"

Fury consumed her, and the more she hurt him, the more her anger sharpened, cutting her from the inside out like a living thing.

It's not enough. I will never be able to hurt you enough.

She grabbed a rock, ready to bash the bastard's skull in—but fast as a night wind, his hand shot out. He gripped her wrist so hard she thought he might crush it.

"Rosalind," he said, his voice quiet.

Not Drew's voice—Malphas's voice.

She caught her breath, staring down at eyes that slowly shifted from green to a pale gray, the color of starlight.

A silver aura curled around him, sliding over her skin like silk. He smelled of lilies.

She stared down at Malphas's bloodied face, and the fury rushed from her body like a mountain stream. Cuts lacerated Malphas's entire body, and blood spattered his forehead.

She gasped, dropping the rock. Her hand flew to her mouth. "Malphas."

He groaned. "I thought you said you were okay."

"What?"

He swallowed hard, as if trying to manage his pain. "You should have been able to control the rage better."

"I'm so sorry," she sputtered. "I thought you were Drew."

The black clouds were still unleashing a punishing torrent of rain.

His lip curled. "You've used too much magic. I asked you if you were losing your mind. Cleo's taking over, isn't she?"

Guilt pierced her chest. "She's been a bit loud, yes."

Malphas's still gripped her wrist—hard. As he stared at her, his eyes darkened, then trailed down her body, studying the tear in her gown.

Uh oh.

His other hand found its way to her waist, fingers trailing over her exposed skin, a touch so gentle she couldn't stop herself from arching into it.

"Malphas," she said. "What are you doing?"

His fingertips trailed lower, just over her hipbone.

Cleo's aura whirled around her, green and vernal.

Ambrose touched me like that once, a long time ago.

I told you I wanted you to kiss him. And you didn't listen.

Now, I take control.

Lightning flashed, and as it did an image slammed into Rosalind's mind.

She stood at the edge of a room. Candles cast wavering light over dark wood walls and tapestries. Guests sat around the table, dressed in fine slips the color of spring flowers.

A feast spread over the table: a roasted goose, a suckling pig, spiced wines, crisp biscuits, fresh baked bread, and steaming pies.

Her stomach rumbled. *So this is how the rich live.*

She didn't belong here. Alchemy didn't pay like it should, and she'd come in a gray, threadbare gown, with yellow cowslips threaded through her hair instead of jewels.

A hand touched her shoulder, and she turned to see him, her breath hitching in her throat. That beautiful, perfect skin. The high cheekbones and soft lips that she ached to feel.

Ambrose. The only reason she'd come, to see those beautiful green eyes—the color of her god.

He grabbed her hand, pulling her into a stairwell where they were completely alone. He moved so quickly, so fluidly, and in the next moment his arms were around her. His fingers gently gripped her hair, tugging her head back, and he pressed his mouth against hers.

His lips were soft and supple. Slowly, his tongue flicked against hers, sending shivers of pleasure through her. Hungrily, he tugged down the front of her dress, his fingers skimming her breasts...

Would he think her a harlot for giving in so easily? Surely she was supposed to play some sort of game—but she didn't want him. She only wanted Ambrose...

"Ambrose," she moaned.

"What?"

The vision faded, and once again, she felt the hard rain pounding her skin. Her lips hovered just inches above Malphas's.

His eyes widened. Suddenly, his fingers were tightening on her shoulders, holding her at arm's length. "Did you say *Ambrose*?"

Her mouth went dry, and she lurched away from him. *What the fuck am I doing?* She leapt to her feet. All at once, her body began to ache from fatigue. "Sorry. I was confused."

Still on the ground, he pushed up onto his elbows. He looked almost entirely healed. *Gods below.* How long had they been kissing for?

He knit his black brows. "I'm sorry. I'm still stuck on this. Did you say *Ambrose?*"

He looked deeply insulted. She couldn't imagine anyone had ever whispered the wrong name over his lips before.

Cleo's aura whirled through her mind. *The fun is just beginning.*

Rosalind pressed her fingertips to her temples. "Be quiet."

In a blur of silver, Malphas rose. "You're out of your mind."

She shook her head. "I thought you were Ambrose. It's fine. Things have... I just have too many memories." She could tell she was rambling, but couldn't quite stop herself. "Caine's and Cleo's, mine and Miranda's... But once I sleep... I need to sleep like the dead, under that heavy dirt where my sister lay."

Stop talking, Rosalind.

His silver aura whipped around his body. "You told me you were okay."

Icy rain poured down her skin in rivulets, and she wouldn't meet his eyes. "I just need some sleep."

He wiped the back of his hand across his mouth as if he was disgusted. "Is that so?"

Tomorrow, I take you to Ambrose, Cleo whispered. *You won't whisper the wrong name then.*

Rosalind squeezed her eyes shut. "I need some bluebells to mute the voice."

The air seemed to chill around Malphas, the shadows thickening. "We're going back to Ninlil. Don't even think of using any more magic until you're ready again. If the shield needs to be strengthened, I'll do it myself. Understood?"

Her body shook in the rain. "Yeah. I get it." She'd pushed things too far. She knew she had.

But they'd all known this was a risk. Humans weren't meant to have this power.

Malphas turned, walking into the forest. She hugged herself as she followed after him. Now that Cleo had achieved her little victory over Rosalind, her voice had gone a bit quieter.

And still, Rosalind craved the thrill of powerful magic.

Her teeth chattered in the cold. She'd left her shawl trampled into the mud back there, and the storm she'd created still lashed them with freezing rain.

As they walked back to the castle, Malphas didn't utter a word, quietly brooding. She couldn't tell if he was more disturbed by her lack of control, or if he was just pissed off that she'd said another man's name while kissing him.

She shook her head, suddenly mortified. What would Caine think if he knew that she'd kissed his brother?

Cleo's aura tingled over her skin as they trudged through the mud. Some of her memories still flickered through Rosalind's mind, but they'd grown duller now, like faded film.

As they approached Ninlil castle, she heard a sharp intake of breath from Malphas.

She glanced up at the castle walls. There, in front of one of the gatehouses, stood Caine, his silver aura glowing like a star.

30

"He's here," she said.

It took only a few seconds for Malphas to get to Caine, moving in a blur of shadows.

Rosalind pulled up the hem of her dress, running to keep up. She still hadn't mastered the art of shadow running.

Still, she cleared the distance as fast as she could, rushing over the muddy earth to Caine.

"You're back!" she shouted, throwing her arms around him, breathing in the scent of thunderstorms and earth.

His hands found his way to her waist, but he was pushing her away. "What is going on here? What have you two been doing?"

Quickly, she stepped away, casting a nervous glance at Malphas.

Malphas frowned. "Come out with it. What happened? What went wrong?"

"Nothing went wrong. I had to fight an army of valkyries, but I found the sigil."

"And?" Malphas demanded.

Caine glared at his brother. "And why did Rosalind give me a panicked mental message about the shield if you were here to repair it?"

Rosalind cleared her throat. "We wanted to make sure you were okay. I thought you were supposed to come back as soon as you could. We couldn't see you through scrying, and using your magic was the only way to know you were making your way out of the House of Shades."

Caine's aura violently slashed the air, and his gaze slid to Rosalind. "You lied to me?"

Her stomach dropped. *Damn, he's scary as hell.* "No. The shield really was thinning. I just didn't mention the part about Malphas being here."

Shadows darkened his eyes. "And what of the first time I loaned you my shadow magic?"

She swallowed hard. "That was something different."

Malphas pushed his rain-soaked hair from his eyes. "Trust me. I've asked her a dozen times. Anyway—what happened to you, Brother? How long did it take you to find the sigil?"

"I found it after journeying through the Tuckomock Forest and fighting an army of valkyries. I spent a little too long in the House of Shades, but you should have had faith in me."

"You found the soul?" Malphas demanded.

"Of course I did." He pulled out a small disc, streaked with different colored metals—gold, silver, copper, tin. A six-pointed symbol had been carved on the front—the sigil of Azezeyl.

He slid it back into his pocket. "Miranda's second soul is trapped in here. Now, we just need a victim to take it on."

I guess Miranda is out of the question.

Rosalind's head throbbed. She felt like she needed to sleep for weeks. "Did you see Drew?"

"No. He wasn't in Maremount. Before you called me here, I was hunting for him in Boston, but he's protected by the Brotherhood army. And more than that, Boston and Cambridge have changed.

Drastically. Drew has practically created an entirely new city with his magic."

Malphas's eyebrows rose. "You defied Ambrose? He told you not to hunt for Drew—that you were to return, and we'd create his army."

Caine shrugged. "His mind is clouded by his obsession with daywalking. I had to make my own decision."

And yours is clouded by your hatred for Drew, she thought.

Caine's icy gaze trailed up and down Rosalind's body. "You haven't told me what you two were doing out here in the rain."

Rosalind crossed her arms, her teeth chattering. Wisps of colored magic still curled from her body like smoke. "Learning gods-magic."

Cleo's voice tinkled in her mind like bells. *Aren't you going to tell him what you did with his brother?*

As if hearing Cleo's voice, Caine cocked his head. "And how loud is Cleo now? Is she drowning out your own thoughts?"

"I just need sleep," she said.

Caine stared at her. "Later, when you're not half-mad, I want you to tell me exactly what you saw when you stole glimpses of my life."

"Fine." She shivered. "I'm going to go inside now. I need to check on—" *Gods below.* She'd nearly said "Miranda." She really *was* losing her mind. "To check on Aurora. She was quite sad about all the funerals."

Caine nodded slowly. But of course the bastard could tell when she was lying.

As she turned to walk past him, he touched her arm, his gaze boring into her. The touch of his fingertips alone sent shivers through her body.

He leaned in, whispering, "And then, I want you to tell me why you smell like lilies."

✤ ✤ ✤

Soaking wet, Rosalind walked down the candlelit hall to her room, each one of her muscles screaming in rebellion.

For the entire walk from the Gelal field to her room, Cleo had resumed shrieking in her head like a demented Banshee. *Find Ambrose. Seduce him, like I asked.*

Rosalind cringed. She'd kissed *both* brothers now. Would Caine understand that she'd been hallucinating the whole time, and that Cleo had taken over?

Or, more importantly—would Caine even care in the first place?

At least he was home. That was the important thing.

Half asleep, she stumbled to her door, then pushed it open. In the dancing candlelight, Miranda paced the floor, chewing on her fingernail. As Rosalind entered, her sister looked up at her, eyes wild.

"*There* you are!" Miranda said. "How long did you plan to keep me locked in here?"

"What?" Rosalind rubbed her eyes. "I thought you had everything you needed."

"I ran out of food ages ago. We need to ask Ambrose for more."

Rosalind sighed. "Fine. No problem."

"I'll go ask him," Miranda said. "I've been desperate to get out of here. I've worn the floor down with pacing."

"Absolutely not." Rosalind wasn't about to unleash her sister on the castle. Not with Caine roaming around. "I'll go. You need to stay in here."

Yes. Cleo cooed. *Go to Ambrose.*

Between her increasingly frenzied sister and the crazy voices in her head, Rosalind wasn't entirely sure she could keep control over anything at this point.

"No," Miranda said, shaking her head. "I don't want to be alone anymore." She pivoted, pacing again. "I'll be fine until morning."

"Are you sure?" Rosalind began peeling off her sodden gown.

"Yeah, it's just this hunger. I can't seem to fill myself. I want food and drink, and... I want to touch things. I want sunlight and grass and everything."

Rosalind dropped her torn gown over the back of a chair. "I guess you're making up for those days you spent dead. Getting all the life you can get."

Miranda raked a hand across her stomach. "This gnawing feeling..." she muttered.

Rosalind's chest tightened. *At least, I hope this is temporary.* She grabbed a towel from the wardrobe, drying herself off. "Well, I have some good news."

"Oh?" Miranda said.

"Caine is back. He has the extra soul."

Miranda's eyes widened. "He does? I want it back."

"I'm not sure Caine will give it to us. Malphas seemed pretty certain of that."

Miranda shook her head. "But I feel like something is missing. That must be it."

There were two people who would know exactly what this meant: Caine and Malphas. And Rosalind couldn't ask either of them.

Miranda looked up, blinking, as if waking from a dream. "But Caine is okay? He's not hurt?"

"He's fine."

Miranda crawled into the bed. "Good. Look, maybe I just need more sleep. And I'm sure you do, too."

"No argument here." Rosalind's muscles shrieked with exhaustion, and her bed called to her.

Go to Ambrose!

"Shut up, Cleo," Rosalind muttered. She crawled into her bed, her eyes already drifting closed.

Go to Ambrose, you faithless whore.

If only the lunatic in her brain would let her sleep.

Miranda peered over at her. "And now that Caine's back, what do you think the chances are that you can slaughter Drew?"

Rosalind swallowed hard. Based on what Caine had said, Drew had the power to create a new city in only a week.

And what had she done with her powers, so far? Some vines and rain. She had a *long* way to go before she could catch up.

Enjoy your life while you've still got it, Cleo purred.

31

*R*osalind woke tangled in her bedsheets. All night, she'd dreamt of Ambrose. She'd dreamt of returning to the stairwell with him, running her hands over his skin. Cleo had let her sleep, but had played scenes from her medieval life through Rosalind's dreams: Ambrose kissing her throat, touching her breasts, standing bare-chested under the starlight.

As the dreams cleared from her mind, Rosalind sat up in bed, letting the sheets fall from her. By her side, Miranda stirred, rubbing her eyes. The smell of freshly-baked bread wafted through the air.

Rosalind smiled. "Good morning, sunshine."

Miranda sniffed. "I smell food."

"Me too." Rosalind jumped out of bed, padding barefoot to the door. She pulled it open and found a basket of steaming baked goods, nestled amongst fruit and cheese.

Her mouth watered, and she lifted the basket. "Look what we have here." She dropped the basket onto a small wooden table by the bed. "And as soon as we're able to leave here, you can have all the food you want."

Smiling, Miranda grabbed a hot roll. "Good. I want to eat while sunbathing. I need daylight like you wouldn't believe." She ripped into her roll. "And I'd like a boyfriend, or at least a lover."

"I'm sure that can be arranged." Rosalind bit into a *pain au chocolate*, letting it melt on her tongue. "At some point."

Cleo's aura began to stir. *Go to Ambrose, you faithless whore!* she shrieked. *Seduce him just once, like you promised.*

Rosalind winced. Sleeping for hours hadn't helped to silence Cleo.

Go to him, Cleo commanded. *You owe me this.*

As if against her will, Rosalind felt herself rising from the bed. She crossed to the wardrobe and pulled it open. She stripped completely, then pulled out a pair of the smallest underwear she could find—sheer black with silver silk ribbons around the hips, and a bra to match.

"Where are you going?" Miranda asked. "In *that?*"

"I need to go somewhere," Rosalind muttered, as if in a daze.

"Where?"

"I need to see Ambrose—"

Cleo stopped her from telling the whole story. Miranda would only try to stop her.

Make up a lie.

"I'm going speak to Ambrose about giving us more food. Then I'll find out about the daywalkers, so we can get out of here."

"Oh. What time is it?"

Rosalind shook her head. "I'm not sure."

In a land of night, she had no clue how to keep track of the time. She pulled on a dress, a pale silver that slid over her legs, billowing slightly in the breeze. The neckline plunged. She snatched a long rope of black pearls from a jewelry box.

Perfect, Cleo purred. *But when you see Ambrose, I want you to look like me. I want him to see me.*

Numbly, she walked to the mirror. Her thoughts had become muddled, swirling with the name *Ambrose.*

Flashes of stars, a wren trilling...

She waited for him to arrive by the forest's edge. But the soldiers came for her instead. And then, the flames.

Through half-lidded eyes, she watched herself paint her lips a glossy red. She blinked twice in the mirror. The crimson shade looked nice with her dark hair. But of course, when she arrived in Ambrose's room, she'd no longer look like herself.

As she crossed to the door, she thought Miranda might have been speaking to her, but she ignored her sister's voice, listening instead to the haunting fragments of Cleo's memories.

They came for me through the shadows, in their tapered hats, with metal prickers in their pockets...

Rosalind pushed through the door into the hall.

Time to make good on your promise, Cleo purred.

She hadn't brought a weapon with her this time. It didn't matter. As she walked down the hall, the vamp's doors stayed shut. Probably still sleeping. She looked down at her long, brown hair, staring in a daze as it flickered to pale blonde.

I used to thread it with flowers...

Barefoot, she padded down the hall, the word *Ambrose* hammering in her skull. She twirled a strand of platinum hair around her fingertips. But somewhere, under the layers of green magic, her own mind began to stir.

What am I doing? I don't want Ambrose. I'm not going to screw him just to keep you happy. You cannot take over my body.

Yet her feet carried her onward. She felt as though she were walking underwater, her movements sluggish and dulled—until her gaze landed on the portrait of Lord Byron.

Caine's room. Even with Cleo trying to control her thoughts, she'd found a way to bring herself here.

Yes, Caine seemed to be able to calm her magic.

No, Cleo shrieked. *You made me a promise!*

Anger simmered, deep in her chest, and she stared down at the blond hair draping over her gray gown. *I'm not letting you take over completely. You had your life. This is mine.*

Rosalind focused on condensing that vernal magic as much as she could. She couldn't go into Caine's room with Cleo's face.

She envisioned the magic constricting into her body. Cleo's glamour slowly disappeared, leaving behind her own dark chestnut hair. She swallowed hard, straining to keep the magic in check. Caine would be able to quell Cleo's power. Whenever he touched her, it seemed to calm Cleo's shrill voice.

It took a few moments for Caine to pull the door open. He stood before her, wearing only a pair of black boxer briefs. Her jaw dropped at the sight of his perfect body—smooth skin over steely muscle. Warm candlelight danced over his tattoos. He leaned against the doorframe, his pale eyes framed by jet-black lashes.

Even Cleo stayed quiet.

"Did you come to tell me what spell you conducted with my magic?" he asked. "A midnight confession?"

Mutely, she shook her head. What *was* she doing here?

Mostly trying to avoid letting Cleo take over my life.

She swallowed hard. "I wanted to talk about the daywalker spell."

He stared at her. "I take it you haven't gotten used to Lilinor's schedule. Everyone is sleeping now."

She shrugged. "Are they? Someone left food outside my door, so I assumed it was morning."

His eyes slid slowly over her body, the thin gray dress that hugged her curves. "Is that really why you're here? To talk about our battle plans?"

She stared at his honeyed skin, the soft curve of his lips, his powerful arms. With him nearly naked, she could hardly remember how to string a sentence together. But she was acutely aware of his electric aura, caressing her skin.

Despite her body's intense reaction to the sight of him, his presence had calmed Cleo's aura. Rosalind no longer had to fight so hard to keep her under control. "And I wanted to know about Boston. You said the city looks completely different. I just need to know what we're up against."

"Admit it." He arched an eyebrow. "You wanted to see me naked. Any minute now, you're going to feign a chill and claim you need to curl up in my bed against the warmth of my body."

Her stomach fluttered, and she waved a dismissive hand. "Don't be ridiculous."

"You do have impeccable taste in men. I'll give you that much."

She rolled her eyes, and he opened his door wider, motioning for her to enter. She strode inside, trying to keep Cleo's aura as condensed as possible. Her gaze flicked to the round bath in the corner of his room. She'd bathed there once, enveloped by the floral scents of Lilinor, while Caine did his best not to look at her naked body.

"Have a seat," he said, gesturing at his bed. It stood against a wall, covered in rumpled silver blankets.

The room was nearly bare, apart from a wooden table with decanters and glasses, and the candles on the walls.

She crossed to his bed, settling down on his duvet. Caine stared at her and folded his arms in front of his chest. He seemed intent. "Before I tell you anything about Boston," he said, "I need to know three things. What spell did you do the first time I let you use my magic, and what, exactly, did you see?"

She swallowed hard. "I'm not telling you about the spell. You clearly don't tell me everything, so you're hardly in a position to demand the revelation of secrets. What's the third question?"

Suddenly, his mood shifted, and the air seemed to thin. The shadows darkened, and candles guttered in their sconces. "Why did you smell like lilies when I found you in the field with Malphas?"

She wasn't going to answer that either. "I'll answer one of those questions. I'll tell you what I saw in the visions. I witnessed you killing the queen. In another vision, I saw a baby with silver eyes like yours. There was a hairpin on a table, like the tattoo on your arm."

Shadows licked the air around him, and his gaze drilled into her. "And what else?"

"I saw your punishment in Maremount, when you were nailed to the stake in front of the fortress."

The rigid set of his shoulders told her not to bring up *Stolas*—that it would be too much for him.

"Is that it?"

"And I saw flashes of what you were doing at the time. The valkyries, the House of Shades. I saw you in Boston."

His aura sliced the air around him, and goosebumps rose on her skin. "Did you learn *why* I was nailed to that stake?" he asked.

"No." But whatever it was, it had to do with *Stolas*.

"I'd never have allowed you to use my magic if it weren't life and death."

Her fingers tightened on the edge of his bed, and she looked down at the floor. She'd already made up her mind that she trusted him, hadn't she? Despite how terrifying he could be, she'd already decided he wasn't going to hurt her. So what was she scared of?

If she truly trusted him—maybe she should just *ask* him about necromancy.

She took a deep breath. "And now I have a question for you." She gazed up at him from below her lashes. "Why have you prohibited bone conjuring?"

Silence filled the room, heavy as dirt. *Maybe this was a bad idea.*

Her muscles tensed, and she ventured, "I don't understand why we can't try to bring Miranda back."

"What do *you* know about it?" he asked.

She took a steadying breath. "Aurora told me you'd forbidden it. I just don't understand why. What's the price?"

"I knew you were leaving out part of the story." His eyes darkened, swirling with shadows and he took a step closer. He leaned down, his hands resting on either side of her hips, like he was searching her eyes for lies. "What else did you see in your visions of my life?"

"What?"

"There is a reason you're asking me about bone conjuring. What did you see?"

What, exactly, does he think I saw? "I didn't see anything from your life about bone conjuring. I wanted to understand why you don't want me to bring Miranda back. That's the reason I'm asking."

He straightened again. "I've prohibited it because death is the province of the gods. The original seven. Even I'm not meant to control it, as a demigod."

"Those are the only details you'll give me?"

Deep in her skull, Cleo began to grow restless again, and Rosalind found her gaze lingering over Caine's muscled body.

Still standing, his gaze pierced her. "Why don't you tell me what happened with you and Malphas?"

Deflect. She frowned. "Is it just me, or are you jealous?" She leaned back on his bed, and let the strap of her dress fall down. She didn't move to lift it again.

As if entranced, his gaze lingered on her bare shoulder and the curve of her breast.

Now, that is how you distract in incubus.

32

$\mathcal{A}$s if lured in by a siren song, he sat next to her on the bed. His arm brushed against her shoulder. The feel of his skin against hers sent her heart racing, and they'd barely even made contact.

"Jealous?" he said. "Demigods don't get jealous."

She frowned. "Lie. I may not read pupil dilation like you and Malphas, but I know that's a lie."

He shrugged. "I just need to make sure you haven't been torturing my little brother again."

"Malphas trusts me, even if you don't."

He studied her. "Why did you come here?"

"When you were gone, I realized something about you."

"What?"

She took a deep breath, and straightened. "We might have a twisted history, and maybe you don't trust me. But you're always looking out for me." Her gaze slid over his powerful body—the rippling muscles and the vicious looking tattoos. She lingered on the hairpin on his forearm. "You've kept secrets from me. And I've kept them from you. And yet, I trust you anyway. I feel like you would keep me safe, even if Esmerelda says you'll dump me in the whore pit when you're through. So maybe you should trust me, too. Even if I don't tell you everything."

"You trust me, now, do you?" Slowly, he reached for her, then ran his thumb over her lower lip.

Her body stirred at his touch.

"I'm glad you're catching on, little Hunter," he said.

She had the strongest impulse to flick her tongue against his finger, but she resisted. "And I came here because you seem to have the power of quieting Cleo's voice."

He pulled his hand away. "I do?"

"Only when you touch me." Her pulse raced. Sitting this close to him, she wanted his beautiful lips on hers—all over her body. "And Cleo was being very loud, so I thought I'd pay you a visit."

He was looking at her so intently, like he wanted to devour her. Like he was holding on to his restraint by a thread. His grip tightened on the edge of his bed, knuckles whitening. She wet her lips, and his keen gaze caught the movement. His muscled chest seemed to rise and fall faster, and his aura curled around her, vibrating over her skin. Her body responded to the feel of his magic.

His gaze slowly raked over her breasts, then lower still. He looked so enraptured, she was sure his gaze went right through the silk to the black lace beneath her dress.

"Why do I feel like you're trying to distract me from the questions I'm asking?" he asked, as if in a daze.

"Is it working? Surely a demigod isn't so easily distracted."

His gaze met hers again. "I wonder, Rosalind. Perhaps there's another way to coax your secrets from you." Slowly, he unclenched his fingers from the blankets, and reached for her.

As he drew his fingertips over her ribs, his touch sent an electric thrill over her skin. Instantly, her back arched at his touch. He stroked her ribs, back and forth, and she swallowed hard.

Tracing lower over her abdomen, Caine leaned in closer. For someone who gave the impression of predatory lethality half the time, she was struck by the unexpected gentleness of his touch—just as when he'd kissed her before in the hall. And it was precisely that gentleness that was going to drive her nuts.

Her breathing shallowed.

As his breath warmed the side of her face, his eyes lost their shadows and returned to their starlit color, burning bright as a dying star. "Tell me about the spells you've woven, Rosalind," he whispered, sliding his fingers over her belly.

Through her gown, heat from his fingertips seemed to inflame her skin. *I'm not telling you a damn thing, but you better keep touching me that way.*

Her body warmed to his touch, heat swooping through her belly.

His fingers stroked lower, over the hollow of her hips. Her entire world narrowed to that thrilling touch. When he stroked just over the top of her panties, his touch painfully light, she had an overwhelming desire to tear off her gown. She was going to lose her mind if he didn't move any faster. She wanted his lips on hers, wanted his hands to grip her harder. He leaned in, but he kept his mouth just out of reach, hovering just an inch from hers.

"Tell me, my Hunter," he whispered.

Cleo's voice had gone completely silent. Rosalind heard only her own heated breaths—and her thudding heart—as Caine's aura caressed her skin.

Caine lowered his face into the curve of her neck, his breath warming her throat. She let her head tilt back, leaning further back on her hands. *Lower, Caine.*

"Tell me, Rosalind," he whispered, fingertips tracing over silk.

Her heart raced faster, heat surging through her core. Was he seducing her to get information from her? Right now, she wasn't sure that she cared. She couldn't even remember what his damn questions were. All she knew was that his fingers were *nearly* where she needed them, lighting her body on fire.

At last, the tips of his fingers slid lower down her silk dress, between her legs, and he drew small circles. Gasping, she let her legs open. She pressed harder against his hand, and a moan escaped her throat.

She couldn't wait for his kiss any longer. She reached up, cupping her hand behind his neck, and pulled him in. He pressed his mouth against hers, claiming her. At first, he kissed her fiercely, hungrily. Slowly, the kiss grew more sensual. Gently, his tongue slipped in, brushing against hers, and he groaned softly. In the next moment, he was gently tugging up her dress, the silk sliding along her legs.

Their kiss deepened, and her body blazed with heat. He slid one of his hands between her knees, fingers hot on her bare skin. Just when she thought she was about to lose her mind, he pulled away from the kiss, breathing hard.

Her lip curled. *How long is he going to draw this out for?*

Gods, she needed him now. She gripped his neck, trying to pull him closer, to press his body against hers. But he resisted, his touch achingly light on the inside of her thigh. "Hunter. You still haven't answered my question."

He was teasing her mercilessly, and her body trembled at his touch. He *liked* his control over her.

"Caine," she whispered, her heart racing. "I don't care about the question."

"But you care that I keep touching you, don't you?" His fingertips moved up the inside of her thigh—glacially slow. As they moved higher, her breath hitched in her throat. He paused—inches away from where she needed him, and he began tracing slow circles again on her thigh.

He was going to drive her insane. *Does he want me to beg?*

"Tell me what I want to know," he said, his voice rough. "Or I'll have to stop."

Her breath came fast, her body dampening with sweat. She didn't want to play his games, didn't even remember what he was asking for at this point. In fact, she wasn't sure she could speak right now, since the entirety of her world was now a few fingers on her thighs.

Maybe he needs some encouragement. She reached down to the hem of her gown, and pulled off her dress. She tossed it to the ground, then pushed the hair out of her eyes.

Caine's eyes slid to her peaked breasts, visible through her sheer bra. His fingers tightened on her thigh. He seemed to take in every inch of her skin, his attention completely rapt. Eyes blazing, his gaze raked lower, between her thighs.

She wasn't sure anyone had ever looked at her the way he was staring at her now, with such raw, animalistic lust. And she liked it. She lay back on his bed, propping up on her elbows. She'd wanted this since... well if she was honest, since she'd first seen him.

His aura whipped from his body in a flash of silver. Once more, he let his burning gaze roam over her body. A look of pure, carnal lust. He wasn't trying to get her to talk anymore. That game was over.

As he lay down next to her on the bed, he cupped the side of her face, kissing her desperately. Slowly, he slid his fingers just under the top of her panties. She groaned into his mouth, her fingers curling into his hair. His muscled body pressed against her, his skin warming hers. Slowly, she ran her fingers down his body, feeling every hard plane until she slipped her fingers inside the top of his boxers, delighting in his gasp.

With a low growl, he unhooked her bra, pulling it off. He kissed her throat, then his warm mouth slowly moved lower over her breasts. She wrapped her legs around his body. As his kisses trailed down to her hips, she arched into him. She tangled her fingers into his hair, her thighs brushing his sides.

With a smoldering glance at her, he ran his fingers over the silver ribbon at the top of her panties, sending shivers through her. He leaned down, kissing the skin just above it, his tongue hot against her skin. A hot thrill rippled through her. She needed him, now.

"Caine," she breathed.

As he hooked his fingers into the top of her panties, she lifted her hips, and he slid them off. Desperate for more of his mouth on hers, she pulled him toward her. He kissed her deeply, hungrily. And when his fingers slipped between her legs, she thought she was going to lose her mind. Her body writhed with pure pleasure, grinding against his hand. He dipped his fingers again and again. She moaned, moving against his hand, demanding more.

Pulling him closer, she kissed his neck. As he touched her, her hands explored his skin. She slipped her fingers into his boxers, pulling them off. At the sight of him, her breath caught in her throat.

He moved between her legs, his eyes burning an intense silver. *I need this now,* she pleaded with him mentally.

She reached up, caressing his face. Slowly—painfully so—he pressed inside her, his gaze locked on hers. *Pure rapture.*

Their hips rocked in movement, and every thrust brought her soaring to a wild peak. They moved together, increasingly frenzied.

With each stroke, she clawed her hands further down his back, pulling him into her, her back arching. Softly, he groaned her name into her neck, and the sound sent shivers through her body.

Their bodies moved in rhythm, a frenzied symphony of gasps and moans—faces dampening, bodies glowing with heat. Every inch of her glowed with pleasure as she felt herself merge with him, until her control began to slip.

A cry tore from her throat, and she shuddered against him with sweet release.

33

*I*n the warm bath, Rosalind lay wrapped around Caine, listening to his beating heart. The smell of lavender filled the air. Caine's chest rose and fell with long, slow breaths, and his hand rested on her hair.

Gently, she traced her fingertips over the faint scars on his chest, the pale white markings. Now she wanted to know the story of each tattoo, each tiny line of scar tissue. She touched the one above his smooth belly, where he'd been impaled on the stake, then moved on to the constellation of scars over his ribs.

"I know there are things you don't want to tell me," she ventured. "Like, everything to do with your relationship with my parents." Or *Stolas*—she wouldn't even mention the name. "But surely there are other things you can tell me."

"Like what?"

"Like why you murdered the King and Queen of Maremount four hundred years ago."

"Ah." He sighed. "That."

Her fingers found the circular scar just below his heart. "Is that a story you can tell me?"

"That was the first time I was imprisoned in Maremount."

"What for?"

"You saw the succubus head on the fountain in front of the fortress—that was Erish's sister. Maremount purged the city of incubi and succubi. Except, the queen had a taste for incubi. So her husband procured one for her, to keep her happy."

Rosalind's throat tightened. "Ah. You said demons were enslaved in Maremount." She felt his heart beating beneath her fingertips. "But how could a human keep you as a slave? You're more powerful than they are."

"An iron collar, with spikes in my neck, chained to a bed. It drained most of my power." His hand covered hers. "And, truthfully, I could have found my way out—except that she threatened to slaughter someone I loved."

She felt her cheeks heat, and anger simmered on his behalf.

And underneath that anger, she couldn't help but wonder who he'd loved.

"No wonder you murdered her."

"I served her against my will for nearly a year, until I couldn't take it anymore. I killed her and the king so neither could make good on their promise."

"The promise to kill the person you loved." Since he was opening up to her, she didn't want to push him too far by asking *who* that person was, though she was desperate to know.

"Exactly."

"That must have been awful for you."

He stared into the distance. "Well. I ended it. I had to slaughter my way free from the city, through a horde of royal guards. And do you know what? That's when I learned I could get a thrill from something other than fucking."

"Killing?"

"I'm quite good at it, as I'm sure you've seen."

"Mmm. You're good at a lot of things." Her head rested on his damp shoulder. "Anyway, I'm glad you made it out safely."

He traced his fingers through the water by her hips. "I left Maremount, and escaped to Lilinor, where I met Ambrose. And I brought with me... the people I needed to keep safe."

"And that's how you became known as the Ravener, the legendary monster of Maremount."

"The children's stories fail to mention the part about me being chained up as a love slave."

Her fingers still covered the scar on his chest, and a twinge of guilt tightened her lungs. *That* scar had come from her. "Um, sorry about the time I stabbed you."

His lips curled in a smile. "I think you've made up for it by now."

Her brow furrowed. "Malphas insisted that the only way I could have stabbed you is if you'd let me. Because your incubus well had run dry, and you probably wanted to gain power through sex."

"Malphas doesn't know everything," he grumbled. "Speaking of Malphas—what happened between the two of you when I was gone?"

Okay. He's not letting this go. She straightened, looking him in the eyes. Droplets of water beaded over his golden skin.

"He was training me. I've worked my way through five of the hells. I have only one left—fire." She swallowed hard. "He was wary of pushing me too far, because of Cleo. So he kept asking if I was okay. He asked if I could hear her voice."

His body had gone tense. "And?"

"And I guess I was craving more power. I just needed to feel more of the gods-magic... We all knew there was a risk, that maybe humans weren't meant to have this power." She was babbling now, she realized. "I didn't let Malphas realize how much Cleo was taking over."

A muscle tightened in his jaw. "Let me guess. You lied to Malphas. Why do I feel like I know where this is going?" Abruptly, he rose from the bath, water dripping down his perfect body.

"Using the gods-magic warped my mind." She folded her arms over the tub's edge, watching as Caine toweled himself off. "I thought Malphas was Drew. I attacked him. And then I was in Cleo's world, getting visions of Ambrose getting frisky in a stairwell."

"According to Malphas, an incubus might put himself in harms way if his well runs dry," Caine said. "Did Malphas's well run dry when he was training you, perhaps? And then, of course, he needed healing."

"I feel like you already know how this story goes."

Caine was already pulling on his clothes. Apparently, their post-coital moment was over.

"You let Cleo take over your mind," he said. "And Cleo has a thing for shadow demons. Whether it's Malphas or me, she's not too picky. Is that about right?"

"Wait a minute—"

"What *exactly* did you do with him?"

"*I* didn't do anything. Cleo kissed him."

"It must be nice to be able to divest responsibility so easily. You're not responsible; Cleo is. How convenient." Caine's gaze pierced right thorough her. "If I were able to divorce myself from the things I've done, what a different person I'd be. Except I don't think the way you do."

With Caine's fury chilling the room, she no longer felt comfortable sitting there naked. Shivering, she rose. "Well, maybe you shouldn't be so hard on yourself." *Or on me.* Maybe if she soothed his bruised ego... "Look, Cleo might have been the reason I kissed Malphas, but she wasn't the reason I came here."

He cocked his head, eyes narrowed, as he buttoned up his shirt. "Oh, really? So you weren't hearing her voice when you knocked on my door?"

She grabbed a towel from the side of the bath. "Well, yes, I was hearing her voice. But she wanted me to see Ambrose. I came here instead, because I wanted to see you."

"Are you quite sure? Do you even know which of your thoughts are yours and which are hers? Did she prompt you to put on that black lace underwear, or was that your idea?"

I thought demigods didn't get jealous. "Obviously you're pissed off."

"I'm not angry. I'm just unclear who I had sex with today—you or Cleo—and I'm not sure who I'll find you with tomorrow." He crossed to a table, pouring himself a whiskey. He didn't offer her any. "Not that it matters. I have plenty of courtesans to keep me busy."

Her cheeks burned as she dried herself off. "I'm sorry I kissed your brother."

"Was it you, now? I thought you said it was Cleo. Anyway, like I said, it doesn't matter." He leveled his steely gaze on her. "But you need to get control of that voice in your head. And in the future, try not to mislead people when they ask if you're losing control." He sipped his whiskey, leaning against his bedpost. "But then, misleading people comes easily to you, doesn't it? I do wonder what secrets I'll learn, when I find out about that spell you seem so keen to keep a secret from me."

As she dried off her body, irritation simmered. "You have more secrets than I have. You and Malphas keep referencing something that happened when you lost your mind. But neither of you will tell me what it is, or how you came into contact with my parents in the first place. And let's not forget that you neglected to mention that little detail about slaughtering my parents until I found it out on my own. I guess misleading people comes easily to *you*."

"Perhaps I have a good reason to keep things from you. Clearly, you can't be trusted."

"That's bullshit. Has it occurred to you that maybe you're projecting a little? You lost your mind, you did something terrible that I'm not allowed to know about, and now here I am to remind you of it all? Who are you really angry at, Caine? Me, or yourself?"

Shadows grew denser and heavier around the room, and the air chilled by ten degrees. Suddenly, the room was freezing, and goose bumps rose on her skin.

"Okay, Rosalind. Let me put this in a way you can't argue with. We can both agree that *Cleo* can't be trusted, and you share at least half of your mind with her."

Rosalind snatched her dress off the bed. The mood between them had been well and truly killed. "Right. I guess it's time for me to leave now."

He sighed, raking a hand through his hair. "Not just yet. We have things we need to talk about."

"Like what?"

"Like how we're going to defeat Drew. His power is immense. I've seen the new city he's built in Cambridge, using gods-magic. Obviously, the Brotherhood are letting him build his empire, working with him. If we're not careful, he'll break through the shields again. Do you have any idea what they might be planning?"

And just like that, he was ready to switch tacks and talk about military tactics. The shift of topic was disorienting.

"Okay." Her dress stuck to her damp body. She shivered, trying to gather her thoughts. "I suppose this is his new empire, for his brainwashed bride. I'm just not clear what the Brotherhood is planning."

"I suspect the Brotherhood may be the true architects of this new empire, with Drew acting as their artisan."

With a shudder, she said, "Tell me what it looks like."

"They're building temples to Blodrial, with great fire pits in the center. For publicly roasting demons, I presume. But I think it's beginning to backfire on them. As much as humans are terrified of monsters like us, they're growing even more scared of the new empire. After all, the Brotherhood are using magic now, and they want to kill heretics in horrific ways. The tide of public opinion is turning against them."

"The change of public opinion might sound like a good thing, but it's dangerous. The Brotherhood will do whatever it takes to turn that around. They're masters of propaganda. As soon as I get through the fire hell, I need to find Drew." She glanced at Caine. "And you'll need to allow Malphas to take on that soul. We can't kill them without an army."

Caine's face darkened. "We don't need to decide anything just yet. You're not going into Boston unprepared."

"You did. You were hunting Drew on your own before we called you back here."

"And I might do so again. But I've been fighting for five centuries. Gods-magic isn't everything. I have the advantage of centuries of warfare."

"Right."

"Malphas and I can keep the shield up, and you'll need to spend some time actually learning how to use the magic. It's not enough to just go through the hells. You have to practice. When it's time, we'll go into Boston together. I'll help protect you." His expression hardened. "Since you're a military asset, I mean. Ambrose wants you alive."

Dick. "And what happens to everyone in Massachusetts in the meantime?"

"In the meantime, The Brotherhood are terrifying everyone. Ordinary people are no longer on their side, and that's a good thing for us."

She shook her head. "They're dangerous when they get desperate."

"How? What are they likely to do next?

Her head throbbed, and she rubbed her temples. "If people are becoming fearful of them, they'll find a way to deflect the terror elsewhere."

"What do you mean?"

"They're going to create monsters worse than they are. Just like they did with the oneiroi. And then they'll execute them publicly, in a spectacle of violence. It serves two functions: keeps the rebels in line, and satiates the mob's fear-driven bloodlust at the same time." She thought of the pale white scars on his chest. "I think you know what it's like to be at the receiving end of that sort of justice."

His jaw tightened. "Right. Well, you'd best get back to your room. You'll need to sleep before you visit the fire hell, otherwise Cleo might have you seducing half the city while we should be fighting Drew."

"You're really irked at me and Malphas, aren't you?"

"Don't be absurd. I don't care what you do. Do you have any idea how many women I've been with? You came here, and removed your dress. I'm an incubus. How did you expect me to react?"

She flinched.

"And I only kissed you in the hall because you asked me to. Don't think it means anything more."

His words felt like a punch to the chest. "I get the point."

"I just want to make sure you stay focused long enough for us to kill Drew, and create the daywalkers. You need to remain sane for that. That is my one concern. Apart from that, I don't care whose room you strip off in."

Well, this went well.

Tears stung her eyes, and she wanted to get the hell away from him before he saw them. "Right. Time for sleep, then." She cast a quick glance around the room for her underwear, but decided to head for the door instead. She didn't want to spend another second in Caine's presence.

She pulled open the door into the drafty hall, and Ambrose's words whispered in her mind: *I would assume he has no interest in you. He has been with many beautiful women before.*

This was absolutely mortifying. A sharp pain pierced her chest, and she blinked away her tears.

34

Rosalind managed to forget about Caine long enough to catch a few hours of sleep. As Caine had so nicely pointed out, if she didn't sleep before visiting the fire hell, she risked seducing half the city.

When she'd woken, Miranda had stirred. Within seconds, she'd literally begun tearing at her hair and ranting about *sunlight*. Rosalind had to run around, collecting an army of candles to recreate some semblance of daylight before meeting Malphas.

Then she'd snuck out through the fortress halls, and through one of the exits.

Now, by Malphas's side, she trod carefully through Edin Woods. He seemed to be leading her back to the rocky ledge overlooking the sea—the place where she'd jumped on top of him and kissed him.

She stared at the thick undergrowth as she walked. Moonlight filtered through the trees, dappling the moss and deadfall with flecks of silver.

If she let her mind go blank, maybe she could forget everything Caine had said to her earlier. That whole *don't think it meant anything* sentiment. Not only was she trying to clear her mind of

Caine's words, but she also wanted to avoid thinking about what lay ahead of her in just a few minutes.

If she thought about the fire hell for too long, she'd flee back to the fortress in complete terror.

As they closed in on the cliff's edge, her mouth went dry, and all attempts to clear her mind failed completely. She dreaded this hell more than the others. She'd already felt the excruciating pain of the flames when Cleo had tormented her. As she walked, her legs began to shake, and her pulse raced at the memory of blistering, blackening skin.

When they reached the edge of the wood, she faltered, swaying. Swift as lightning, Malphas slipped an arm around her back to steady her.

He peered down at her. "Are you all right?"

"I'm not looking forward to burning."

"I know. Just try to remember that it's not real. It's your mind playing tricks on your body."

"But I came back from the shadow void with a giant gash in my stomach."

"True," he said. "The mind is a powerful thing. But if your body starts to burn, I'll stop it. You just need to trust me, okay?"

She swallowed hard. "Right."

"Look, you don't have to do this if you don't want. You've already been through five of the hells. Maybe you don't need fire magic if you've got five types of gods-magic already."

She shook her head. "Drew will have fire magic. And I think we need all the power we can get on our side. Don't you?"

"Probably, yes." He cocked his head. "On the plus side, flames won't hurt you after this. The Brotherhood can put you in one of their fires, but you won't burn."

"Really?" Now that was a serious plus.

"The fire goddess can't burn."

She took a deep breath. "Well, let's get this over with, then."

Malphas grabbed her by the hand, leading her to the cliff's edge. He pulled a flask from his back pocket, unscrewing the top. "An important tool for fire spells." He took a sip before handing it to her.

She took a long swig of whiskey, letting it burn her throat, before handing it back to him.

"Good," he said. He was studying her closely, almost as if he was unsure if *he* wanted to go through with this. The sea wind picked up his dark hair, toying with it.

"What next?" she asked.

"I need to create a sigil around you. Just stay where you are." He began pouring the whiskey on the rock around her, encircling her with alcohol. When the circle had been created, he poured a triangular shape in the center, trailing over her skin. Cold rivulets of whiskey dripped down her legs and toes.

Concern flickered in his eyes, and he handed her the flask again. "You should take another sip. Or two." He cleared his throat. "Maybe finish the rest."

"I thought you had no compunctions about exposing me to pain, after I tortured you?"

"I may have changed my mind."

As she took the flask from him, her hand shook so hard she could hardly get the thing to her lips. Her throat burning, she drained the flask, then wiped the back of her hand across her mouth. She was about to learn exactly how it felt to burn to death, to let her body burn like a lonely bonfire on a dark cliff's edge.

I don't think I gave you enough of the flames before, Cleo whispered. *This will be good for you. Now you'll know how it truly feels.*

Rosalind swallowed hard. "Okay. I'm ready."

"It won't last long." Malphas pulled a lighter from his pocket; his hand shook nearly as bad as hers.

"Just do it," she said, her heart skipping a beat.

He flicked the lighter. She braced herself as he dropped the lighter to the ground.

Instantly, blazing hot sunlight burned the darkness from the sky, and a wall of flames erupted around her, searing her skin. She threw back her head and screamed.

Then she wasn't with Malphas anymore, but standing in a city square. Her arms had been tied behind her, fixed to a stake. Bundles of wood surrounded her, and smoke curled around her body. White-hot pain ripped her mind apart, and she unleashed another agonized scream. When her vision focused again, she stared through the dancing flames.

A braying mob surrounded her, their faces contorted with fury. A man with a black beard screamed *Witch! Witch! Witch!* Spittle flew from his mouth.

She looked down at her body. Black pitch covered her skin and clothes, and flames climbed up her legs. The smell of burning flesh filled her nose. Agony seared her nerves.

Her long hair caught in the flames—blonde hair. *Cleo's hair.*

This was where she'd die, surrounded by dark wrath.

Sobbing from the pain, she scanned the crowd, searching for another face, until her gaze landed on him. His hair a vibrant red, his eyes green. He was screaming for her, his arms pinned by three men.

Richard.

He would be next.

The flames reached her waist, scorching her skin, and another scream tore from her throat. She wanted to call for Richard, but her lips would form only one name: *Ambrose*. Ambrose the Betrayer.

In the next moment, her vision went dark. The flames disappeared. Instead, icy water enveloped her skin. Her eyes snapped open. Under the water, pale streams of moonlight illuminated Malphas's face, close to hers.

He gripped her around the waist, swimming with her in his arms.

When her head breached the surface, she gasped for air. Her legs had burned; the skin was raw. But it was all over.

It was night again here in Lilinor, where the stars gleamed in the sky like jewels. She'd never been so happy to see the night sky.

Dizzy, she wrapped her arms around Malphas's neck as she caught her breath. "What happened?"

"Your body was burning. It seemed like an intense vision. I couldn't stop it with my shadow magic."

They bobbed in the gentle waves. "So you jumped into the ocean, with me in your arms."

"Well, you're not burning anymore, are you?"

She unclasped her hands from his neck and began swimming for the rocks.

As they closed in on the shore, her feet touched the rocky ground. "Do you think the spell worked?"

"It looked like it worked to me. What was it like in the hell?"

She pulled herself up onto sludgy rocks, grimacing with pain. Her shoes had been burned, and her pants hung in threadbare tatters around her legs. Blisters covered her skin, and she winced as the salt stung her raw wounds.

Malphas hoisted himself up next to her.

"I saw Cleo," she said at last. "I *was* Cleo. I was in her body as she was burned in front of a mob. They were screaming about witchcraft. She was screaming for Ambrose. And Richard was there to watch it all."

Malphas grimaced at the sight of her legs. "Hold on, let me heal you."

He leaned closer, and she caught the scent of lilies. He traced his hand just above her legs, letting his silver magic soothe her skin. His aura enveloped her legs, caressing her skin. Instantly, the pain began to ebb away as her skin healed, and she heaved a sigh of relief.

When he finished, he met her gaze. "And who, exactly, is Richard?"

"Caine's second soul. Cleo has spoken of him before. I think the three souls might have been in a coven of sorts. I think Cleo and Richard were lovers, until she left him for Ambrose."

"I see." He nodded at her legs. "Does your skin feel better now?"

"Completely cured."

Her stomach still churned at the thought of what had happened to Cleo. No wonder the old witch had some emotional problems. That had been pure, unadulterated agony, and a terrible injustice.

Rosalind swallowed hard. "If we don't stop the Brotherhood, they're going to bring back the old ways. The screaming mobs, the women burning like torches in town squares."

Seawater dripped off Malphas's porcelain skin. "We'll get there, Rosalind. You've impressed me already, more than you know."

"If we manage to defeat the Hunters, I'm sure I won't be doing it alone. You, me, and Caine—we'll create the daywalkers together, and together we take on Drew. It's the only way this will work."

Malphas arched an eyebrow. "Richard and Cleo, reunited. Not sure I want to get involved in all Cleo and Richard's drama. Perhaps I'll avoid the soul Caine brought back."

"Do you think you could handle a second soul?"

He shrugged, looking out toward the sea. "Better than I could handle half a soul."

"What does that mean?"

He shook his head. "Never mind. Let's get you home. You still need to practice, and Caine and I need to bolster the shield in a few hours."

Half a soul. And there it was. Another tantalizing hint of the Mountfort secrets, with no explanation. She rose, hugging herself in the cool sea air. The waves lapped gently over the rocks.

As she walked with Malphas along the Astarte shoreline, an image burned in her mind: her blond hair catching in the flames, all those years ago. After Ambrose had betrayed her.

She blinked hard, trying to clear the image.

Not me, she reminded herself. *Cleo.*

35

Standing in her room, Rosalind peeled off her soaked dress. Seawater pooled on the floor below her bare feet, and her sister stared at her.

Purple smudges darkened the skin below Miranda's eyes. "What were you doing outside?"

"Preparing to fight our cousin."

Miranda cocked her head. "Preparing how?"

Shivering, Rosalind pulled on a lilac gown—with long sleeves, to keep her warm. "Malphas has been helping acquire gods-magic."

Miranda heaved a sigh. "Did you touch him?"

"What do you mean?"

"I haven't touched a man in far too long."

Rosalind crossed her arms. She'd never had this sort of conversation with her sister, and the eerie way Miranda was staring at her didn't make her want to start now. Still, she had to tell *someone* what had happened with Caine.

She crossed to the bed, sitting cross-legged at the edge. "Well, the thing is—Cleo has been confusing me. She's been sending me visions of Ambrose, demanding that I go see him. One of these nights, when I used powerful magic and Cleo started to take over, I ended up kissing Malphas."

Miranda bit her lip, her eyes wide. "What's it like to kiss a demigod?"

"I can't tell you what it's like to kiss Malphas. I was too busy hallucinating."

"Oh." Miranda ran her finger back and forth over her lips, as if she was thinking about Malphas's lips on hers. "That's disappointing. I want to know what it's like to be with a shadow demon."

Rosalind raised her eyebrows. "Well, after that, I went to Caine's room. And that time, I wasn't hallucinating."

Miranda lunged forward, a hungry look in her eyes. "What was *he* like?"

Rosalind thought of the light touch of his fingers over her body, his deep kiss, the way he looked in the warm candlelight.

And then, the positively frigid look in his eyes as he'd told her she didn't mean anything to him.

The memory still stung. Worst of all, she was pretty sure the experience had ruined her for life. How could she ever settle for a normal, human man after that?

"It was pretty much perfect, until it wasn't. He'd smelled Malphas on me, and wanted to know what had happened between us. I ended up telling him. And then he was like, 'well, I don't really care, because none of this meant anything, and I have tons of courtesans.' And he basically wanted me to leave the room and never speak to him again unless it was about military stuff."

For a moment, it almost looked as though shadows were swirling in Miranda's eyes. "Ah. Well. He's probably still upset about Stolas."

The word *Stolas* sent a jolt up Rosalind's spine. She was suddenly very alert. "What do you mean? Who is Stolas?"

Miranda blinked, as if awaking from a dream. "I don't know. I don't know why I said that."

Rosalind's fingers tightened "It's very important to Caine. Where did you hear the name?"

"I told you, I don't know!" Miranda shouted, her cheeks pink.

"Lower your voice!" Rosalind whispered.

"The word Stolas was just a stray thought, floating through my head like a feather on the wind." Miranda reached out, grabbing Rosalind's arm. "I need to get out of here. I want to find a shadow demon of my own."

"We don't need shadow demons. I thought we were just going to get out of here and get a house of our own in the woods or something. You, me, and Tammi. Abominatonia."

Miranda had that hungry look in her eyes again, and she clutched her chest. "It won't be enough. You know it won't be enough. You want Caine, even if he's hardened his heart to you. And I want..." Her fingers tightened on her dress. "I want *everything*. I need to feel alive again. Don't you understand? I need to feel the rain on my skin, and I need to feel the rush of a first kiss. I need to taste everything. And I belong with the shadow demons now."

Oh. Shit. Maybe this wouldn't go as smoothly as she'd hoped. She rubbed her temples. "It's just that Caine has some kind of prohibition against raising people from the grave."

"Well, you've got to figure something out. You've just found the best lover you could ever hope to find, and you can't lose him."

Her chest ached. "That's a dead end. He doesn't want to see me again anyway."

"Okay, fine. But I want to see the world again. You've taken me from one coffin and buried me in another."

She took a deep breath. She *really* didn't want to face Caine again after her last humiliating encounter. "I don't know, Miranda."

"Just tell him," Miranda said. "Then I can get the hell out of this grave of stone and actually see the world."

Rosalind bit her lip. "I suppose I could broach it gently, again. I tried before, but it didn't get very far."

Her temples throbbed, and Cleo mentally slapped her with an image. Not Ambrose's naked body this time, but Caine's golden skin, skimming against hers.

"Stop it, Cleo," she muttered.

Your sister is right, Cleo purred. *Broach it with Caine. See what happens. After all, you said you trusted him, didn't you? Are you changing your mind just because he doesn't love you?*

Rosalind stood. Maybe it was worth a shot, at least to feel out his reaction. "Fine. Both of you, settle down." She pointed at her sister. "But wait here, please, until I get back."

Miranda grunted, her lip curling. "Get me out of here."

Rosalind grabbed a knife in a holster, strapping it around her waist, then crossed to the door.

As she walked through the hall, her footsteps echoed off the ceiling, and her mind flashed with images of Cleo's death: the dancing flames, the horrified look in Richard's eyes.

When you're in love, you can't escape the fire.

Rosalind flinched. Maybe Richard had loved Cleo, but things were a little different between Rosalind and Caine. In fact, Caine didn't find her particularly special. He'd made that clear enough.

She pulled open the door to the stairwell. How *exactly* was she going to phrase this question to Caine?

She didn't imagine taking her dress off a second time would do the trick.

In the corridor, candlelight and shadows dancing over the dark flagstones. She stopped at the door near the picture of Lord Byron. For a few moments, she steeled her resolve, then knocked on the dark wood.

After a moment, she heard his muffled voice through the door. "Who is it?"

"It's Rosalind."

A long pause. Then, "Is there a reason you're here?"

I don't have a good feeling about this. "I need to ask you something," she ventured.

The door unlatched, and swung open. Caine must have used his magic to open it, because he was on the other side of the room. He sat in a gray armchair by his window, sipping bourbon from a tumbler. His glacial eyes sent a chill through her blood. He didn't exactly look happy to see her.

She stepped over the threshold anyway, then took a seat on the edge of his bed.

"What do you want?" Ice tinged his voice.

Might as well dive in. "I need to know what you would do if I raised Miranda's body from the grave."

"I'd kill her."

His words cut her to the bone. "Why? Why would you do that?"

"Because the dead are supposed to stay dead." He took another sip from his tumbler. "Was that your only question? I'd prefer you didn't remove your dress again, because I have a dinner guest arriving soon."

Her heart constricted, and she scrambled to think of a response, but before she could get another word out, the door creaked open.

Esmerelda stepped into the room, her red hair cascading over a stunning crimson gown.

She shot a furious look at Rosalind. "What's the human doing here?"

"She's leaving." Caine glared at Rosalind. "Do you mind? I don't have much time with Esmerelda. I'll need to leave to work on the shield again."

His words felt like a punch to the gut, and Cleo whispered in her mind. *I told you, Rosalind. A shadow demon can't really love. Or at least, he'll never love a human.*

Tears stung her eyes, and Rosalind rose. "Right. I'll be on my way."

As she walked to the door, she tried to ignore Esmerelda's victorious smirk.

Maybe she'd been wrong to trust Caine. How much did she really know about him, anyway? How much did she really know about demons at all?

Kill them all, Cleo sang. *Dance in their blood.*

A part of Rosalind wanted to let Cleo take over, to see what destruction the old witch could wreak on the place, but she kept her grip on the spirit this time.

Still, as she walked down the halls, she caught her reflection in the silver sconces: stunning long blond hair, and green eyes. *Cleo's eyes.*

36

$\mathcal{R}$osalind pushed through the door to the Gelal Fields, on her way to practice the gods-magic.

Her muscles burned. Over the past few days, while Caine and Malphas had kept the shield in place, she'd been practicing shadow running—moving from one place to another like a phantom wind. Thrilling, but exhausting. On top of that, she'd been trying her hand at the other types of gods-magic, like calling vines from the earth and shooting fire from her fingertips.

As if the magic weren't draining enough, there was the Miranda problem. With each day, her twin grew more desperate for freedom. Rosalind had snuck her out twice while the vampires slept, so Miranda could feel the sea air on her skin, and let the salt water run over her legs.

But it hadn't been enough. She seemed so *hungry,* like she couldn't get enough of the world.

Today, after practicing magic all morning, Rosalind had snatched a few hours of sleep while Miranda paced the room, gnawing through cakes.

Now, Rosalind glanced up at the cloudless sky, admiring the stars etched in the dark. She was definitely *not* going to think about how they reminded her of Caine's eyes. She hadn't seen him at all over the past few days, and she had an agonizing feeling he'd been spending time with Esmerelda. Rosalind's *least* favorite vampire.

Long grasses tickled Rosalind's legs as she walked, and a chorus of crickets chirped around her. *I'm not thinking about Caine. Or Ambrose. Or any other shadow demons. I'm just gonna focus on the storm I need to raise.*

As her eyes adjusted to the dark, she could see a pale silver glow of magic, just at the edge of the forest. *Caine?*

So much for her plan not to think about him.

She crossed her arms as she walked through the fields, and glanced at the sky again, at the faint shimmer of silver magic that protected the kingdom. Already, around the moon and the Big Dipper, the shadow magic had thinned again.

A shudder crawled up her spine. Drew was close to breaking through, and they were running out of time.

Her heart tightened. She still hadn't mastered most of the magic she was supposed to use. She couldn't quite get the rocks to obey her commands, couldn't call up a large enough flame to burn a twig. It hadn't exactly been easy to concentrate the past few days. While she'd been practicing all the new gods-magic at her fingertips, Cleo had been invading her mind with visions of torture and burnings, alternated with Ambrose-porn. Rosalind was pretty sure she could pick out Cleo's fondest memories: screwing in a castle, in a meadow, and up against a tree.

Not big on beds, those two.

As she drew closer to Caine, her heart began to speed up. Pathetic, really. She was going to turn into Cleo, obsessed with the memories of sex with a shadow demon—his exquisite kisses replaying on a loop in her mind for the rest of her life.

She should run the other way. And yes, despite herself, her pace quickened.

But when she'd come within twenty feet of him, she felt a flicker of disappointment.

Not Caine.

Malphas.

For the best, anyway. I have no idea what to say to Caine right now.

Pale magic curled from Malphas's body, snaking up to the sky like silver smoke.

She snapped a twig as she approached, and Malphas broke his focus, his pale eyes landing on her. The silver tendrils of magic snapped back into his body.

"Sorry to disturb you while you're working on the shield," she said. "How's it going?"

"Not well. I'm not sure how much longer I can hold it in place. Caine should be helping me, but I'm not sure where the hell he's gone."

"With Esmerelda, perhaps?"

"What?"

"Never mind. So what do you think Caine is doing, then?" she asked as casually as she could.

"Arguing with Ambrose again, I think. He won't produce the sigil we need. And he keeps threatening to go back into Boston on his own to slaughter Drew without us. He's certain he can solve this whole problem on his own." Malphas frowned. "He no longer seems keen to include you in his plans. Care to tell me why?"

"You'd have to ask him. But once I'm done practicing this storm spell, I'm going to have a word with him. Going to Boston on his own is the last thing he should do."

"Why?"

"They're looking for a scapegoat." Dread welled in her gut. "And Caine's the perfect specimen. He's powerful, demonic. The Brotherhood already hate him. He'd be a great coup for them. Granted, so would you and I. But we're going to have to look out for each other. No one is going alone."

"You think they could be waiting for him?"

"It wouldn't surprise me. Maybe they're trying to lure him out—first Caine, then me. Drew knows I'd go after Caine. He'd have everything he needed: his scapegoat, his revenge, and his mind-controlled wife to torture for the rest of her life."

Pale moonlight washed over Malphas's skin. "When do you think you'll be ready to fight him?"

A sigh slid from her. "I'm getting there. I just feel like I need a few more weeks. And I need Cleo to shut the hell up, so I can focus. She's quiet now, but when I'm using the magic her voice gets louder. She wants things that I can't give her."

"What does she want?"

Ambrose. "It doesn't matter."

As soon as the words had left her mouth, Cleo assaulted her with a vision of Ambrose kissing her naked hips. Rosalind nearly groaned at the image, and the hot flash of need that seared her body.

Her jaw tightened. "Not now, Cleo," she muttered.

Malphas stared at her. "That's not a good sign."

"I've got it under control," she snapped. "I don't have time to keep resting. Look, I've got to go practice the storm magic. And as soon as I get back, I'll have a word with Caine about his plan to go into Boston—"

A loud crack interrupted her sentence, and her gaze flicked to the sky. "The shield," she whispered.

Below their feet, the ground began to rumble. Once more, a geyser of water surged from the field by the castle wall.

"Help me fix the shield," Malphas shouted. "Now!"

She stared at the moon, letting the shadow magic spiral from her body. She could feel Drew's power just on the other side of the shield, the tendrils of colored magic snaking along the dome of shadow magic. When she closed her eyes, she saw a vortex of stars and night. On the other side of the portal, Drew's horde of Hunters waited to invade, ready to slaughter everyone she cared about.

Nyxobas's magic charged her body, and she let it flow from her, mingling with Malphas's. As the earth trembled below her, she lost herself in the surge of power, melding with the night sky and the jewel of Nyxobas.

I am the darkness. I am the eternal void.

When she opened her eyes again, three Hunters were crawling from a muddy portal. Filled with Nyxobas's power, Rosalind and Malphas shadow-ran to them, flying on the wind in just a few seconds. Despite moving at an intense speed, she took in every detail of the Hunters' faces: a woman with freckles and a round face; a man with a trim black beard, no more than twenty-two; and a bald man with a square jaw.

They weren't monsters, but they'd chosen the wrong side of this war. All three would be dead within seconds.

The woman raised her gun, and Rosalind's fist connected with her jaw—once, twice, three times, her head snapped back. Fast as the night wind, Rosalind grabbed the gun from her, turning it on the woman.

She cocked the gun, and fired.

One for Miranda. Two for Cleo. Three for me.

Three Hunters fell to the ground, bullet holes in their chests.

Malphas stared at her. "I guess you're getting better at this."

She tucked the gun into her belt, still buzzing with night magic. "I guess I am." She looked up at the shield, examine the sterling sheen of magic. "I need one more practice session with my magic skills. But soon you, Caine, and I will just need to go into Boston. I could feel Drew's power on the other side of the shield, and he's desperate to break through."

37

*R*osalind stood on the cliff's edge, staring out at the Astarte sea. A damp breeze kissed her skin, and she licked the salt off her lips.

She swayed slightly on her feet. The sea wind toyed with her hair, and she drank in the briny scent of Dagon. She closed her eyes, trying to gather the energy she needed for a storm spell.

But as soon as her eyelids fluttered closed, Cleo greeted her with a vision of Ambrose kissing the tops of her breasts, her back flat against the wooden wall, dress hiked up around her waist. His firm hands gripping her waist.

Richard will be upset...

Rosalind shook her head to clear the vision. "Not now, Cleo. I need to practice."

Cleo slammed her with another vision—her legs around Ambrose's muscled waist, her back against the rough tree bark. He kissed her milky white neck, and her body writhed against his...

Rosalind's fingernails dug into her palms. *I don't need to be a voyeur into someone's sixteenth century sex life.* "Stop it. I get it. You liked fucking Ambrose. Can we move on?"

Her legs were shaking, and her gaze flicked to the starry sky. With the daywalker plans in complete disarray, they had few defenses against Drew. She'd have to master her abilities, or they'd all die when he invaded the city again.

She held out her arms to the side. Gusts of marine wind whipped at her hair. This time, she had no incubi to attack. It was just her and the vast skies. She arched her back, opening her body to Mishett-Ash, imagining a storm simmering on the horizon. An electric thrill surged through her limbs.

This is working.

Her eyes snapped open, and she stared up the stars, watching as dark clouds rolled in. An ancient, wrathful power vibrated through her body. Maybe she *was* mastering this magic after all. She narrowed her eyes at the sky, watching as the clouds covered the moon, blotting out the light. Far below, the sea began to seethe like a dying beast, slate gray and angry.

An electric thrill charged her muscles. She flicked her wrist, and lightning pierced the dark sky. *I can do this.*

A second flick, and the clouds opened, unleashing a torrent of rain.

Fat raindrops soaked her clothes, and the distant call of a valkyrie pierced the air. Filled with a soul-deep assuredness, Rosalind stepped off the edge of the cliff, and took flight into the air. Gray magic whorled around her body, and she soared over the frothing sea, dark as bitumen.

Thunder rumbled over the horizon.

Cleo whispered, *It feels good to wield the power of nature, Rosalind, Doesn't it? Glorious. Until they punish you for it.*

Rosalind swooped lower, letting the ocean's spume wash over her, tasting the salt. Cold wind whipped at her skin, tearing at her dress and hair. Finally, she'd wielded the gods-magic successfully.

Too much power now. They'll burn you, too.

Her heart began to pound harder when she thought of Cleo burning in the funeral pyre, of Richard watching. But she couldn't think about that now—not with Drew eating at the shield, ready to invade the city and slaughter everyone.

Rosalind pushed the memories of Cleo to the back of her mind.

She swooped back over to the cliff's edge, landing with a hard roll on the jagged rock. She grunted, then righted herself, dusting off the gravel. Cold magic still rushed through her veins, dulling the pain from her landing's impact.

As she stood on the cliff's edge, another crack of lightning flashed in the sky. Reaching out toward the sea, she focused on the salty air, letting Dagon's magic curl from her fingers. Her mind flickered with an image of Dagon in his bestial form, his tentacles sliding over her skin...

She flicked her wrist, then watched as the ocean convulsed. Slowly, the tide retreated from the shore, leaving behind sludgy black rocks,, hammered by the storm's onslaught. Dagon's phantom tentacles curled tighter around her body, encircling her waist as she used his power.

As watery magic surged through her blood, she flicked her wrist again, and the sea returned once more—this time, as a wall of black water, rushing for the cliffs. Rosalind stared, wide eyed, as a small tsunami rushed for the cliff's edge.

But before water met rock, Cleo seized her mind.

Rosalind faltered, her vision going dark. Then, a shocking burst of green—Cleo's aura.

The green aura thinned, giving way to a sycamore grove. In the heavy spring night, she stood, dressed in her thinnest white dress—the one Ambrose liked, because he could see through the fabric when the sunlight hit it from behind.

Her blond hair tumbled over her shoulders—Ambrose and Richard were the only men who'd ever seen her with her hair down, threaded with flowers. Bluebells for peace of mind.

She sighed, leaning back against a trunk. She'd eaten dinner with Ambrose last night, at his manor. She shouldn't have gone to him like that, so recklessly—not with the witch hunters roaming Fife. But she couldn't resist his beauty, nor stay away from his touch.

She plucked a petal off a bluebell. Ambrose drew her to him like a moth to the flame. Some nights, she just stood outside his window, watching him. Trying to draw his attention to her, making sure his love wasn't false. She was sure he saw her, too.

But last night had been different. She'd stood in the garden just outside his manor. She'd needed to see him, needed to feel his hands all over her. But when she saw him with that other woman, the one with the raven hair, beautiful as a goddess—

Their quarrel had been terrible. She'd said things she regretted, and she was sure he'd never want to see her again. But then, he'd invited her to dine with him, just the two of them. Roasted quail, venison, strawberry pudding, and malmsey wine— enough to drown a man.

But they hadn't finished eating. Just as she'd finished her second glass of wine, Ambrose had pushed the food off the table, and he'd taken her right there. He'd laced his fingers through hers, and he'd given her the most amazing love of her life.

She hoped she'd see him again tonight. He knew he'd be able to find her here, and she was certain he'd want to see her again. Already, her body was warming—getting ready for his touch.

The sound of footsteps turned her head, and her heartbeat sped up. *He's coming.*

But as she stepped through the grove, looking for her love, the world seemed to tilt below her feet. It wasn't Ambrose coming for her.

How did they know I was here?

There were three of them, their black caps peaked, iron tools gleaming in the moonlight. It was the *Hunters*.

Her heart skipped a beat. *Ambrose and Richard are the only ones who know I come here...*

Her heart thudded, and she lifted her hand to begin a spell. But before her lips could finish the first Angelic word, an iron arrow struck her in the chest. She fell to the earth, pain screaming through her shoulder. Grief cut through her.

Ambrose turned me in to the Hunters.

A hunter kicked her hard in the gut, another slammed a boot into her ribs.

Ambrose is sending me to my death.

One of the Hunters—his face red as a devil's—tore the front of her dress, and she screamed.

Ambrose wouldn't come to save her.

Ambrose had sent them here.

As the storm raged above, Rosalind clenched her fists tighter, until her fingernails pierced the skin. A hard wave slammed against the rocky cliffs. The black clouds seethed in the sky, dark as the smoke from a witch's pyre.

Cleo's wrath was hers now—and she had a score to settle.

Ambrose, you faithless prick.

She turned, rushing back toward the fortress.

Fury ripped through her nerves, colder than a valkyrie's rage. Ambrose had been Cleo's lover, and then he'd sent the Hunters for her. Instead of meeting her himself, he'd left her to be beaten and raped.

And then he'd let her burn.

Wrath shook her body.

Why had Ambrose done this to Cleo? Because she'd been too much trouble for him? Because he didn't know how to get rid of a lover he no longer wanted?

Shadow demons aren't capable of love.

No wonder Cleo hated the fucker. No wonder she wanted to light him on fire.

Rosalind's feet pounded through the forest. Her breath was ragged in her lungs. She ran, carried on the wind, and gusts of cold air billowed around her.

But Cleo had said something else. *Richard* had known where Cleo would be. He was a jilted lover. What if it had been him?

And what if Richard's angry soul had poisoned Caine's mind against Rosalind?

She lifted the hem of her dress, running faster through the Gelal Fields. She needed to get to the bottom of this, once and for all. She was sick of all the secrets.

But before she got to the fortress walls, a loud *crack* boomed over the horizon. Flicking her wrist, she flung open the entrance to the castle. She sprinted through a dark hall. As she ran through the candlelit corridors and up the stairs, her mind flashed with images of the fire.

Ambrose sent me to the flames, Cleo screamed.

He'd burned his lover. He'd left his wife to rot in a prison.

Demons can't really love, Cleo whispered. *They will use you, then kill you.*

Gasping for breath, Rosalind sprinted up the stairs to the White Tower. She knew where she'd find Ambrose: toying with another courtesan.

At the top of the stairs, she rushed through the long hall, her gaze on the two guards at the door. Two near-giants, large as vikings, wielding axes designed to separate intruder's necks from their bodies. But she didn't feel so intimidated anymore.

"Stop!" One of them shouted, readying his weapon.

She held out her hands, and two sharp bolts of lightning shot from her wrists, finding their marks in the guards' chests.

Good, Cleo purred. *Vengeance is glorious.*

Stalking past their unconscious bodies, Rosalind climbed the stairs. She flicked her wrist, flinging open the door. Blazing with power, she stepped into Ambrose's chamber. With the storm raging above, a glass dome covered the open ceiling, and rain hammered against the clear glass.

Ambrose stood, naked, by one of the windows.

Before she could even register surprise, he had her pinned against the wall, his hand around her throat.

38

*H*e pressed his muscled body against hers. Cleo seemed to thrill at his touch, wanted his hands all over her waist—but Rosalind heard nothing but the angry roar of blood in her ears.

Either you or Richard gave her up to the Hunters.

She slammed her fist into his cheek, knocking him away.

His head whipped to the side, and he touched his mouth, dabbing at the blood. He eyed her warily. "You've changed your tune."

"What did you do to Cleo?"

Rosalind felt her body shifting, lengthening. Her hips narrowed, and from the corner of her eye, she watched her dark hair lighten to a pale gold.

Ambrose's eyes widened. "Cleo," he whispered.

Rosalind's fingers twitched, fire magic sparking at the tips. "You better tell us now, vampire," she spoke, half in her own voice, and half in Cleo's. "Because we know what it feels like to burn. I'm not sure you do, but we can change that real fast."

His jaw dropped.

Despite her fury, Cleo's lust simmered, and Rosalind found her eyes scanning Ambrose's chiseled body. She could almost understand why Cleo had become obsessed with him.

Almost, but not quite.

"I won't speak to you in that form," he growled.

Now, Rosalind understood what Cleo wanted from Ambrose. It wasn't simply sex or vengeance.

She wanted a confession.

"Tell me the truth!" she shouted, her voice mingling with Cleo's.

In a fraction of a second, his hand was at her throat once more, squeezing ever so slightly. "I won't ask again."

Coolly, she surveyed him. Now she had the power to fight him—but she wasn't here for a slaughter. She was here for a confession. She let her body transform again, growing petite once more, her hair darkening. "If you don't give Cleo what she wants," Rosalind said. "I will turn into her once more and flay your skin from your bones. Are we clear?"

Slowly, he backed away. "I need to get dressed for this conversation." He crossed to his bed, pulling on a pair of black underwear. His clothing littered the silky sheets, and she had the distinct impression he'd been banging someone not long ago.

"Where'd your latest lover go?" she asked, taking another step closer. "Did you hire an army of thugs to burn her to death?"

As he stepped into his pants, Ambrose's gaze was positively glacial. "You really have completely lost your mind, haven't you, Rosalind?"

She shook her head. "I've just come to understand why Cleo hates you so much."

"You've lost your wits. You're no good to me if you're insane."

"Don't you get it?" Rosalind shouted. "She's not going to let my mind rest until you tell me the truth." She stepped closer to him, letting the flames spark from her fingertips. Smoke curled to the ceiling. "Confess what you did."

Still bare-chested, Ambrose gestured to the bed. "Sit."

She curled her lip. "I'm not sitting on sheets you just screwed on."

He took a step closer, his dark magic curling from his body. He was angry. Furious, even.

But he didn't scare her anymore. "Tell me what you did," she demanded.

He took a deep breath. "I met her in the 1590s. I had moved to Scotland nearly a hundred years before."

"Why?"

His eyes darkened. "You don't need to know that. You only need to know that it was the darkest period of my life—until I met Cleo."

Deep in Rosalind's chest, Cleo's aura sparked.

"She was different. A female philosopher. Smarter than any woman I'd ever met. She had a lover when I met her."

"Richard." Rosalind swallowed. "That's Caine's soul."

"Hmm. I guess that explains what happened earlier."

"What do you mean?"

He arched an eyebrow, jaw tensing. "You know what I mean. Anyway, I'd meet her in the sycamore grove, or among the wildflowers at night. She was an amazing lover. Passionate beyond belief."

"Believe me, I've seen the mental video."

"But she always wanted more."

"So?"

His aura darkened the air around him. "You have to understand that in Scotland at this time, the whole country was overrun by prickers. Hunters, you'd call them. More powerful than at any other point in their history, except now. Anyone found guilty of witchcraft would be burned at the stake. I wasn't as powerful then as I am now. I hadn't taken over Lilinor yet."

Rosalind crossed her arms. She was losing patience. "And why did you give her over to the Hunters?"

"She'd become obsessed with me. She needed to see me every night. If I wasn't there for her, she'd send wisteria vines all over my manor, clinging to the brick. She'd practice magic in my garden. The people who lived nearby had begun to notice. There were rumors."

She swallowed hard. Cleo's magic roiled sharply in her gut. "So you turned her in?"

"Not until she spied on me one night. She caught me speaking to Erish in my home. It was before Erish and I had married, but Erish had... an interest in me. The jealousy ripped Cleo apart. She threatened, then and there, to turn me in to the Hunters. I tried to calm her. I invited her in for dinner. I thought I'd made her happy again. I thought I'd stopped it. But she was too unpredictable. She didn't forgive me. Because the next night the Hunters came for me. And there was only one way out of it. It was me, or her. They wanted a witch, and I gave them one."

Rosalind's fists tightened, fury still blazing through her blood. "She didn't turn you in."

His eyes had darkened to a pitch black. "She was trying to get me killed. And after what I'd already been through, I wasn't dying for a crazy woman."

"She didn't turn you in. Maybe they saw all the wisteria." Cleo's anger seethed, and Rosalind nearly punched him again. "They raped her, you know."

The room grew positively frigid.

"She didn't turn you in." She shook her head. "You said the Hunters were all over Scotland. Maybe they just came for you anyway. Or maybe they'd heard about the vines. Or, you know, the fact that you drink people's blood."

Ambrose seemed to pale, shadows thickening around him. "Are you certain she never sent the Hunters for me?"

"She thought you'd be coming for her in the sycamore grove. She was certain of it."

He dropped his gaze, staring at the floor. "When they burned her, I hid inside the nearby church, and I forced myself to watch the whole thing. She cried my name, over and over. And Richard screamed hers. He was the next to burn."

Bile crawled up her throat.

Cleo's voice had gone quiet.

"Those are the old ways that the Brotherhood wants to bring back," Rosalind said quietly.

"I'll never forget the sound of her screams."

Rosalind shook her head. "What did you mean about Richard's soul? How it explains what happened earlier?"

He glanced at her quizzically. "Caine's outburst, of course. His jealous rage."

A pit opened in the hollow of her stomach. "What outburst?"

"When he found you with me here earlier. You do realize that the only reason I didn't slaughter you for bursting in here is that you were the best shag I've had since... well, since Cleo. That, and the—"

Her mouth went dry. "I was here earlier?"

"You really don't remember?" He pinched the bridge of his nose. "I'm not sure if I should be insulted or concerned. I didn't know Cleo had taken over your mind that badly, or I never would have allowed you to seduce me."

Oh shit oh shit oh shit. Rosalind's breath caught in her throat. Cleo had compelled her to seduce Ambrose while she was in some sort of a haze. Maybe while she thought she was sleeping? She shook her head. "I don't remember anything about it. What happened? What did Caine do when he found me here?"

Dark magic whorled around Ambrose. "He knocked on the door, and you answered it. Naked. It seemed to upset him. He turned into the Ravener once more. It really doesn't ring a bell?"

She swallowed hard. "And what did he say?"

"That he should have known not to trust an Atherton."

Her stomach twisted in knots. She'd confirmed everything that Caine thought about her.

With adrenalin burning through her veins, she turned to flee from the room.

39

Her feet pounded over the stone floor as she raced to Caine's room, heart thudding hard against her ribs. Her sodden clothes still clung to her legs, slowing her pace, and she lifted the hem. She didn't know what she was going to say when she found Caine, but she had a desperate need to talk to him. *Now*.

When she got to the painting of Lord Byron, her heart sped up. His door was *open*. Why would he leave his door open?

She rushed inside, but the place was empty. The storm winds rattled the window, and only a guttering candle lit the room.

What the hell was she going to tell him, anyway?

Panic gripped her chest, and she began pacing the room.

And as she paced, her mind stopped racing, and started actually working.

Maybe she'd gone to Ambrose's room and shagged him stupid while she was in a fugue state.

Or maybe she wasn't the only person walking around this place with her face on.

What if it hadn't been her? What if it had been Miranda? Ambrose had still been naked when she'd burst into the room, which meant it hadn't happened that long ago...

Miranda. Her stomach twisted in knots. It was worse than she thought. *Something is going very wrong with my sister.*

Maybe the spell had gone wrong, or living after death took some serious adjustment. Who the hell knew? This was completely uncharted territory, and the one person who could guide her hadn't told her a damn thing.

She needed to find her sister. Now.

Her pulse racing, she tore out of Caine's room and down the hall. With ragged breaths, she stormed down the stairwell. She pushed through the door into the darkened hall, where candlelight wavered over the flagstones. As she sprinted toward her room, a figure rounded the corner at the other end of the hall, silver magic curling from his body.

Her heart skipped a beat. *Caine?*

No. As her eyes focused in the dim light, she made out Malphas's features.

Shit. She wouldn't be able to go into her room with Malphas lingering around here. Miranda could be just on the other side of the door. She slowed her pace, trying to act calm. *Nothing to see here. No undead sisters, no postcoital drama with Caine and Ambrose.*

Malphas didn't slow his pace when he saw her. In fact, he sped up, moving toward her in a blur of shadows.

Her blood turned to ice. What the hell was happening now?

In the next moment, he was standing over her, silver eyes piercing in the dim light. "There you are," he said, his magic whipping around his body.

"What's happening?" *I mean, apart from the fact that your brother caught my undead sister screwing his boss?*

"Caine told me he was leaving Lilinor on his own, just to gather information. Maybe to find a human for us to use as a host for the mage's soul. He said he wasn't going after Drew." He narrowed his eyes. "But something seemed off with him. Like he wasn't telling me the whole truth. I tried to slow him down, but he went through the portal."

A growing sense of dread welled in her gut. "What do you mean, something seemed off with him?"

"He wouldn't look me in the eye. He seemed... angry."

Rosalind's gaze flicked to her door. She had a terrible feeling that, at any moment, her sister might burst from the door and try to bang another demon. Why stop at just one?

Malphas cocked his head. "What's distracting you?"

She swallowed hard. If Malphas spoke to Ambrose, he'd quickly learn what had happened. Might as well come clean with the truth now. Or at least, the fake truth.

She folded her arms, cheeks burning with humiliation. "He was upset when he found me in Ambrose's room."

Malphas took a deep breath. "And why was he upset?"

She cleared her throat, staring at the floor. "See... Caine and I had a moment—"

"A moment?"

"We slept together."

Malphas's eyes darkened, his icy aura whipping the air around him. "Ah. And then you had a moment with Ambrose?"

"I felt terrible when I realized what was happening, and when Caine found us. But Cleo is obsessed with Ambrose. I think she's settled down now, after she got what she wanted."

"Sex with Ambrose."

"A confession."

"Well that is unexpected." Malphas scrubbed a hand over his mouth. "You know that I can tell when you're lying. I'm just not entirely sure which part you were lying about. Probably the part about how you felt awful."

Well, now I definitely feel awful. Her gaze darted to the door again. What was Miranda up to?

Malphas crossed his arms, leaning against the wall. "Is this conversation keeping you from something important? It's just that I think my brother may have just run to his death. You know his theory about how emotional attachments are a liability? This is what he means."

"I don't know why he cares so much. He was with Esmerelda in his bedroom the last time I saw him. He pretty much kicked me out so they could have dinner."

"She works for him—she's a spy. I doubt it was romantic."

She took a deep breath. "Okay, well, we have to go after him. He's the perfect scapegoat for the Brotherhood. And if they're waiting for him outside Lilinor..." She let her sentence trail off. She couldn't even imagine what horrors Drew and the Brotherhood would have in store for Caine.

"We don't have daywalkers. We don't have an army. It's daylight in Boston. Our rescue force consists of two people: you and me."

She bit her lip. "And if anyone is waiting on the other side of the portal, they'll still be there."

Malphas nodded. "We'll lower the shields, just for a few minutes. Long enough to do some scrying. We'll ask about danger that awaits us on the other side. If it's clear, we can slip into the city quietly, using shadow magic. We'll drag his arse back here until we can make our army. Okay?"

She glanced at her door again. "I need a few minutes to change and get my weapons ready. I'll meet you by the portal."

"The one in Ambrose's room?"

She grimaced. She didn't want to face Ambrose again. "Gods, no. The one outside."

He glanced at her door, as if he knew she kept her darkest secrets locked behind it.

Her stomach clenched. "I'll meet you outside," she repeated.

He gave her a wary look before turning. Shadows thickened around him, and he disappeared like smoke on the wind.

She took a deep breath before opening the door to her room. Miranda sat on the floor, wrapped in a silky white bathrobe. Half-eaten cakes littered the ground around her, and custard and jam smeared her mouth. Her eyes looked wild, empty.

Rosalind's blood ran cold. *Something is definitely not right.*

"You've finally come back for me," Miranda said. "I thought you might have abandoned me."

"I told you I was coming back. I had to practice the magic I'm learning."

Miranda wiped a hand across the back of her mouth. "And how come I'm not allowed to have this power?"

Irritation simmered. "I told you why. No one is supposed to know you're alive. And you nearly ruined everything by running into Ambrose's room to shag him. Caine said he'd murder you if he found you. The only reason he didn't kill you was that he thought you were me. And now he's run off to Boston to get himself killed."

Tears glistened in Miranda's eyes, and she rose. Her body looked tense, her arms stiff. "And why is it that Caine has forbidden people from bone conjuring? Do you know?"

Dread crept around Rosalind's heart like wisteria, crushing the life out of her. "Aurora said he considered it a blasphemy."

Miranda inched closer, grabbing her robe just over her heart. "Or maybe it's because he understood what it would do to a person. There's a void in my chest that can never be filled, and if I don't get enough of the world it will consume me alive until there's nothing left but the darkness. You can't keep me in here, Rosalind—in this prison."

Rosalind's legs had begun to shake. "I won't keep you in here. But when Caine caught you with Ambrose, he rushed into Cambridge on his own. I'm worried Drew could have been waiting for him. I need to get him back."

"You always have something important to do. Don't you, Rosalind? While I wait here, in darkness. Ripped apart by loneliness."

Rosalind held out her hands, as if calming a wild beast. "I'm going to Cambridge, and when I get back we'll figure this out." Surely there must be another spell that could help heal Miranda's mind.

After all, what the hell was the point of magic if it couldn't solve your real problems? What use were grimoires and auras if they couldn't heal broken minds and dead bodies, if they couldn't overturn humanity's fundamental curse?

"We'll fix this," Rosalind said, more to reassure herself than anything. She pulled off her soaked dress, crossing to the wardrobe. "We'll get our house. Abominatonia. We'll have our fireplace, our paintings. You'll have as much life as you want."

Miranda's lip curled. Her look was ferocious. "I want oak trees, and the smell of the ocean. I want to hear the call of a golden-crowned sparrow. I want sunlight, and the feel of water on my skin. I *need* these things."

"You'll have them." Rosalind pulled out her fighting gear: black leather pants and a tight top. "And you can sleep with as many vampires as you want."

"Oh really?" Miranda said tonelessly. "And when will this happen? After you save the world?"

Rosalind stepped into her clothes. "I'm trying the best I can, Miranda. We're in the middle of a goddamn war. You died. Drew killed you. I'm trying to fix that, but he's going to kill a lot of other people if I don't help to stop him."

Miranda sat on the edge of the bed, hugging herself. "I spent years wandering the streets, looking for you. I slept in train stations. I ate discarded food. I kept to myself," she muttered, seemingly lost in her own thoughts. "I just want a chance at the life I deserved."

Rosalind zippered up the front of her jacket. "I know. And you will. That's why I brought you back. Please just stay in here for a little while longer. We'll get out of Lilinor soon."

Staring at the floor, Miranda nodded wordlessly.

Why do I have the terrible feeling this isn't going to work out well? Grabbing her weapon belt, Rosalind pushed those worries to the back of her mind. Instead, she ran Miranda's mantra through her mind: *Sunlight, the smell of the ocean. Oak trees. Water on skin. The call of a golden-crowned sparrow.*

Mentally, she repeated these words as she strapped her weapons to her thigh.

They would have life again, once they left Lilinor.

She cast one last look back at Miranda as she reached for the door. "Please stay here. I'll be back for you. Get some sleep."

Miranda's gaze met hers for just a moment, and the pain in those dark eyes pierced Rosalind to the bone.

Dressed for battle, Rosalind walked toward the fountain in an abandoned square at the edge of Lilinor. Her heels clacked over the cobblestones, and the shadows around her seemed to creep and writhe like half-living creatures. The rain had stopped, but rivulets of cold water ran through the stones and dripped off the steep-peaked roofs.

As she approached the gently trickling fountain, she caught sight of two figures. Aurora stood by Malphas's side, dressed in an emerald-green gown, and dripping with silver jewels.

Rosalind took a shaky breath, her nerves burning. This was where it had all begun—where Rosalind had first entered Lilinor all those weeks ago, when she'd recklessly chased Caine through the portal. Now Caine was the reckless one. Apparently, emotions *were* a liability, though she had no real clue how he felt about her. His actions certainly didn't match his words.

As she approached, Malphas stared at her, his eyes blazing with cold light. "Are you ready for this, Ros?"

Aurora traced her finger in the pool's dark water. "When you're ready to lower the shield, I can help you both with the scrying. You two control the shield with shadow magic, and I'll chant the scrying spell. Got it?"

Rosalind nodded. "Thanks." She swallowed hard. "Before we start, Aurora, I want to talk to you for a minute." She glanced at Malphas. "In private."

Malphas scowled. "You really need to talk about your lovers' quarrel now?"

She glared at him, and Aurora raised a hand, dismissing him. "Give us a few minutes."

Malphas made sure they saw his eye roll before he turned, slipping into the shadows of a nearby alley.

Aurora cocked a hip. "What happened now?"

An ache spread through Rosalind's chest. She wasn't sure how to put her thoughts into words. "Caine told me that if I raised Miranda from the dead, he'd kill her."

Aurora crossed her arms. "Bloody hell. That's a bit much, isn't it?"

"Thing is, Miranda hasn't been acting right. She's talking about a void, and being lonely. She's desperate to get out of our room. And then, when I wasn't watching her..."

"What did she do?"

"She had sex with Ambrose. And Ambrose, Caine, and Malphas think it was me. Malphas thinks that's part of why Caine left the city."

Aurora's eyes widened. "Are you kidding me? Let me guess. You shagged Caine before all this went down."

"Sort of. Yes. And he was already mad because..." Her fingers tightened. *Maybe I should leave out the bit about Malphas.* "Anyway, he was already mad."

Aurora shook her head. "Woman, trouble's all over like moss on a grave."

"But I'm just wondering if there's more to Caine's prohibition than sacrilege. What if it's because... people don't come back quite right?"

"We knew that was a risk when we started. I told you—she was dead to start. If she came back wrong, she'd end up dead again. No worse than when she started."

Rosalind's chest tightened. "I'm not saying we should kill her. She deserves a chance."

Aurora nodded at the fountain. "We have time to figure it out after we find out what happened to Caine. Okay? I can't go with you into Boston—not with the daylight. But I'll be here when you get back." She turned to the alley. "Malphas! We're ready to go."

Malphas slipped from the shadows, crossing the rain-slicked cobbles to Aurora and Rosalind.

He shot a wary look to Rosalind. "We can only let the shield down for a few moments, just long enough to ask what danger awaits us on the other side. Any longer, and we risk letting Hunters in—or Drew and his army of godsforsaken demons."

"I've got it," Rosalind said. "Let's do it."

She leaned against the fountain, feeling its cool water over her fingertips. She closed her eyes, and Malphas's aura began to crackle the air around her. The smell of burnt air enveloped her, and electric shadow magic began creeping over her body. She arched her back as her own magical stores began to well within her. A hollow opened in her chest as a cold and ancient power ignited in her veins. She opened her eyes, staring at the shield's silvery sheen in the sky, just below the lingering storm clouds.

A deep, silver aura curled from her body, snaking up to the sky. Her magic curled around Malphas's, intertwining like lovers' bodies. Power flooded her muscles, and she watched as their magic ate gaps in the shield. As she stared up at the dark sky, a painful image flashed in her mind: sitting in an empty room, her own dead face pressed against the other side of the glass. She shuddered as the image cleared.

As the shield above her began to thin, she heard Aurora chanting in Angelic. A new magic rippled over her skin, smooth as silk. "Nyxobas, show us the danger that awaits these two as they travel into Cambridge," Aurora said.

Rosalind glanced down at the fountain's rippling surface, watching it swirl with silver and black magic.

Slowly, an image began to form—a face so beautiful it pained her. Golden skin, perfect lips—and eyes black as pitch. Caine's lips were curled back in a vicious snarl. The face of an angel, twisted with wrath. The bestial look in his eyes sent ice through her veins.

As the image clarified, her panic worsened. Bathed in milky white sunlight, black wings arched behind his back. He moved with a terrifying grace.

Rosalind's heart sped up. "What's going on?"

"We need to close the shield," Malphas said. "We can't leave it open."

Caine seemed to be stalking toward someone, like a beast of prey. The image clouded again.

"Rosalind," shouted Malphas. "We need to close the shield!"

Her pulse raced, and she looked up to the skies again, letting Nyxobas' power flow through her like a river of shadow. Magic surged to the skies, curling over the gaps in the shield.

What happened to Caine? He'd hardly even looked human. She had the unsettling feeling that she'd just seen his true face— and it was terrifying. She closed her eyes as the magic whirled from her body, and her head throbbed.

Caine was in trouble—deep trouble. How had everything become so royally fucked up?

Drew. It all came down to Drew, and the power-hungry maniacs like Randolph Loring. Had she really looked up to him once? When she found the bastards leading the Brotherhood, she wanted to burn them. A flame for Caine, a flame for Miranda. One for Cleo. She'd sow a garden of pyres across the city.

She could feel Cleo's purr of approval at the thought of burning Hunters. At least Cleo's voice had gone quieter—ever since Ambrose had made his confession. Maybe she wouldn't have to fuck him and burn him anymore.

Malphas touched her arm. "Rosalind. That's enough for now."

She glanced at him, her breath coming hard and fast. "We still don't know anything. We know Caine's in danger, but not what we're heading into. According to that scrying spell, the danger that awaits us is Caine."

315

Malphas's face had gone pale. "I can believe that Caine is the most dangerous thing on the other side of the portal."

"What do you mean?" Rosalind asked. "Why would he be dangerous to us?"

Malphas stared at her for a moment before nodding slowly. "I've seen him look that way before. Once, after your parents gave him the second soul."

"When he lost his mind." Her stomach sank. "You think it's happened again?"

"Maybe Drew is controlling him," Aurora said. "He can control his mind with that charmed iron."

Rosalind wanted to be sick. "He wasn't wearing a necklace. Maybe they've given him a scar, like mine."

Malphas shook his head, "Whatever the case, we've got to go after him before they decide to execute him."

"I'm ready," Rosalind said. Already, she was climbing to the fountain's edge. She dipped her feet into the icy water, and Malphas climbed up beside her.

Aurora touched Rosalind's arm. "Please bring him back in one piece."

Rosalind nodded. "I will. I promise."

Before she plunged into the icy water, a dark thought flickered through her mind. *Maybe I should stop making promises I don't know I can keep.*

She let go of the fountain's edge, letting herself sink beneath the water's frigid surface.

40

She plunged deeper through the portal, until her lungs burned.

But water couldn't hurt her anymore, not with Dagon's power flooding her veins. As she sunk lower, Dagon's phantom limbs snaked around her, caressing her skin. And when she let her chest unclench, it stopped hurting. Under the water, she no longer needed air. She could stay under the surface as long as she wanted.

Except she had a psychotic incubus to rescue. Her gaze flicked to Malphas, who swam beside her, his eyes beginning to bulge. *He* couldn't breathe down here.

A thin stream of light pierced the surface, and she grabbed Malphas's hand. Kicking her legs, she dragged him up to the light.

When her head breached the surface, she wrapped an arm around Malphas's chest, pulling him up with her. He clung to the ledge on either side of her, his body pressed against hers. Coughs racked his body.

"Thanks," he gasped.

"No problem." She scanned the crypt. Sunlight streamed through latticework over the crypt door. Lucky for them, no one seemed to be lying in wait here. "We should hide ourselves before we go out. We can use the invisibility spell. And as soon as we get out of here, let's move quickly, using shadow magic. I think this cemetery is dangerous. The Brotherhood might be watching it."

Water dripped down his face from his drenched hair. "Where are we going?"

"There's a hill in Huron Village, away from the Brotherhood's headquarters. Hold my hand, and I'll take you in the right direction. And then I'm gonna do a sweep of the city from the air so I can figure out where Caine is."

Malphas body still floated dangerously close to hers. Incubi just couldn't help getting close. "Sounds like you have a plan."

He blinked, as if waking from a dream, then began chanting the spell for invisibility. She felt his magic kiss her skin, and watched as his face shimmered away.

In the icy water, her teeth began to chatter. "Are you ready?" she asked.

"Let's go."

She hoisted herself out of the water, then reached down, feeling for Malphas's arm. She pulled him out, and water splashed to the floor. Grasping his hand, she said, "As soon as we're through his door, I'm taking us to the old Gallows Hill."

"What is it about that name that unsettles me?"

Ignoring the comment, he pushed through the door into the sun. For a moment, the sun blinded her and she blinked hard, trying to adjust. She hadn't seen proper light in weeks.

Then, clutching Malphas's hand, she let Nyxobas's power flow through her body. Shadows whispered through her bones. She focused on a point about twenty yards away, and let the magic carry her on the wind.

She knew that too much shadow running would burn the energy right out of her body, but it was a major rush. With

Malphas's hand in her own, she shifted from one spot to another through the winding cemetery paths. As she moved, a warm, floral breeze rushed over her skin, toying with her hair.

Gods, it feels good to be in the light again. Even as she got power from the god of night, the sunlight felt glorious on her skin. With Malphas by her side, she rushed through the cemetery gates, down Mount Auburn street to Brattle, and further up Avon Hill, whirring past the towering wood-frame houses.

At the top of the hill, her muscles burned, and fatigue pulsed through her body. They stopped by a dark wooden mansion, and Rosalind caught her breath.

By her side, Malphas's broad form began shimmering into view. "You're already becoming visible," he said.

"So are you."

"The invisibility spell won't hold long when you're burning through power like that."

Her pulse raced. "Well that's a real fucking liability. I can't be flashing into the Hunters' view while I'm expecting to be invisible."

"You have the power of seven gods now. Just like Drew. Maybe you don't need to be invisible."

True, but a thought nagged at the back of her mind. "I've seen how Caine operates. He stays focused on his objective, and he doesn't let the enemy know more about him than they need to. When we were imprisoned together in the Chambers, he took pains to make sure they had no idea what his powers were. He didn't want them to know his strength. We're here for one reason, and one reason only, right?"

"To drag Caine back to Lilinor."

"We're not here to defeat the Brotherhood and Drew. We'll do that when we have an army together. So I don't want to let Drew know I have this power."

"What exactly do you have planned?"

She felt a flicker of vernal magic stir in her chest. "I'm going to let Cleo fight this battle—or at least it will look that way." She let Cleo's magic snake over her body, curling over her skin and hair.

"Come out to play, Cleo." As the magic wound over her dark hair, she watched as it lengthened and turned blond. She felt her legs elongate, her hips narrow.

When she looked at Malphas, his eyes had gone wide.

"How do I look?" she asked.

"Like someone completely different. I had no idea you could do that."

"Cleo's been desperate to come out." She gazed down the hill, looking for any signs of chaos or destruction, but everything seemed normal on Mass Ave. Maybe she'd taken them too far from the Brotherhood's headquarters. She'd need a proper aerial view. "I'm going to find Caine. I'll signal to you with lightning, okay? When I find him, shadow run in the direction of the striking lightning."

"Do you really have that much control over your powers?"

"I created a damn fine storm not that long ago."

She glanced up at the cloudless sky, then closed her eyes. A cool wind rippled over her skin, and she held out her arms. Mentally, she called to the storm-god, and his ancient magic pooled in her body. Raw power ignited her veins, and she opened her eyes to find the sky churning with dark clouds.

A cold wind whipped at her pale hair. Or rather, Cleo's hair.

As she arched her back, the heavens opened, and a hard rain began to fall, soaking her clothes. She cast one last look back at Malphas, then let the wind rush through her body, lifting her with it. She swooped into the air, soaring over Cambridge's wooden houses and brick buildings, racing over Mass Ave. As she soared further along, a wave of horror washed over her. The city had changed completely closer to the square. Gone were the old wooden houses and squat buildings that lined the street; now it was all towering stone edifices, built to look like roman temples and colosseums.

And the closer she got to the Brotherhood's Chambers, the more a sense of unease began to crawl over her skin.

The good news was that no one was looking at her. The bad news was that they weren't looking at her because they seemed to be fleeing from Harvard square—not unlike the time that the keres had attacked.

Rain battered her skin, and she soared over Harvard, flying in the opposite direction of those fleeing. She was moving south, toward the Charles—the river that the Hunters had named after their witch-killing king. At least the river had a tactical advantage. If Nyxobas allowed it, she'd be able to use the water as a portal back to Lilinor.

But as she soared toward the river, her blood turned to ice. Wooden stakes jutted from one of the stone bridges that arced over the Charles, just waiting to burn the bodies of heretics. No wonder the people of Cambridge were terrified. And no wonder the Brotherhood needed a scapegoat to keep everyone in line.

As she swooped along the river, horror punched her in the gut again. There, on the road that gently curved round the river's side, she saw the pale silver glow of Caine's magic, curling from his body. He stalked down the center of Memorial Drive, black wings swooping from his back.

Around him, cars had smashed into each other. Black smoke curled from the wrecks, and shattered glass littered the pavement. And worse– broken and bloodied human bodies lay strewn on the ground in pools of blood. Had Caine done this?

She flicked her wrist at the clouds, letting Mishett-Ash's magic race through her fingertips into the sky. A sharp spear of lightning touched down on the river, illuminated the sky. Instantly, thunder cracked over the horizon.

She flicked her wrist once more, calling forth another sharp crack of lightning.

As the rain battered her body, she circled overhead, searching Caine's face for clues. His eyes were black as the void, his lip curled disdainfully. The way he prowled the street, muscles coiled, he looked like an angel of death.

And he wasn't wearing a necklace.

Had Drew managed to carve the mark of Azezeyl into his skin? Or had he lost his mind again—like he had in Maremount, all those years ago?

She circled again, watching with a growing sense of horror as he ripped off a car door. He pulled an injured man from the passenger's seat. The crash had crushed the man's legs, and he screamed in terror at the sight of Caine.

Okay. Time to stop this.

Rosalind swooped lower. Slowly, Caine's gaze slid to her, and he cocked his head. As he did, he snapped the man's neck, letting him fall to the ground.

She landed in front of him, her body buzzing with the icy fury of a valkyrie. Caine's aura blazed from his body, slicing the air around her. He took a step closer. A part of her felt terrified at his cold gaze. A part of her wanted to run—or fly—as fast as she could from his bone-chilling demonic rage.

But the valkyrie's strength coursed through her blood, cold and ancient as Caine's own power. She didn't want to fight him—but she could if she needed to.

"Caine," she said. "It's me. Rosalind."

A low growl escaped his throat. In a blur of shadow magic, he reached for her throat—but she was faster. She leapt out of his way, jumping back again and again—until she slammed into the back of car.

Shit.

In the next second, Caine's hands were around her throat, ready to snap her neck. She raised her arms, slamming them into his forearms with the full force of Borgerith's strength. He dropped his grip on her, surprise alighting in his eyes, then moved toward her again.

Letting Nyxobas's magic whisper through her blood, she lunged for him, landing a punch at the speed of a hurricane gale. Her fist slammed into his jaw, knocking him off balance. He staggered back. She wanted a chance to see what she was up against—if he'd lost his mind, or if Drew had marked him.

Swift as the wind, she rushed at him again, ripping through the front of his shirt. She scanned his skin—just long enough to see his smooth abs, free from Azezeyl's mark—and in the next moment, his hands were around her throat again.

Okay, so he's lost his mind. Her heart thrummed.

And then she realized: Maybe he didn't know who she was.

Cleo, drop the glamour.

Instantly, she felt Cleo's aura flush from her blood. She felt her body shift, watching as her blond hair darkened in the corner of her eye. As it did, Caine's eyes widened, his fingers loosening on her throat.

"Caine," she said. If he *had* lost his mind, she actually had no idea how to cure it. She had neither the time nor the expertise to act as his psychotherapist right now. "It's me. It's Rosalind."

He leancd in closer, his body warming hers. It didn't seem like he wanted to rip her throat out anymore. But he definitely wanted *something*. He thrust his fingers into her hair, tugging back her head. He growled again, low and animal, and his teeth skimmed her throat. His fingers found her waist, gripping her tight. He had her pinned to the car, but at least he wasn't trying to kill her anymore.

"Caine," she said. "This isn't the time."

The wail of sirens pierced the air, and her heart began to race. They were coming for Caine.

She reached up, gripping his face, trying to get through to him. "Caine. What the hell is going on with you? I need to take you to a portal. I think we can use the river."

His eyes narrowed, but she wasn't convinced he understood a word she was saying.

Fuck it. She'd have to use her new brute strength. She cupped her hands around his neck, then slammed the top of her head into his face.

He staggered back again, dazed just for a moment. As she wound up again for a punch to his jaw, he caught her wrist, twisting it behind her back. He slammed her against the car, pressing against her.

Shit. Maybe she'd underestimated *his* brute strength.

"Caine!" she shouted. "You're acting like a psycho! Stop it or I will beat the shit out of you!"

Okay. So maybe that wasn't the most subtle of psychological techniques, but it was all she had time for. Caine leaned in again, growling, and his breath warmed the side of her face. He seemed to be enjoying this. In fact, from what she could feel pressing against her back, he was *definitely* enjoying this.

She raised her foot, smashing it down onto his. He grunted, but kept his grip on her.

The wailing of sirens drew closer, and she heard the screeching of brakes just behind her.

"Caine!" she shouted. Where the hell was Malphas?

In the next second, a hail of bullets ripped through the air, and Caine's body jerked against hers. Her world tilted, and the pure panic seizing her mind. *Iron bullets, probably.* They'd do some damage to Caine. She was damn lucky the bullets hadn't pierced through his flesh to hers, or they'd be stranded here without magic.

She turned to Caine, ready to shadow run with him to the river. But just as she wrapped her arms around his slumping body, a team of Hunters ripped him away.

And, in the next moment, Drew stepped from an armored vehicle, dressed in a black suit. He flicked his wrist, and Borgerith's magic shot from his fingertips. All the air left Rosalind's lungs, and she felt the weight of a ton of rocks pressing on her chest, pressing her in place. She stared, wide-eyed, as a team of black-clad Hunters dragged Caine toward the bridge.

As her ribs threatened to snap and pierce her lungs, one thought blazed in her mind like a torch in the night:

They're going to burn him.

41

*D*rew clasped his arms tightly around her, still pressing the air from her lungs. She had magic now—the same as he did. But he'd had a lot more practice.

He dragged her to the bridge, her feet scraping over the pavement. As he did, she closed her eyes, focusing on pushing the tendrils of copper magic from her body—just enough that she could gasp for air. When she opened her eyes again, Drew gripped her chin, forcing her face to look in the direction of Caine.

The Hunters were chaining his slumped body to a stake. A crowd of onlookers had gathered at the Bridge's southern entrance.

I need to get us out of here.

She had no clue what was going on with Caine, but she wasn't going to let the Hunters burn him.

He didn't have a scar marking his skin, wasn't wearing any iron that had been specially treated with magic. And yet, he'd just slaughtered all those people. He'd attacked her, too. Sure, the man had secrets, but she just couldn't believe that this was really him.

She watched the Hunters pile wood on the pyre, and she strained to muster her magic as Drew crushed her lungs. If she could summon Borgerith's power like Drew could, maybe she could fight him back. She struggled for another breath, trying to force the copper tendrils from her body.

But it was kind of hard to summon powerful magic when you couldn't breathe.

Her heart threatened to jump out of her chest. The rain had slowed to a dull trickle, not enough to douse the flames—especially not now, as the Hunters doused the wood just below Caine's feet with gasoline. Pure panic ripped through her mind.

Drew leaned in close, whispering into her ear, "Now you'll get what you deserve, my wife. You'll get to watch your lover die. Slowly, painfully, and without dignity. I want to watch the pain in your eyes as his skin blackens. Perhaps I'll make you light the flames to burn your lover."

She tried to suck in another breath, watching as Drew pulled a syringe filled with dark liquid from his coat pocket. A single thought struck her, like a bullet to the brain: *There's iron in blood.* Not a lot—not enough to extinguish magic. But maybe it was enough for Drew to control someone if the iron had been charmed.

Drew gripped her wrist, ready to inject.

Her pulse raced. She couldn't let him do this, or she'd have no chance of getting Caine out of here. *Maybe I'll have better luck with Druloch. Come on, Cleo.*

Green magic simmered over her skin.

As Drew lifted her sleeve, a rope of vines shot from her wrist, wrapping around Drew's neck. He clutched at his throat, and the magic crushing her chest lifted from her.

She glanced at Caine. To her horror, flames already curled around his feet.

A Hunter pointed a gun to her head. "Stop the spells!" he shouted.

Not a chance.

Her gaze flicked to the river, and she let Dagon's power ripple through her body, vibrating through her bones. The river churned, then roared as an enormous wave crested over the bridge, knocking the Hunters off balance. Black smoke curled into the air as water doused the flames.

So much for keeping my magic hidden.

She shadow ran to Caine. Using the strength of the mountain goddess, she tore the iron chains from his body. Already, the Hunters were mustering again, and Drew was breaking free from his chokehold.

She let vernal magic simmer in her body, then unleashed it on the bridge. In the next moment, vines sprouted from the bridge, weaving around the Hunters and Drew. A blur of shadow moved through them, and she heaved a sigh of relief. *Malphas.*

He stopped just before her, catching his breath.

"Use the river as a portal!" she shouted. "Take Caine to Ambrose, and tell Ambrose to drain his blood."

Malphas was already dragging Caine across the bridge. "You want him to *what?*"

"Just trust me! Drain his blood. He'll recover."

She watched as Malphas leapt over the side of the bridge, with Caine in his arms.

This was it: her chance to kill Drew, while he was completely within her control. She turned to her cousin, watching the tendrils of colored magic whirl from his body. She lifted her hand, and Emerazel's fire sparked from the tips of her fingers.

Deep in her chest, Cleo's aura thrilled at her power. *Roast these bastards alive.*

But just as the golden magic roared through her blood, Drew

broke free from the plants' constraints. Moving on the wind, he leapt for her, punching her in the head with a loud *crack*.

Dizzy, she staggered to the edge of the bridge.

The portal is still open. It must be.

From behind, Drew gripped her hair, but she pulled away from him. As fast as she could, she climbed over the edge of the bridge, and leapt into the churning dark waters below.

As she plunged below the chilly surface, she felt a powerful hand grasp her leg, and her stomach sank.

42

Rosalind swam below the water's surface, trying to free herself from Drew's iron grip. Shadow magic whirled around them.

The shield wouldn't let Drew into the city.

Unless—if Drew was clinging to her body, would the shield let him through?

She didn't want to find out.

Frantically, she tried kicking her way free of him, but he climbed higher up her body, wrapping his arms around hers. And even as she squirmed and writhed in his arms, she only kicked herself further toward the surface, until pale moonlight began to pierce the murky water.

It wasn't until they'd reached the air that she was able to gain enough leverage to wiggle one of her arms free—but by then, Drew had already breached the shield. She hammered his face hard with a volley of punches, until he dropped his grip on her.

I'm gonna have to fight him on land.

She grasped for a rocky ledge, pulling herself out into the cool night air, and launched over the fountain's edge—the same one they'd used to leave Lilinor. She landed hard on the cobblestones and yanked an iron knife from her belt, widening her stance.

I'm ready for you, cousin.

In the next moment, Drew burst from the fountain. Before his feet could even land on the pavement, she hurled the knife at his chest. His green eyes opened wide in shock, and he staggered back.

But it only took him a fraction of a second to rip the knife from his chest. He lunged for her, his movements too fast for an ordinary human to track. But with Nyxobas's power flooding her body, she saw him coming. She kicked him in the face, cracking his nose with her foot. Immediately, she dodged back. As he swung for her, she ducked, bringing up her fist into his groin.

She rose, letting the power of seven gods soar in her body.

I can take you, Cousin.

While he hunched over, in pain, she kicked him hard in the gut. He grunted, clutching his stomach.

But when he raised his green eyes to her, a chill rippled over her. There was no longer anything human in his gaze, just the senseless wrath of insane gods.

She pulled another knife from her belt, ready to throw. But with a tremendous roar, Drew leapt for her, knocking her back onto the pavement. The full weight of his body pressed on her, and he gripped her hair. Screaming like a wild beast, he smashed her head into the pavement—once, twice, three times.

Pain ripped through her skull, so sharp she thought she'd die. Dizziness surged over her, and she struggled to push him off.

Drew tightened his fingers around her throat, squeezing hard. Blood ran from his lip. Through gritted teeth, he said, "My wife. I know how to make you behave. I know how to make you serve me."

He pressed on her throat harder, threatening to crush her windpipe. How many seconds did she have before he crushed the life out of her? She needed to muster her magic—her strength. *Borgerith*. She envisioned the copper magic welling in her belly.

But just as she was starting to build her strength, Drew reached into his pocket. She stared in horror as he pulled out another syringe.

"I know you can be a sweet wife, when I tame you." He stabbed the needle into her chest. "I need to punish you, and break your will. Then you'll be my little toy."

He depressed the plunger, and panic ripped her mind apart.

But there's iron in blood.

And Borgerith controls magnetism...

As soon as Drew pulled the syringe from her skin, she focused on letting Borgerith's copper magic whirl around her chest, trying to draw the iron from her own blood, through that tiny hole in her skin. But even as she tried to focus, her thoughts began to move slowly, as ice seemed to encase her mind.

What *was* she trying to do?

Drew unclenched his grip on her neck, leaning down to stare into her face. Gently, Drew stroked the side of her face, then he leaned in closer to lick her cheek.

Somewhere, beneath the ice of her mind, she recoiled.

"Do you know," he purred, "I feel very close to you. I think I even understand some of your worst fears. I can see them in your dark eyes. We've got rid of Miranda, haven't we? But it wasn't enough. I have something even better in mind for you."

He gripped her hair, cracking her head against the stone once again.

She woke, flat on her back, in the bottom of a grave, staring up at the starry sky.

No—not quite the bottom of a grave. She couldn't quite clarify her thoughts, but she had a vague sense of lying on top of soft, rotten limbs. *A mass grave.*

The thought moved slowly under her mind's frozen surface, like an ice floe.

As a powerful stench registered, another thought simmered dimly under the ice: *I'm in the whore pit.*

Horror stole her breath, but she couldn't quite remember what she needed to do, or why she was here. She didn't seem to be able to control her own body.

A man leaned over the grave's edge. The moon formed a silver halo around his head. His green eyes pierced the dark, beautiful and intense. And yet, the sight of his face curdled her stomach.

"Comfortable, are you?" He frowned. "Is this what they call the whore pit? I'll wager they buried your sister here." He narrowed his eyes. "Now which rotten body is she? Do you suppose you're on top of her?"

The words sent a cold shiver up Rosalind's spine. There was something she needed to do—some way she could get out of this, but she couldn't formulate a clear thought. Not with all this ice encasing her mind.

The man shrugged. She thought his name might be Drew.

Suddenly, his face contorted with rage. "Fitting, isn't it, for my wife? The whore pit. After what you did with Caine." His face turned red, and panic gripped Rosalind's chest.

"When I break your mind," he continued, "you'll serve me eagerly, or I'll rip your bones from your body. Do you understand, little whore?" Spittle flew from his mouth.

Would anyone hear him yell?

She stared up at the night sky as Drew began flinging earth on top of her. Her chest tightened. Desperately, she tried to pick out clear thoughts, but they slid under the surface or her mind. Somewhere, under the glacier, she formed a thought about the bodies beneath her, slick and rotting. About the stench turning her stomach.

Thump. A clump of dirt hit her in the face, and she gasped.

Another thought bubbled to the surface. The one about how she wouldn't be able to breathe with all that dirt covering her. How she'd die down here in the whore pit. There was something she needed to do to break free...

Thump. The earth felt heavy from the recent rain—more mud than dirt.

She glanced to her right, vaguely registering a woman's half-rotten arm.

A long time ago, someone had told her it would end this way. *Buried in the whore pit.*

Thump. Particles of dirt slipped into her mouth, trickling down her throat. As the earth rained down, her body began to shake, that one phrase burning clearer under the ice. *Buried in the whore pit.*

Drew hurled another shovelful of dirt onto her face, and she gagged at the mud trickling down her throat.

This wasn't how it was supposed to end.

Sunlight, the smell of the ocean. Oak trees. Water on skin. The call of a golden-crowned sparrow.

She moved her head back, just an inch, and gasped for air. Within a few minutes, inches of dirt covered her body, until she couldn't see, could hardly breathe. And yet, under the dirt and the ice, rage began to simmer, burning away the ice.

Now, Miranda's words began to ring in her mind, clear as a bell. *Sometimes, what's buried doesn't stay underground.*

Before the glaciers had gripped her mind, she'd been trying to free herself. She'd had some kind of plan. *Get the iron out of your blood.*

Her body wasn't quite moving like it should, but her mind was clearing. Maybe Borgerith's magic *had* worked just enough to clear some of that charmed iron from her blood. Under a thickening layer of earth, she focused on the coppery magic in her body, letting it churn within her ribs. Then she imagined the copper magic drawing out that black liquid in her chest—a magnetic pull through that tiny hole in her skin.

Slowly, Borgerith's magic leached the iron from her blood, and she began to grow dizzy. Still, even as she grew lightheaded, she was able to move her muscles purposefully once more—curling her toes and fingers.

Sometimes, what's buried doesn't stay underground.

She let the magic flow through her muscles, charging her body with power and the speed of Nyxobas. A hot thrill rippled thorough her as the gods-magic began to blaze through her body. *I'm going to tear your bones from your body, Drew.*

In the next moment, she burst from the grave, dripping with fetid dirt. She leapt over the pit's edge, wind rushing over her skin.

And as her feet hit the ground, her gaze landed on Drew.

She was back from the dead, here to wreak a vengeance of her own.

This time she was moving with the speed of a god, her gaze locked on her prey. She must have looked like a true angel of death, because Drew backed away from her, his eyes wide.

But she wasn't letting him get away.

She rushed for him, slamming her fist into the side of his head, reveling in the crack of bone. She hit him again and again, and his head snapped back. Full of Nyxobas's icy power, she kicked him hard him the gut, and when he bent over, she hammered the back of his skull with her elbow.

He fell to the ground. Quick as a storm wind, she was on top of him, raining down blows onto his face, trying to smash his bones. In the distance, she heard the cry of a valkyrie, and the storm god's fury filled her body. *Go in for the kill.*

She gripped his throat tight, squeezing hard. It would only take a few seconds—

Water magic burst from Drew's body, and in the next second a small pond filled the space around them.

She tightened her grip on his throat. *Fine with me. I'll drown you in a ditch.*

But as the water began to rise higher, shadow magic whirled on its surface.

He's creating a portal.

The bottom seemed to drop out of the earth beneath her, and in a rush of murky water, she lost her grip on Drew.

Holding her breath, she swam for the surface, her fingertips finding purchase in a muddy ledge. She pulled herself out, her heart racing, and backed away from the portal.

She let out a roar. She'd been so damn close to killing him. But she couldn't go after him now. Not now, when she had no clue where that portal went—she'd made that mistake once before, and learned her lesson.

Still, she'd come for him soon enough.

Nausea gripped her gut, and she fell to her hands and knees in the mud, vomiting.

After another minute of catching her breath, she rose and stared at the small pond, still whirling with shadow magic. She wanted to make damn sure Drew wasn't coming back in anytime soon. With the last of her energy, she let shadow magic flow through her fingertips, sealing up the muddy gateway. When she'd finished, the ground had sealed over again—a slick of mud covered with a silver sheen.

She turned to walk back to the fortress, her entire body shaking.

As she walked along the path, a spray of purple-headed flowers caught her eye. Their long, thin petals pierced the air like fireworks, surrounded by green leaves. She reached for one, but as soon as she touched one of the leaves, the plant seemed to fold into itself, shrinking away from her.

Rosalind didn't know the name of this plant, but Cleo did.

Morivivi.

I died. I lived.

She plucked two blossoms from the plant—one for her, and one for Miranda.

These are for our new crowns—the ones we deserve.

43

$\mathcal{W}$ith shaking legs, stepped into the candlelit hall on Caine's floor. Filthy mud covered her body, and she looked like a swamp monster.

She crossed through the hall toward Caine's room. She didn't particularly want him to see her caked in mud and puke, but he had a bath in his room. Plus, she wanted to see how he was doing after Ambrose drained his blood.

Raw fatigue burned through her body as she walked the corridor, and each step felt like agony. It was a good thing she hadn't followed Drew through the portal, because she was pretty sure she didn't have a single drop of magic left in her body right now.

Drew had nearly killed her out there. Nearly suffocated her in the whore pit.

Mass grave, she mentally corrected herself. No need to insult the dead.

Her sodden feet left muddy tracks over the stones. At last, her gaze landed on the portrait of Lord Byron.

The door stood partially ajar—just the way she'd left it—and she pushed it open the rest of the way. *Empty.* No one lay on his silver sheets, and a single candle flickered in a sconce.

She dropped her two *morivivi* flowers on a wood table, then crossed to the bath.

Exhaling with relief, she turned on the hot water. As the steam rose from the bath, she pulled off her filthy clothes, dropping them onto Caine's floor. She'd clean all this up later, once she'd washed herself.

As she stepped into the bath, the warm water soothed her aching muscles. She submerged herself in the water up to her waist, and the caked dirt and blood lifted from her body, muddying the water. She pulled the soap from the edge of the tub, rubbing it over her skin, breathing in the soothing scent of lavender.

She still had to find a way to work things out with Caine. She couldn't tell him Miranda had slept with Ambrose.

Then again, maybe there was no point in correcting him. It wasn't as if anything could happen between her and Caine again. For one thing, he'd told her he didn't really care. And for another, he'd never be able to know about Miranda.

She rinsed her hair under the faucet, clearing the mud from it, watching it swirl into the water. She was basically bathing in mud at this point.

She uncorked the drain, letting the filthy water swirl down, then rinsed her limbs again under the faucet. She grabbed a cloth from the side of the bath, scrubbing at her skin until it looked raw.

Bending down once more, she rinsed her face again under the tap, scrubbing off all the muck with a ferocity that would wake the dead. As she washed her face, it occurred to her that she hadn't brought anything to change into, but she'd just have to borrow a long shirt from Caine.

With the last of the muck rinsed from her skin, she straightened, and her heart skipped a beat.

While she'd been washing herself, Miranda had crept into the room. She now stood by Caine's bed. As if on a ghostly breeze, her torn and blood-stained nightgown billowed around her. Her knuckles were bleeding, her fingernails chewed down to the bone.

The look in her sister's eyes unnerved Rosalind, and she shivered. "What are you doing here, Miranda?"

Miranda cocked her head. "Where did you go?"

Water dripped down Rosalind's skin, and she hugged herself, shivering. "I went after Caine in Boston. Drew seized control of his mind, then tried to burn him." She stepped from the bath.

"And he lived?" Miranda asked, her voice dull.

As Rosalind stepped from the bath, water splashed onto the floor. "Malphas dragged him back here through the portal. I'm guessing he's in Ambrose's White Tower. He should be able to make a fast recovery." She crossed the room to the wardrobe, trying to ignore the unsettling feeling of the hair raising on the back of her neck.

She should probably ask about the blood on her sister's hands, but she didn't want to.

I'll just pretend everything is normal.

"What's all the dirt from?" Miranda asked.

Rosalind pulled open Caine's wardrobe, and pulled out a towel. "Drew tried to bury me in the mass grave."

"You were luckier than I was, since you made it out alive."

Rosalind wrapped the towel around herself, trying to ignore the guilt nagging at her mind. "That's certainly true."

"Maybe you shouldn't have brought me back," Miranda said, her voice breaking.

"Why?"

"There's something wrong with me." A tear rolled down her cheek. "I'm empty inside, and I can't fill the void no matter what I do."

Rosalind shook her head. "We can fix this. There must be a spell to heal your mind."

Miranda's forehead crinkled, as if she was confused, and she pulled up the hem of her gown. Strapped to her thigh was a knife, which she pulled from its sheath.

Rosalind's heart thudded.

Miranda cocked her head, her eyes filling with tears. "But you can't fix me." She hurled the knife at Rosalind, striking her in the chest. Rosalind staggered back, dropping her towel. Pain ripped through her chest, and she stared down at the blade protruding from her body. Blood gushed from the wound.

"Miranda!" she shouted. "Why are you doing this?"

Panic stole her breath.

I need to pull it out.

She reached for the hilt, but Miranda was already kneeling before her, yanking the blade free. She reared back her arm to stab again, but as she did a blur of silvery shadow magic streamed into the room.

Rosalind stared in horror as Caine pulled Miranda off her— then, swift as a phantom wind, snapped her neck with a loud *crack.*

The one blunt sound ended Miranda's life for the final time.

The world seemed to fall from beneath Rosalind.

"Caine!" she shouted, tears stinging her eyes.

He leaned down, scooping Rosalind up in his powerful arms and carrying her to his bed. Brow furrowed, he said, "I told you not to bring her back."

Tears spilled down her cheek. "You killed her."

Gently, he laid her down on his bed. "I had to," he said softly. "I need to heal you."

She shot a glance at Miranda, whose body lay crumpled on the floor. "What was wrong with her?"

Caine's fingertips traced along the perimeter of the gash on the front of her shoulder, and magic curled from his fingertips. "I once raised someone from the dead. But I soon learned it was a mistake." His eyes glistened as his hand hovered above her chest. "I regret it, even now. When you raise a body from the dead, there is a price. And the price is that Nyxobas keeps some of their soul in the void."

"Why didn't you tell me this?"

His eyes clouded with unspoken grief. "I can't bring myself to talk about it."

Deep sorrow pierced Rosalind's chest. "So part of Miranda is still in the shadow void?" No wonder she'd felt empty.

Caine's gaze met hers. "Yes, but I can help. It took me years to learn how, but I can travel to the void and free her."

Caine's magic soothed her muscles, healing the tears and leaching away the pain. Faintly, Miranda's voice rang in the back of Rosalind's skull. *Sunlight, the smell of the ocean. Oak trees. Water on skin. The call of a golden-crowned sparrow.*

"When I traveled to the shadow void, I saw my own face there. Dead." A hot tear spilled down her cheek. "Maybe it wasn't me, after all. Maybe it was a vision of Miranda."

Caine wiped the tear from her cheek. "We're going to hold another death feast. You'll tell Miranda's story. And when you're finished, I'll claim her soul back from Nyxobas." He leaned in, touching his forehead against hers. Her heart had broken, but Caine's soothing aura dulled some of the pain. He pulled away from her, glancing at the mud spattering his room, his hand cupped around her neck. "What happened to you?"

"Drew followed me through the portal into Lilinor. He injected me with that iron. Like he did to you."

"He was waiting for me when I came through." Caine's eyes darkened, the candle dimming. "Is he still here?"

She shook her head. "No. He tried to bury me in the whore—in the mass grave. Flung dirt all over me. But I got the iron out."

Caine traced his thumb over her cheek. "So you did better than I did. I didn't make it out of there on my own."

She glanced at Miranda again, and raw grief washed over her.

Caine pulled away from her, covering her in his soft, silver blankets. "Close your eyes," he said. "I'm going to take Miranda away."

"I've left the remnants of a grave all over your room." She shivered, then a thought sparked in the back of her mind. "Caine? Why did you say I was lucky, after Miranda died? What was lucky about it?"

He touched her shoulder, and her mind began to calm again. "Get some rest, Rosalind. tomorrow, you need to speak over your sister's grave, and then we'll free her soul."

She wasn't sure she'd ever sleep again—not after the horror of tonight. But after Caine carried Miranda's body from the room, fatigue claimed her mind, and she drifted into a deep sleep.

44

*R*osalind stood, flanked by Caine, and Tammi. Moonlight streamed through the yew, dancing over the black casket deep in the earth. Behind them stood Ambrose, Malphas, and Aurora.

In one hand, Rosalind clutched a fistful of morivivi flowers—in the other, the dried wreath Miranda had woven from bluebells, ivy, and poppies. She turned from the grave, walking to the yew. Her finger shook as she tied the wreath with a shimmering blue ribbon marked with Miranda's name. Clutching the flowers, she turned back to the open grave.

Caine rested his hand on her back for reassurance, letting his aura wash over her.

She took a deep breath. "When she first died, I didn't remember our past. She died, and she lived again. And when she did, she told me the stories about us I didn't remember. How we built ships of wood, and we'd sail them in Athanor Pond. About her meadowlark named Poppet, and the little bird's viking funeral in a flaming boat."

As she spoke, the memory suddenly blazed in her mind: the tiny wooden boat, floating out in the dark waters of Athanor Pond; Miranda standing by her side, holding her hand.

"You told me we'd sneak out at night with Malphas, and we'd lay in the dandelion beds watching the shooting stars. For years, you wandered the cities, looking for me. Your own dream stayed constant as the North Star—our own little house, our own family."

Rosalind closed her eyes, breathing in the scent of muddy earth and the yew's boughs. She could nearly feel the bluebells in the grass beneath her, when she'd lay next to her sister. She plucked one of the morivivi flowers from the bunch, tossing it in the grave. *One for sunlight. One for the ocean.* She tossed them in, one by one. *One for the oak trees, and for water on skin. One for the call of the golden-crowned sparrow.*

She swallowed hard, turning from the grave. Grief pressed hard on her chest as she trod the path through the cemetery. Silently, Caine walked by her side.

She'd laid her sister in the cold earth for the final time, before Miranda had gotten the chance to really live. Drew—and her parents—had robbed Miranda of the life she deserved—a family and a home, where Miranda would paint portraits and thread her wildflower wreaths. Where she'd feel the rain on her skin, the warmth of the hearth. Where she could, at last, have lived among people who loved her.

Rosalind's chest ached.

As they walked up the path, Rosalind lost herself in visions of what might have been. The other life. The one that should have existed, but didn't...

Making tea. Talking about dates. Drinking too much on the weekends. They'd been so close to that reality that it almost seemed tangible, even now—as if somewhere out there, another Rosalind and Miranda sat on a sofa in a small house in the woods, laughing at each other's stupid jokes, bickering over who got to shower next.

As the others silently walked inside the fortress, Rosalind stood outside the castle walls, staring up at the night sky. It didn't seem quite right to leave Miranda in that cold field by herself. Caine remained quietly by her side—silent, but just close enough for the heat from his body to warm hers.

After a while, clouds began to gather on the horizon. Somewhere, below the sharp pang of grief, rage began to simmer.

"Caine?" she said at last.

"Yes?"

"I want to destroy the Brotherhood for what they've done to Miranda. And to Cleo, and all the countless others."

"You will," he said quietly. "And I'll be right by your side when you do."

Thanks for Reading

Dear Reader,

We hope you enjoyed Blood Hunter. While you're waiting for the next book, we think you might enjoy our novel **Infernal Magic.** It takes place in the same magical universe.

Yours,
Christine & Nick

Also by

C. N. CRAWFORD

The Vampire's Mage Series
Book 1: *Magic Hunter*
Book 1.1: *Shadow Mage*
Book 2*: Witch Hunter*

Demons of Fire and Night
Book 1: *Infernal Magic*
Book 2: *Nocturnal Magic*

The Memento Mori Trilogy
Book 1: *The Witching Elm*
Book 2: *A Witch's Feast*
Book 2.1: *The Abysmal Sea*
Book 3: *Witches of the Deep*

About

C. N. Crawford is not one person but two. We write our novels collaboratively, passing our laptops back and forth to edit each other's words.

Christine (C) grew up in New England and has a lifelong interest in local folklore - with a particular fondness for creepy old cemeteries. Nick (N) spent his childhood reading fantasy and science fiction during Vermont's long winters.

In addition to writing fiction, we love to hear from our readers and can be reached at any of the following links. We always reply to our readers.

Acknowledgments

As always, we'd like to thank our wonderful editor Tammi Labreque; our cover designer Rebecca Frank; and our proofreader Sara Pinnell. We also thank our ARC team, Crawford's Coven, and Author's Corner for their inspiration and moral support.

Our beta reader Mike Omer already got the book dedicated him so a further acknowledgment seems excessive. Okay fine, we would like to thank Michael here, too, for his amazing feedback.

Made in the USA
San Bernardino, CA
15 January 2017